TAKEN GIRLS

BOOKS BY CAROLYN ARNOLD

Detective Amanda Steele series

The Little Grave

Stolen Daughters

The Silent Witness

Black Orchid Girls

Her Frozen Cry

Last Seen Alive

Her Final Breath

Brandon Fisher FBI series

Eleven

Silent Graves

The Defenseless

Blue Baby

Violated

Remnants

On the Count of Three

Past Deeds

One More Kill

Detective Madison Knight series

Ties That Bind

Justified

Sacrifice

Found Innocent

Just Cause

Deadly Impulse

In the Line of Duty

Power Struggle

Shades of Justice

What We Bury

Girl on the Run

Her Dark Grave

Murder at the Lake

Life Sentence

SARA AND SEAN COZY MYSTERY SERIES
Bowled Over Americano
Wedding Bells Brew Murder

MATTHEW CONNOR ADVENTURE SERIES
City of Gold
The Secret of the Lost Pharaoh
The Legend of Gasparilla and His Treasure

STANDALONE
Assassination of a Dignitary
Pearls of Deception
Midlife Psychic

TAKEN GIRLS

CAROLYN ARNOLD

bookouture

Published by Bookouture in 2023

An imprint of Storyfire Ltd.
Carmelite House
50 Victoria Embankment
London EC4Y 0DZ

www.bookouture.com

Copyright © Carolyn Arnold, 2023

Carolyn Arnold has asserted her right to be identified
as the author of this work.

All rights reserved. No part of this publication may be reproduced, stored in any retrieval system, or transmitted, in any form or by any means, electronic, mechanical, photocopying, recording or otherwise, without the prior written permission of the publishers.

ISBN: 978-1-80314-788-8
eBook ISBN: 978-1-80314-787-1

This book is a work of fiction. Names, characters, businesses, organizations, places and events other than those clearly in the public domain, are either the product of the author's imagination or are used fictitiously. Any resemblance to actual persons, living or dead, events or locales is entirely coincidental.

PROLOGUE

The girl looked beautiful, sitting in the chair, her arms and ankles bound. She'd put up little fuss as he'd dressed her in the gown, but the drugs he'd given her had helped with that. They'd relaxed her, turning her limbs into flexible putty and making it so she could barely form words. She was helpless while he worked his magic, yet she watched him with judgment. As if he were garbage.

He wanted to rip her eyes from her head!

"Plea... se." Tears fell down her cheeks.

"Don't stress. Soon you'll be where you belong." He smiled at her as she trembled and tried to pull from her restraints. But there was no give.

He grabbed a tube of superglue from a nearby table and unscrewed the lid. She freaked out when she saw him coming toward her, swaying her head wildly side to side.

The drugs were wearing off. He had to work quickly.

"Don't move." He grabbed her jaw, fixing her in place with his vise-like grip, and started to paint her lips with the adhesive.

She squirmed and screamed; the sound trapped in her throat. Based on the smell, she'd vomited in her mouth. He had sealed her lips just in time. The bile rolled back down her throat, bulging out like a snake swallowing a rat, and she jerked as if she were choking. Shortly after they started, the throes of panic subsided.

"Just a few seconds for it to set." He stood there, continuing to hold her jaw in place, her lips pursed together. Tears spilled down her cheeks, and the light dimmed in her eyes. She was losing her will to live.

Just give me more time, and you'll be begging for death...

While she sat suffering, as she deserved, he felt more alive than he had in years.

She needed to know how girls like her affected those who didn't measure up to perceived standards. People like him were viewed as different and treated as insignificant. The fact she was a byproduct of an ignorant society was no excuse. Everything in life was handed to this type of girl—their cliques, their Prince Charmings, their high-paying jobs, whatever they desired. For them, life was but a dream, sweetheart. With their perfect little lives that fit within the accepted confines established and enforced by society. But he'd never squeeze into that mold or be accepted no matter how "tolerant" people claimed to be. He'd always be seen as different, a freak, an outcast. Even by those who considered themselves open-minded and woke. They were actually the worst—treating him one way to his face and speaking of him cruelly behind his back. Though some were blatantly rude to his face. Truly, open-mindedness and acceptance were things society as a whole paid mere lip service to, nothing more.

But he had no choice but to play along, to claw through life while sacrificing a bit of himself every day. He dared not confront these bigots with their narrow-minded thinking. No rocking the boat. That was, until now...

"There." He released her and watched as she tried to pull her lips apart.

They didn't move.

Her eyes widened and she protested vehemently—nothing more hitting his ears than mumbles. He should have cut out her tongue... But too late now. Oh well. He was still in control. For once, he would say what happened.

He grinned again, unable to help himself. But his amusement was cut short. Those eyes were watching and judging even after showing her he was the one with the power. How dare she challenge him?

A torrent of rage pulsed through him, and he grabbed a length of chain from the hook on the basement wall.

"Stop looking at me!" he screamed as he wrapped the chain around her neck and pulled it tight.

Little resistance, and it was all over.

He was left breathing like he'd experienced an orgasm. Relief settled over him, calming his heart rate. He stepped back to admire his work.

Her eyes were still staring through him—from beyond the veil of death. Mocking and condescending.

"No!" He looked around for something to remedy the situation, and his gaze fell on paint cans, brushes, and rollers stacked on a shelving unit. They came with his job. But he'd also had to patch up some drywall.

He laid his hand on the perfect tool and returned to the girl. Her eyes were still staring, judging. Not for long.

ONE

The house felt empty this morning, and Amanda was bored. The fact it was a Saturday and even her seven-year-old daughter, Zoe, had plans made her lack of any even more pathetic. Zoe was staying at a friend's house for another night, and Amanda's boyfriend, Logan Hunter, had cleared out about an hour ago. He had to make a ten o'clock tee time with friends at a local country club. But he'd be back later.

Still, she had hours to pass. She must have been delusional to think some alone time might be nice. She imagined kicking up her feet and reading a book, but who was she kidding? Now it felt like she was facing a gaping void she needed to fill.

She thrummed her fingers on the arm of the couch. The novel in her other hand wasn't offering much, and she'd read the same line ten times. Nothing was going on outside her living room window either. She might as well be watching paint dry.

In all fairness, she'd shift the blame to her job in the Homicide Unit of the Prince William County Police Department. It normally kept her so busy that she wasn't left with free time to take up any hobbies.

She could scratch cleaning the house off the list of possibilities. It was spotless in preparation for Logan's visit. Not that he cared about such things, but she did.

What to do...? Preferably something that passed the time and accomplished something. One idea came to mind. It ticked off both boxes *and* it had been on the to-do list for a long time. The question was, could she bring herself to do it?

It had been nearly eight years since her husband, Kevin, and daughter, Lindsey, had died in a car accident. Amanda had been in the vehicle that day but was left to live, to grieve and shoulder survivor's guilt. The scattered images and sound of crunching metal could be recalled on command. Though sometimes they surfaced on their own, at unexpected and unwelcome times. But even more crippling was her injuries had also taken her unborn baby and stole her ability to have children in the future. It was as if God hadn't punished her enough and needed to inflict just two more blows.

But then, two years ago, Amanda had met Zoe Parker. She had lost her parents to murder, and Amanda fell fast. They had an instant bond, and Amanda adopted the girl. Confronting any residual grief head-on was no longer an option—it was necessary. She had to clean out Lindsey's room for Zoe. It had been a healing experience. But there was one thing Amanda had yet to tackle. The garage.

Kevin was supposed to organize it, a promise he'd made numerous times, but it had never come to fruition. Boxes had been dumped there when they first moved in, and most of them never left. After the accident, it was easier to shuffle all the junk aside than face what it really meant. The stuff in that garage was the only tangible connection she had left of Kevin and Lindsey. To rid herself of these items was to fully let go of them. But it was time to fully accept that her family was gone and never coming back.

It is time to move forward...

She stepped into the garage and let her gaze go over the

mass of cardboard boxes and totes. It might be best if she put this project off until she had a dumpster in the driveway. But she recognized the procrastination tactic.

She took a deep breath. *Think first steps...*

To start, she'd move everything to one side of the garage. Then, she'd sort through everything, making stacks for garbage, for donation, for keeps. She expected little would remain in the latter category, but she couldn't arbitrarily trash it all either.

Just the first part turned out to be hard work that had her sweating like mad. It might only be the third week of May, but summer-like weather had already arrived.

Amanda popped open the garage door for air flow. It let in a warm, slight breeze, but it helped knock off the heat.

As she stood catching her breath, she noted her efforts were already starting to pay off. She could see past the clutter enough to imagine her Honda Civic tucked away inside. The garage would actually be used for what it was intended for. *What a concept.*

But it was too soon to get excited. The next step would be even more time-consuming and emotionally taxing. It wouldn't just be moving a package from here to there. She'd have to look closely inside each one.

Time to face any demons that may be waiting...

She headed inside to grab a glass of water and a snack. The clock in the kitchen told her it was one in the afternoon. Time was flying. She grabbed a Coors Light from the fridge.

Kevin would always say there was nothing like a beer on a hot day, and then drink three.

But she had nowhere she needed to be. It wasn't like she had plans to drive. She twisted the cap just as her phone rang. Caller identity showed it was Amanda's fourteen-year-old niece, Ava. It wasn't common for her to call. "Hon, everything okay?"

"No." There was a gasp for breath that sent shivers up Amanda's spine.

"What's happened? Where are you?"

"I need you to come to Prince William Forest Park."

"Are you okay? Your mom? Dad?"

"I'll tell you once you get here. Meet me down near the carousel in the kid's playground area, the one near the Potomac River."

"Give me ten minutes." Amanda shut her fridge, popped out and lowered the garage door. She was sweaty and filthy, but none of that mattered right now.

If her niece's plea told her anything, it was that something was terribly wrong.

TWO

Amanda found Ava and another young girl about her age, right where Ava told her she would be. Her niece's jeans were soaked through to the knees, and she was holding on to a phone with a flashy case.

"I can explain," Ava jumped in, as she must have noticed the question in Amanda's eyes.

"I'm sure you can." Amanda turned her attention to the other girl—brown hair, freckles dusted across her nose, and a stud in her bottom lip. Her eyes didn't meet Amanda's for long, and based on first impression, Amanda would say she was shy. "And who are you?"

"Nadine Thompson, ma'am." Her voice was small, dispelling any tough-girl image the piercing might have given.

"She's my best friend, Aunt Amanda, since forever."

"What's going on, Ava?" Amanda's heart was thumping away, fixed on her niece's deer-in-the-headlights look and recalling her panicked tone on the phone.

"Nadine's sister has been missing since Wednesday night."

The skin tightened on the back of Amanda's neck. She had sensitivity when it came to young girls disappearing. Chalk that up to a sex-trafficking ring in Prince William County she'd brought down the better part of two years ago. She might have knocked out its key players, but she lived on eggshells fearing that more would rise in their place and operations would resume. "This is a matter for the police. Has your mother reported her missing?" she directed at Nadine.

"I don't think so."

"Aunt Amanda, you *are* the police. That's why I called you. We found this. It was in the river." Ava handed Amanda the phone and pointed to a spot along the riverbank. "I went into the water after it."

That explained Ava's wet pant legs...

"It's Reese's." Again, Nadine's voice was tiny, childish, inward.

Amanda turned the phone over. Blue rhinestones on the case were laid out to form the letters *RT*. Reese Thompson. "I'm going to need more information, girls." Reese had been missing for three days and the police hadn't been notified? Surely there was a reasonable explanation for that. Were Nadine and Ava making more out of Reese being AWOL than her parents? Then again, Amanda didn't know what kind of parents they were. They might be absent from their lives, letting the TV be the babysitter as they shuffled from one job to the next, moving through their lives like zombies.

"Mom and Reese had a nasty fight," Nadine began. "Reese stormed out the door, screaming that she never wanted to see Mom again."

It sounded like a teenager trying to assert her independence. "How old is your sister?"

"Eighteen. She was voted prom queen. The prom is tonight, and I haven't been able to reach her since she left."

This tidbit had Amanda feeling a bit more worried again. What would cause a prom queen to up and disappear before her big moment? It didn't sound like it would be something she'd have done willingly. Unless it was a dramatic attempt for more attention. "Reese might be staying with a friend. Have you talked to any of them?" She pushed away her niggling worries, opting to be the picture of strength and reason.

"They say they haven't seen her," Nadine said, her posture taller, more composed.

Amanda considered that it was possible one of them was sheltering Reese, not talking to the younger sister on directions from Reese herself. And there was an age difference that the older girls wouldn't ignore. They were high-school seniors, whereas Nadine was only in grade nine, assuming she and Ava were in the same year.

"Something's wrong. I know it here." Ava clenched a hand into a fist and held it to her stomach. "And doesn't Grandpa always say to trust your gut?"

Amanda's father, Nathan Steele, had served as police chief for the PWCPD, a path she would gladly follow—one day to its conclusion. He had retired about seven years ago. "He does say that."

"Then, please, listen to me," Ava said. "Reese is in trouble."

"Has she ever run away before, Nadine?" Amanda asked.

"Yes, but she always comes back after she's cooled off. And she always takes my calls."

Amanda assembled the limited pieces of intel together— prom queen runs away days before the main event *and* tosses her phone? It didn't make much sense. "All right, let's get you home, Nadine." She wanted to know what argument had Reese running, but she'd leave that question for the mother. "Girls, get in my car." Nadine's sister had been missing for three days. An innocent explanation might exist, but the churning acid in Amanda's gut told her otherwise. Something very bad had befallen Reese.

THREE

Amanda followed the directions she'd received from Ava and Nadine. She glanced in the rearview mirror at the girls in the back seat, feeling for them. Logic told Amanda that Reese hadn't tossed her own phone. Amanda had taken precautions by securing the device in an evidence bag she'd plucked from her trunk. No need for gloves at this point. The phone had taken a swim in the Potomac. The best hope for a lead would come from what was on the SIM card. And if digital forensic techs failed to resuscitate it, the service provider might come through when they provided records and the GPS history. The latter would let them track the girl's last movements. "Do you have any idea how your sister's phone might have ended up in the river?"

"She wouldn't have done it," Nadine said.

"Does she go to that park often though?"

"Uh-huh. To think and be by herself. That's why we came here... to look for her. Then we just happened to see the phone in the water."

"Has she ever tossed a phone before?" Another attempt to

review past behavior. Amanda glanced in the rearview at Nadine.

"She'd never." Nadine bit her bottom lip, and the flesh whitened.

Poor thing... "Okay, we'll see if we can find out some answers. In the meantime, try to stay positive."

"Kind of hard, Mrs. Steele," Nadine said. "The prom starts in a few hours."

Ava whispered to her friend, correcting her.

"*Ms.* Steele. Sorry."

"It's fine. You can call me Amanda." She had let the form of address wash over her, an understandable assumption. But having just been boxes deep in memories of wedded bliss, her heart cinched. It also brought a twinge of regret at not taking Kevin's surname, James, as per tradition. She'd opted to remain with her maiden one, thinking it might aid her career ambitions with her father blazing the trail ahead. She glanced at the clock on the dash. 2:12 *PM*. "When does prom start?"

"Doors open at six thirty," Nadine said.

"Aunt Amanda, I think someone took Reese, and she's..."

Amanda glanced over her shoulder, admiring her niece's confidence and instinct. But she was putting on a bold, brave front for the sake of her friend. "Let's work everything out, okay? I'll speak with Nadine's parents and go from there." One of the first things she was going to suggest was they file a missing person report.

"It's just Mom where we live," Nadine said. "Dad lives somewhere else."

That sparked hope. "Any chance that Reese went there?"

"Nope. I checked his place. He was at work... where he always is." Nadine rolled her eyes.

The rest of the drive was quiet. Amanda looked in the rearview mirror a few more times and once spotted her niece reaching for her friend's hand. It was lovely to watch Ava growing into such a great person. To think that Lindsey would be about her age now if not for the accident. There was only eleven months between them, with Ava being the eldest. What would Lindsey have been like? But Amanda pushed that thought aside, focusing again on Ava. Her biggest concerns should be schoolwork, recreation, boys, how to style her hair, and what clothes to wear. Ava certainly shouldn't be worried about the welfare of a friend's sister. The fact she obviously was, though, further endeared her to Amanda.

She pulled into the driveway, and Nadine jumped from the car and headed into the house. Ava and Amanda walked up to the door together. She wished to shelter her niece from the ugliness in the world, but she feared it was rushing right for her.

She put her arm around Ava, and her niece turned to her.

"Please, find Reese."

"I will do all I can." Amanda normally handled homicide cases, but she'd ask for an exception to be made. Since she was close with her sergeant, she'd use that to get the necessary approval to proceed.

"Ava... who is this?" a woman said as she stepped back to let Nadine inside. The girl hurried down a hallway. "And why is Nadine crying?"

"This is my aunt. She's a police detective. Is Nadine going to her room?"

"I assume so." There was a slight tremor in her voice, and she avoided making eye contact with Amanda.

Ava hugged the woman and retreated into the house.

In the following silence, the woman offered up small talk. "Ava's such a good kid. And a great friend to both my girls. So, you're a detective?"

"Amanda Steele." She held out her hand but drew it back when the woman didn't take hold. "You're Nadine and Reese's mother?"

"Yeah. Clarissa. Did something happen to Reese?" Her eyes flicked up to meet Amanda's.

"Not sure yet, ma'am, but when did you last see her?"

"Wednesday evening." Clarissa's eyes pooled with tears. "If something happened to her, it's all my fault. I should have let her have her way. But she's run away before. She's always come back. How could I have known?" She was shaking and rubbing her arms.

"May I come in?" It might be best that Clarissa get off her feet before they discussed Reese any more.

"Sure. This way."

Amanda walked past a wall filled with framed photos, many of which were of Clarissa with her girls.

Clarissa pointed one out to Amanda. It showed the three of them posed in front of a Christmas tree. Reese's grin was wide, and her eyes were bright. Amanda could almost hear the girl laugh.

"This was taken for Christmas cards just six months ago. She has an incredible smile."

"She does."

Once they got settled in the living room, Amanda pulled out the evidence bag with Reese's cell phone. "The girls found this in the Potomac River this afternoon. They tell me it's Reese's. Can you think of why she might have thrown it into the water?"

Clarissa blinked slowly, matching her gaze with Amanda's. "That doesn't make any sense."

Amanda agreed. Her gut was telling her that this story might not have a happy ending. Clarissa's eyes begged for a positive spin. To give one would equate to a lie, but Amanda wasn't going to lay out the worst-case scenario yet either. "I recommend that you file a missing person report, and I'm going to speak with my sergeant to see if I can get the clearance to investigate."

Clarissa rocked back and forth. "I can't believe it's come to this. I just thought she was ghosting me. Isn't that what the kids call it, when people just stop talking to you? But now"—she pinched the tip of her nose—"some perv might have her."

"Let's not leap to that conclusion." Amanda spoke as calmly as she could, doing her best to mask her own fears.

"Please, you have to investigate this. Find her. I trust you as Ava's aunt."

With that declaration, duty, responsibility, and hopeful expectation all landed on Amanda's shoulders. But what if she couldn't deliver? What if the answers weren't good ones? What if Reese was dead? "I'll do my best. To start with, I'll ask that you file a missing person report."

Clarissa nodded.

"It would help to know a few things about your daughter—where she likes to hang out, names of her friends, a boyfriend, if she has one. I'll also need to speak with her father."

"*Pft*. That man is maddening. Works all the time. He used to throw money at the girls. As if that can make up for him not being around."

"I'm sorry to hear that. Separated?"

"Divorced. Four years ago. Thank God."

When Amanda was married to Kevin, it never escaped her how blessed she was by stability and a faithful partner, a spouse who was her best friend. So many people didn't have that. "Do you know where Reese might have gone after she left here?"

"Laurel Wilkinson is her best friend. I'd imagine she would have at least texted her about our fight. Vented, whatever you want to call it."

Easy enough to confirm with Laurel or through Reese's phone records. "Is Reese on your phone plan?"

"She is."

"Okay, I'll be putting through a warrant to request her information, correspondence, that type of thing."

"Of course. Go ahead."

"And her social media accounts. Which ones is she active on?"

"Oh, it would be best to ask Nadine about that."

"Will do. In the meantime, I'm going to get an officer here to file that missing person report."

"Can't you do that?"

Amanda laid her hand on Clarissa's forearm. "I'm going to start looking for your daughter."

Seconds passed. Clarissa eventually nodded and blinked, tears squeezing from her eyes and running down her cheeks.

Amanda called dispatch and requested an officer come out. She was advised one would be around in ten minutes. She hung up and passed this message along to Clarissa. "And just keep positive. That's the best thing right now." She'd said the same to Nadine but saying it to the mother felt shallow and meaningless. No amount of positive thinking could bring the girl to the doorstep. Just like Amanda's optimism never had her family walking away from that car crash.

"I need to make another call." Amanda stood and stepped outside. She pressed the contact for her sergeant. He'd just returned to the job earlier that month after being off for a year and two months to recover from brain surgery to remove a tumor. His voice calmed her when he answered. "Hey, boss," she said.

He groaned—just slightly. "Amanda? You do realize it's Saturday, one of your days off?"

"What makes you think I'm calling about work?"

"The *boss* bit gave it away."

"Ah, right." She was smiling, unable to help it. Scott Malone, family friend for as long as she could remember, and a best friend to her father as they both worked their way up the ranks. Malone had been content to stay at sergeant, unlike her father, who had his eye on police chief from the start of his career. "Well, something has come up."

"Do you seek out things to investigate?"

"It's a teenage girl, Sarge." It felt amazing calling him that. While he was convalescing, a transplant from the New York City PD, Katherine Graves, was brought in—a woman with a hard edge. She'd just started to grow on Amanda when Malone's return pushed her out. But Graves was more than happy to go. She'd turned down a transfer to another unit, relinquished her badge, and took an early retirement package. She was still in Prince William County, but had reinvented herself for the next chapter of her life.

"Go on."

"She's missing and—"

"We're not Missing Persons, Steele, you know that. And you said teenage girl, right? Flights of fancy, all that."

"She's been missing for three days. We both know the likelihood of finding this girl alive now is slim to none." This is part of the reason Amanda had made this call outside of Clarissa's earshot. She needed the ability to talk freely.

Malone grumbled something that was incoherent.

Amanda continued. "The girl fought with her mother just before, but I'm telling you something is off here." She shared that prom was that night and Reese had been voted queen. "Her family can't reach her. Don't know about friends yet or her father, but the girl's phone was pulled from the Potomac River."

"Who found that?"

Amanda realized she'd possibly talked herself into a tight corner, approaching close to a conflict of interest. But it wasn't like she knew the Thompson family before today. She told Malone about Ava and that the missing girl was her friend's sister.

"What I'm hearing is Ava's out there playing investigator. Sounds like she might be the next with Steele blood to wind up on the payroll. But, I agree, this isn't sounding good. Has the mother filed a missing person report?"

"She will be. But I wanted to clear this with you, because I'm investigating." She framed it in the affirmative and held her breath. Malone had a soft spot for her, but he wasn't a pushover.

"Huh. Well, then, why even call me?"

She smiled. A person who didn't know Malone well might assume he'd be ticked off by her presumptuousness, that he'd view it as an insult against his authority. She was armed with knowing his admiration for initiative. "I wanted to keep you in the loop."

"Why thank you."

"You're welcome." Another twitch of a smile. "I want to bring Trent in to help." Trent Stenson was her work partner of over two years now.

"Oh, just leave Trent to his weekend. Before you lecture me on how callous that sounds, the girl may be staying lost of her own initiative. I trust you can figure out whether that's the case on your own."

Nothing like pressure... This was the second time in a matter of minutes someone had expressed confidence in her abilities. "I'll do everything I can. But if I need more help, I'll be calling Trent."

"Uh-huh."

She'd take that as approval. "Actually, I could use help with that phone I mentioned. It needs to go to the lab for processing. Unlikely that it will give us prints since it's been in the river, but we might get something from it. In the meantime, it would be advantageous to get a warrant for her phone records."

"Get it done, then."

"While I'm actively searching for the girl? How is that possible?" Ideally, Trent would be working on securing the warrant at the same time.

Silence stretched across the line, drawing out for longer

than she was comfortable with. But she had to bite her lip and remain quiet, play to its power.

"Fine," Malone eventually huffed out. "Give Trent a call, but afford him some leash. He might have a life this weekend."

Ouch!

"Amanda, good luck finding this girl. Keep me posted."

"Thanks, Sarge." She ended the call with a quick thank you. To those who didn't know him well, Malone would have sounded like his relaxation trumped a missing girl, but it was a protective mechanism he used to keep his emotions from clouding his judgment. She was quite sure her call had just wrecked his weekend.

She next selected Trent's number from her favorites. It rang through to voicemail. Apparently, he did have things going on this weekend. She left a message, asking that he call as soon as possible. Even then could be too late to save Reese. Heck, now might be.

But she'd take her own advice to the Thompsons. She'd cling to that teeny glimmer of hope inside that Reese was still alive. It would give her fuel to fight for a happy ending.

A police cruiser pulled up, and Officer Cochran got out of the vehicle. Amanda couldn't have made a better choice for this job. Traci was empathetic with a solid head on her shoulders. It might also help for Clarissa to speak with a woman.

"Detective Steele," Traci greeted her as she reached the front door. Her expression was grim, pre-armed with why she was there.

"Hi. I'll advise Ms. Thompson you're here and make the introductions."

After doing that, Amanda went to speak with Nadine and Ava. Clarissa directed her to the second bedroom on the right.

Amanda stopped next to the first one though, looking inside. A gown hung from a hanger over the top of a closet door. *Reese's prom dress...*

Amanda entered for a closer look. It was a pale pink, the bodice fitted, and the skirt flared out like a mermaid's tale. Sequins enhanced a lace pattern in shimmering thread that flowed the length of the dress. It would have transformed any teenage girl into a princess, or in this case, a queen. She touched the fabric, her fingers barely grazing the material, and she closed her eyes and made a wish that Reese would have the chance to wear it.

"Aunt Amanda?" Ava stopped at the doorway. "I thought I heard you telling Clarissa you were wanting to speak with us."

"Good ears." A tense silence budded, and Amanda added. "I got sidetracked, noticing her dress. It's stunning."

Ava looked past her, eyes widening as if she were seeing the gown for the first time. "It is." Her niece frowned. "I'll take you to Nadine."

They left Reese's room and found Nadine sitting on her bed, a tissue bunched in her hands. Her face was blotchy and pink, tears having made tracks down her cheeks and leaving their mark. Amanda's heart fractured at the sight. The girl must be terrified.

Ava sat next to her friend.

"Nadine, your mother is in the living room with an officer filing a missing person report for your sister." She was matter-of-fact, successfully presenting a much-needed strong front.

Nadine sniffled and looked at Amanda. "Where is she? She wouldn't ghost us like this. At least, I can't believe she would. Do you think she hurt herself or that someone took her?"

The girl had clearly given thought to her sister's fate, and Amanda was stuck on her first theory. "Was Reese unhappy?"

"I don't think so." Nadine nudged a shoulder into her cheek.

"Do you think that Reese could have hurt herself?"

"No idea. But she'd never throw out her phone. She was

mad at Mom, not me. She'd never leave me." This admission started a fresh crying jag.

Amanda gave the girl a few moments. "Sadly, we can't know what's going on in a person's mind. Was your sister depressed or distant before she ran away?" She thought she'd try again. There had to be some reason Nadine would mention suicide, or was it just denial that someone else had intended her sister harm?

"Nah. I don't know what I was thinking. Reese was always happy. She had every reason to be."

"Such as?" Amanda asked.

Nadine didn't look at her when she replied. Her gaze was fixed on her hands in her lap. "She was popular. Prom queen."

"Ah, I see." Amanda didn't take Reese's popularity to mean she was above depression though, and it was noteworthy that Nadine had suggested it. The girl's body language was a mix of sadness and possible jealousy. Did that mean anything or was it merely sibling rivalry? She'd dig deeper to unearth why Nadine had even mentioned suicide. Was it as Amanda thought, an unwillingness to accept some monster might have hurt her sister? "Did Reese ever try to hurt herself before?"

Nadine glanced down at the floor, swaying her legs. Ava shuffled along the edge of the mattress and put an arm around her friend. "It's okay, you can talk to my aunt Amanda. She's here to help."

Nadine slowly nodded.

"When was this?"

"After Mom and Dad's divorce went through."

"Four years ago?"

Nadine looked at Amanda and nodded. "Reese ended up in the hospital. She, ah, cut her wrist. But the doctors said the nicks weren't deep. Mom thought it was for attention." Nadine picked at the tissue in her hand, pieces of it snowing down on her lap.

Amanda bristled at that remark. How could Clarissa have callously disregarded her daughter's call for help? "Well, no matter how deep, your sister must have been hurting."

"She was. We both were."

"Nadine, do you know of anyone who might have reason to hurt your sister?" Amanda hated going there, but she had to ask. Broaching the difficult questions came with the job. Without the answers, there were too many uncertainties. Just suspicions, hypotheticals, and best guesses.

"Why?" Nadine spat. "She was popular, and my sister wasn't a bully." Nadine met Amanda's eyes, defiance filling them.

The girl's quick defense left Amanda wondering if she'd used it before. By extension that might mean that at least one person had considered Reese a bully. And anytime there was a vote for prom queen, someone's feelings were hurt. Popular people attracted enemies. "Do you know who else ran for prom queen?"

"Makayla Mann."

Amanda pecked the name into the notepad app on her phone. "Do you have a number for her, by chance?"

"No, and she wasn't anyone Reese hung around."

That tidbit had Amanda wanting to speak with her. "All right. What social platforms was your sister on?"

"All of them, but she spent most of her time on Snap VidPic."

Amanda was familiar with the app from a previous investigation. It encouraged picture sharing with little text.

Nadine added, "She's obsessed with taking selfies. She's a little self-absorbed at times."

"Well, that's good to know." Amanda smiled gently at Nadine, to set her at ease. But all of this was helpful. If Reese was a self-absorbed bully, that elixir opened the potential for injured parties. "I'll need to know all her social handles, but could you show me her Snap VidPic profile right now?"

"Ah, sure." Nadine pulled a cell phone from a pocket, moved her finger around on the screen, and handed it to Amanda.

She scanned down the profile, noting immediately the last post was from Wednesday, presumably following her storming from the house. It was a picture of Reese scowling with the hashtag: Momssuck.

Before that update, it appeared Reese shared pictures one to three times a day. Nadine was right about her sister and the selfies. Every post included Reese's face, whether alone or with friends. It was daunting to think Amanda might meet everyone on this feed. That's if the investigation dragged out.

Was it too much to hope Reese would come walking through the front door with some elaborate story?

FOUR

I love her. Staci is my best friend, and she is so beautiful to look at. So much of what I'm not. She is west side while I hail from the wrong side of the tracks. She is surrounded by white-picket fences and wears designer jeans. I live in a mobile home with my mother and alcoholic father and am a regular customer of the thrift store. I had been hopeless, living in a world of darkness before I met her.

She turned my life to color. She is my salvation and way out from the pit of my otherwise pathetic life.

She smiles at me with this wild spark in her eyes and says, "You're amazing, Moon Pie."

Her nickname for me, natural to her as she moved up to Prince William County from Texas. If anyone else dare called me that, I would have thrashed them, but when it comes from her mouth, it makes me stand taller, inhale deeper. "Thanks."

"Don't mention it. We're going to be fabulous. And I'm going to nominate you. I will, I swear."

Her nominate me? The most popular girl in the school, and me nothing. This could be one way to get closer to her. "And I'll nominate you."

We hugged to seal our pact. I knew then I didn't want to live without her in my life.

The memory hurls through him, threatening to rob his newfound joy. At that time in his past, he had been granted reprieve from the war that carried on within himself, the little voice that constantly told him the world would see him as some sort of freak. But Staci, in that sweet pocket of time, had melted his worries and he felt like he belonged. That peace was not to last though. Staci ended up betraying him and hurting him more than he would have imagined possible.

He released his clenched fists, reminding himself he had a reason to be grateful now.

The girl was tucked away in the van, secured, and ready for her debut. And, oh, how beautiful she was.

He fussed with her curls, fingering this one, then the next, so they all laid perfectly. They circled her face as a mane. Her delicate pixie-like features—upturned nose and rosebud lips. He'd painted her face. She was, for the most part, flawless.

If he had planned this for weeks, it couldn't have come together any better. Though he might have shown more restraint. If he had, there wouldn't be drops of blood on the nape of her gown.

She wouldn't be presented *just so* as he had in mind. But she would attend her prom and be the belle of the ball. She'd sit on her throne, elevated above her humble classmates who would cower at her magnificence...

He laughed, not able to take the narrative in his head seriously. But it came down to this fact: tonight would be his show. Even if he was confined to the shadows, unable to claim credit. Regardless, he knew.

He'd have the last word.

FIVE

Two hours had passed, and Trent still hadn't returned Amanda's call. In that time, Amanda had dropped off Reese's phone to the PWCPD's Digital Forensics Unit, also termed Digital Crimes. They worked out of the Eastern District Station, located in Woodbridge, just like Central Station where Homicide was assigned. She hoped the detectives there could work their magic and get the device operational again. Regardless, a warrant for the records would be requested. Still, despite the game plan, Amanda's mind served up doubts. Would all this effort amount to anything that helped find the girl?

Amanda also popped by Central and looked up the information for Reese's dad. His name was Melvin Thompson, and he lived in Dumfries. She checked out a department car and dropped by his house, but found no one home. Trying to reach him by phone landed her in voicemail. But she left a message and stressed the urgency that he call her immediately upon receipt.

Before leaving Nadine, her mother, and Ava at the house—who had begged to stay; Clarissa promising to make sure she got home—Amanda had obtained a list of the teen's friends and the name of her boyfriend. Next up was Reese's best—and oldest—friend, Laurel Wilkinson. She was the girl most often featured in photographs on Reese's Snap VidPic page.

Laurel's mother had directed Amanda to the teen's bedroom. The door was shut, and Amanda knocked.

"Go away!" a voice said from inside.

Laurel probably thought it was her mom or dad. Best to clear that up right away. "I'm Detective Steele with the Prince William County PD."

There was silence, then thumping. Footsteps bounded toward the door, and it was flung open. A hairbrush in one hand, head cocked. "What do you want? Prom's in, like, a few hours, and I need to get ready." She tapped a foot.

"I'm here about your friend, Reese Thompson."

"Gah, I don't have time for this." Laurel retreated into her bedroom and ran the brush through her blond hair. "She always does this. Makes everything about her. I bet she's going to show up and wow us all. She's like that."

Interesting reaction... Though also telling. Based on the picture Reese's best friend was painting, Reese sounded selfish, but Amanda chose a more delicate spin. "She has a flair for the dramatic?"

"Ah, yeah." She set the brush on her makeup vanity and leaned in to look at herself in the mirror. The girl was dressed in jean shorts and a tank. Her cosmetics were done, appearing like they had been plastered on with a spatula. Her hair was wavy and shiny. She looked like an eighteen-year-old going on twenty-five, but her scowl disclosed displeasure with her reflection. "No. No, don't tell me..." She moved in closer to the mirror, angling her head this way and that, her fingers stretching her left cheek taut.

"If I could just get your full atten—"

"Gah. A pimple. This is just great." The teen threw up her arms.

Amanda would laugh if the situation wasn't serious. "You do know that your friend, Reese, is missing?" Stressing the situation *might* pierce through the girl's obsession with a blemish that Amanda couldn't even see.

"She's not missing. She's seeking attention. All for her big reveal." Laurel waved jazz hands, then returned to checking her appearance.

Amanda stiffened. "Laurel, I need you to take this seriously. Reese hasn't been seen or heard from for three days. Unless there's something you can tell me. When did you last see or talk to Reese?"

"Ah, Wednesday. She had a fight with her mom. It happens." She poked at her perceived imperfection as she spoke.

"You should probably leave it alone." Amanda flailed a finger toward her, inferring the pimple.

Laurel paused her expedition and shot her daggers through the reflection in the mirror.

"It will get worse if you fuss with it." Amanda had been there, done that. But for some reason, most teenagers wanted to discover everything for themselves. How advanced would civilization be if knowledge from prior generations was simply accepted and built upon?

"Yikes. Well, I don't need that." Laurel grabbed a tube of concealer and dabbed it over the pimple, smoothed the cream with her fingertip. "Might get away with it, if the lighting there is crap tonight."

"Could you just sit for one minute? We need to have a serious conversation about Reese." Amanda was tiring of the girl's dramatics.

"Fine." Laurel dropped into the chair in front of the vanity.

"Is that all Reese said to you, that she fought with her mom? Did she say what it was about?" Amanda realized now that she hadn't asked Clarissa.

"Nope, but she said she wasn't going home until she cooled off. She asked to stay here, but I turned her down. Mom would have a flippin' bird."

Amanda hoped Zoe would stay a little girl forever. She wasn't sure if she had enough bandwidth to cope with a teenager. With less than six years to go, she best start preparing her mind now, though. To think, Lindsey would have been thirteen last June. "Why would your mother be upset?"

"I'm not using up favors on Reese. My mom kept holding the prom over my head. 'Laurel, you straighten up your act or you won't be going.' Jeez. Like seriously. I'm going to prom. Period." Her gaze drifted to the mirror again, her eyes landing on the zit, which Amanda could now see as a faint red dot despite the concealer.

"Do you know if Reese ended up staying with one of her other friends?"

"No clue. But Hailey and Ella are part of our little *sisterhood*." She took time from her self-scrutiny to tag on finger quotes.

"That's Hailey Garner and Ella Maxwell?" Amanda asked, recalling those names from the list of Reese's friends.

"Yep. But like I said, I have no clue if she bunked with them. This week has been *in-sane*. But I don't think you need to worry about Reese. She probably *disappeared* to get attention. I doubt she's in any real danger. Oh, actually. She did text me on Thursday."

"What time and what about?"

"Think it was in the afternoon. I can check."

"Sure."

Laurel grabbed her cell phone off the vanity and swept her finger across the screen. Soon, she was holding it in Amanda's face.

It came in at 12:12 PM on Thursday and read, *Everyone's going to be jealous on Saturday—even you. I'll show everyone.*

"This was from Reese?"

"I mean, yeah, her number." She didn't say it, but her tone added *duh*.

"Can I see your phone for a minute?"

"I guess..." Laurel handed it to Amanda.

She scanned up and read other messages from Reese. They were full of abbreviations and emojis—teenage communication reverting to the days of the caveman, who had their pictographs. But the last message was a full, grammatically correct sentence. It was possible Amanda was seeing what wasn't there, her experience with the dark nature of humanity hindering her perception. She gave the phone back to Laurel and thanked her.

"I wouldn't expect differently of Reese, though. Being prom queen is her moment in the spotlight, and she's going to lord it over everyone."

"Even her close friends?"

"Ah, yeah, us especially."

"Were you, Hailey, or Ella running for prom queen?"

"You're kidding, right? No way. That would go against the code. We decided as a group, she'd represent."

"I understand she was up against Makayla Mann."

Laurel curled her lips like she'd eaten shit. "She never stood a chance. You either have it or you don't. Makayla doesn't. She's all school paper and band. Reese is football quarterback. Makayla got some votes from the losers, but not enough. The only reason she got runner-up was because no one else had the nerve to go against Reese."

Amanda imagined that the popular kids could have intimidated some of their classmates to sway votes in Reese's favor. She was struck by Laurel's statement though. "No one else ran for prom queen?"

"Nope."

Amanda would be talking with Makayla at some point. Her

next step would be Reese's other close friends and the boyfriend, Adrian Savage.

She handed her card to Laurel. "If you hear from Reese, call me immediately."

"'K, but don't expect one. From now until tomorrow at noon, you won't be hearing a thing." She shot up from her vanity, headed for her closet.

Amanda left the house with a quick word to Laurel's mother to let her know she'd finished speaking with her daughter and thanked her for her cooperation. At least the stop hadn't been a complete waste; she was leaving with a few valuable leads.

One, Reese wasn't the golden child. It would seem she let her popularity roost in her head.

Two, Reese may have stayed at Hailey's or Ella's, and the girls kept her cover.

And three, it would seem Reese had her phone until Thursday, when she'd messaged Laurel. But why the change in writing style? Also, why avoid her sister's calls and texts when she never had before?

SIX

Amanda stopped by to see Hailey Garner and Ella Maxwell, Reese's two other closest friends. Even though they swore they never brought Reese into their homes, Amanda had applied pressure. She'd separated them from their parents, curious if they'd cop to sneaking their friend in. Both stuck to their story and were anxious for Amanda to leave.

She would have preferred to keep going, but her stomach wasn't being cooperative. She hit a drive-thru and scarfed down her food in the parking lot.

Her phone rang, and she said, "Finally," at seeing the caller ID. She answered, "Trent, where have you—"

"It's Saturday. Technically a day off work."

"Sure, unless there's an active case."

"Didn't think we were in the middle of one. You realize there are other detectives in the unit? Do you ever take time off?"

"No time for that right now. There's a missing teenage girl, and I need your help."

"Amanda, I have company here and—"

"If you were going to point out we don't work missing

persons investigations, know this one is different. It's a friend of Ava's." A minimal stretch of the truth, but Ava likely thought of Reese as a friend too, especially considering how long she'd been friends with Nadine.

"Is Ava okay?"

"She's fine. It's her friend Nadine's eighteen-year-old sister who is missing. She's been gone since Wednesday evening. Apparently, a friend got a message from the girl on Thursday, but—"

"You suspect someone else sent it?"

Sometimes it was scary how well he read her inflections. "It was rather formal compared to previous messages. Though I may be reading too much into it."

"I think you need to, until you know she's safe."

"Very true." Amanda told him the phone was found in the Potomac and had already been dropped off to the Digital Forensics Unit.

"Seems unlikely she'd have tossed it. Teens live on those things."

"I know. I fear we're not going to find a happy ending to this one. The girl, her name's Reese Thompson, by the way, is set to be crowned queen at prom tonight. It really doesn't feel right she'd choose now to disappear."

"What can I do to help?"

Amanda let out a breath. She should have known better than to think Trent would start letting her down now. "Work with a judge, do whatever necessary paperwork. We need to get a hold of her phone records and tracking history. Currently, I'm boots on the ground, reaching out to everyone in her world. All her closest friends haven't seen her. I'm thinking I'll speak to the runner-up prom queen next. Could be she's holding Reese somewhere so she can step up and wear the crown." Amanda hoped it was that simple.

"Who got the message on Thursday?"

"That would be her best friend, Laurel."

"All right, well, what about a boyfriend?"

"Yeah, she had one. Adrian Savage."

"I'd speak to him next. I assume he's the prom king?"

"Possibly." She hadn't confirmed that yet.

"Either way, girls like to tell their dates what to wear, when to show up. If anyone has heard from Reese, it would be him."

Amanda resisted the urge to ask if his knowledge came from firsthand experience; it sure sounded like it had. "Good thinking."

"Okay, I'll get my company sorted then get over to Central and start on the paperwork."

"Thanks."

"Don't mention it. I just hope we find the girl and she's okay."

"Makes two of us." She ended the call and pulled up the address for the boyfriend. Time to get moving.

"I haven't seen or heard from her in days. I was thanking God." Adrian Savage was a good-looking boy, thick chest and lean. His mom boasted that he played quarterback for the Potomac High football team and was tonight's prom king within two minutes of Amanda entering the home.

"Adrian," his mother said, her tone firm, as she popped her eyes.

Amanda appreciated the woman was likely appalled at his attitude toward Reese, especially since a cop was there asking about her.

"I swear, I have no idea where she is," Adrian repeated.

Amanda was in the living room with the boy and his mother. The father was out in the driveway polishing a black Mercedes sedan. She wondered if it was for himself or for Adrian and prom night. If the latter, brave man.

"How long have you and Reese been a couple?" Amanda asked.

Adrian pulled back, sinking farther into the couch. "Yikes. Couple?" He choked on the word. "You make it sound serious. It's not like we planned on getting married or anything. We hung out."

"They've been dating for a few months, Detective," the mother volunteered.

Adrian shook his head and looked away, drew a deep breath. "Hung out," he spat. "But I haven't heard from her since earlier in the week. Though I didn't expect to."

Amanda narrowed her eyes. "Why is that? Did you have a fight?"

"I guess. She was going overboard with this whole king-and-queen thing. Far over the top, even for her. She kept pestering me about my rental tux and blah, blah, blah. I told her she was making far too much out of it. She stormed off. Haven't heard anything from her since."

"When was that?"

"Tuesday. What is it with girls anyway? They make a freaking ordeal about prom."

"Was it unusual for her to ghost you after an argument?"

Adrian met Amanda's gaze, mouth gaped slightly open, as if he were surprised at the lingo she'd used. "It was her thing," he said.

Amanda got the sense the heat in the romance had fizzled out. "Were you and Reese happy?"

"Honestly?" Adrian glanced at his mother, back to Amanda. "I planned to end things with her tomorrow."

How chivalrous...

"Hey, if she's not going, do I have to go?" Adrian pleaded to his mother.

"Damn straight you're going. This is your high-school prom, and you only get one."

He flailed his hands. "See? Girls..."

Amanda barely remembered her high-school prom. It belonged to another lifetime. Her memory had purged what her dress had looked like, but she recalled how handsome Kevin had been. Even more momentous, he had given her a promise ring that night.

"Detective, if that's all, Adrian needs to get ready."

"Sure, that's fine," Amanda said.

"Mush now." His mother swept her hands in a hurrying gesture toward her son, and Adrian got off the couch.

"I don't have to be there the second the doors open."

"You're prom king. Move it."

Adrian left the room.

"He's probably right, Detective. These things mean a lot more to us girls."

The reiteration of this had a horrible feeling washing over Amanda. Adrian had said prom had been a huge deal to Reese specifically. She wouldn't miss prom if she could at all help it. Was it too much to hope in the validity of that text message—that Reese would be there tonight and *show everyone* in a good way?

SEVEN

Ava had called her Mom at about four o'clock and was given permission to stay over at Nadine's.

"Are you sure you don't need me to bring you anything?" her mom asked.

"No, I'm good. Nadine has pajamas I can borrow."

"Do you need me to pick you up in the morning?"

"No. Nadine's mom said she'd take care of that."

"I should talk to her—"

"I'd have to wake her up. She's taking a nap right now. She's been working long hours and is tired these days. There's no need to bother her. Besides, she's told me before I'm always welcome." That part was true. The rest was a misdirection. There hadn't been an actual conversation about tonight. But if her mother spoke to Clarissa, she'd find out about Reese and freak out. She'd smother Ava with good intentions.

"If she's as tired as you say, she might not want another kid to look after."

Shoot, I didn't think this through... "Mom, I'm not a kid, and it will be okay. Trust me."

"All right," she dragged out. "But isn't Clarissa admin staff for an insurance company? She's been working overtime?"

Her mother's mind was a vault that retained everything, even if she just heard it once. "Ah, yeah, but... Well, they had some big thing happening and her boss needed her to, you know, sort paperwork. Come on, Mom. Have I ever given you reason not to trust me?"

The ensuing pause lasted long enough to poke a dagger into Ava's heart. Was her mother giving serious consideration to the question? She'd always done as she was told, a model daughter. Her grandfather told her she was mature beyond her years. That might be why the situation with Reese had her aching to be an adult. She wanted to do grown-up things like investigate and get answers. It might also have to do with the cop blood running through her veins. Then again, it might be the simple fact she wanted to make Nadine happy again. Yes, that was the most important thing. "Please, Mom. I'll be home tomorrow by midmorning, in plenty of time to make family dinner tomorrow night." Everyone with Steele blood had dinner at her grandparents' place on Sundays.

"All right. Fine. You can stay."

"Thanks, Mom."

"Uh-huh. And be on time tomorrow. If Clarissa can't drive you home, call me to come get you."

"Will do." Ava ended the call, guilt tightening its grip.

"Ava, I'm going to call you a taxi." Clarissa rounded Nadine's bedroom door and leaned against the frame, but she appeared to be unsteady. She gave her a lazy smile, like Ava's dad sometimes did when he'd been dropped off by a cab after a night at the bar with his friends.

"I thought I'd stay with you guys tonight," Ava told her. "Figured Nadine might like the company. My mom says it's okay."

"Oh, that was nice of your mother to allow that. We love having you here. You're a good kid."

Another jab to her bleeding conscience. It would have had her buckling if the stakes weren't so high. She trusted Aunt Amanda to do her part, but Ava wasn't just going to stand by and wait to see what happened next. She wasn't wired that way, probably due to her role models all being ambitious people who got things done.

"Thank you, Clarissa." She had been told to use the woman's first name a long time ago. It had been an awkward adjustment at first, but now it rolled off her tongue.

"You betcha." Clarissa headed back toward the front of the house, and Nadine shut her door.

"I thought you'd look good in this." Nadine opened her closet and pulled out a pant suit.

"It's not a dress..." Had that escaped her friend's notice?

"You hate dresses."

"I do." This time Ava managed to pull off a smile. How thoughtful of her friend to take her preferences into consideration.

"No big deal. I had it because Mom bought it for me to wear to some stupid Christmas party her boss had. Why she thought I'd like it more than a dress, I have no idea."

Seeing her friend carrying on lightly infused some hope into Ava. They could be jumping to the worst-case scenario for no reason. She and Nadine may very well walk into that country club and find her sister all decked out for prom. But if so, why was the pink gown still hanging in the room next door? Surely, Reese would have come back for it.

Ava put on the pant suit while Nadine took off her shirt and jeans and slipped a blue dress over her head. She smoothed down the fabric and looked at Ava. "So...?"

The shade of the dress ignited the color of her eyes.

Normally azure, these days they were more a deep aquamarine —common when Nadine was tired, sore, or depressed.

But still, Ava had to compliment her friend. "You look amazing."

"Thanks." It was a half-hearted response, but Ava appreciated that Nadine's mind was distracted.

Ava took her friend's hands. "We'll find her, okay?"

A half bob, then Nadine pulled her in for a quick hug. "I don't want to ruin my makeup."

"That would be a tragedy." Ava attempted a smile that fell short. Neither of them were much concerned with cosmetics, but they needed to make themselves look older tonight if they'd have any hope of getting into the prom.

"You look amazing too." Nadine smiled, but the expression stopped short of her eyes.

"Thanks." Ava had been doing so well, looking ahead, anticipating, but she hadn't seen this coming. The guilt was chewing her up inside. Clarissa was already going through enough with Reese missing. Would she notice later that Nadine was gone too? And then what? "Maybe we shouldn't do this."

"Ava, I need to find my sister. My heart is broken." Nadine's voice cracked, and it refueled Ava.

"Okay, let's do this. But we'll be quick and get back as fast as possible. If she's not there, we'll figure something else out."

"If she's not there...? I don't even want to think about that. Then it really will take your aunt to bring Reese home." Nadine sniffled.

Ava hugged her friend, rubbed her back. She wanted so badly to make everything better for the people she cared about.

EIGHT

By the time Amanda finished with Adrian Savage, the doors for prom would be opening in thirty minutes. She didn't feel like she was anywhere closer to knowing where Reese was. At least Trent had gotten somewhere with his efforts. The request for the warrant for Reese's phone records was sitting with a judge for review.

She was reversing out of the Savages' driveway when her phone rang. Caller ID told her it was Logan. *Shit.* "Sorry, I got caught up." She was supposed to meet him at her place and have another night in with him. "Did you let yourself inside? The key is in the—"

"I know where the hide-a-key is, considering I gifted it to you for Christmas."

"Right." Long story, but it was something he'd used himself for years and bought her one for Christmas. But he had paired the practical gift with diamond earrings. She loved them because they were from him, not that she knew where or when she'd have reason to wear them.

"Where are you?"

"It would take a while to explain."

"You can tell me tonight over dinner and wine."

She hesitated just a moment too long. She had planned to drive up to Manassas and stand by at the prom. Hopefully, Reese Thompson would be there and this living nightmare would end.

"We are still having dinner and wine?"

"I don't know. A friend of Ava's is missing, and it's not looking good for her," she rushed out.

"Oh? Shit."

"Yeah. At this point I'm worried that something bad happened to her." She didn't share the facts of the case with Logan, but the pitstops of her day played out in her mind. All the way back to how it had started, with her sorting out the garage, and that had her feeling like a sweaty grub. As soon as she'd received Ava's call, she'd been on the move. "I'll pop by home for a few minutes. A brief distraction might do me a world of good."

"Huh, I like the sound of that. See you soon."

She heard his smile on the other end of the line before she ended the call. Fifteen minutes later, she was in the shower with Logan. As she had suspected he had no objections to being her "distraction." They didn't get out until the water ran cold, while their bodies were warm.

Amanda wiped at the steamed-up mirror with her towel.

"Is there anything I can do to help?" Logan came up behind her and wrapped his arms around her, pressing his naked flesh against hers.

She detected notes of concern in his voice and loved that he'd asked. Her career as a cop had caused a rift between them in the past, even led to a temporary breakup, but he was in full acceptance mode this time around. It made her want to stay with him. After all, there was nothing saying she had to go back out. Reese would show up or she wouldn't—both outside Amanda's control.

Amanda dropped the towel on the counter and turned in Logan's arms. "You know what? I think I'm going to stay in."

"Really? I shouldn't challenge this, but are you sure?"

"Yep."

He smirked, a lopsided expression that was mischievous—and sexy as hell—before he moved in and took her mouth.

They got dirty again, then took another shower.

After which, she held up a hand in front of herself. "It's been fun, but one more shower and I'll be waterlogged."

"Worse things." He reached for her sides, and she squealed.

"Cut it out. Let's get dressed, pour a glass of wine, pick a movie to watch, and settle on the couch."

"I could get behind that."

And that's what they did. They cracked open a bottle of merlot, and Logan had just poured it out when her phone rang.

Not again, she thought, flashing back to the undrunk Coors Light from that afternoon. It felt like forever ago.

"You should get that," he told her.

He was right. For one, Zoe wasn't home, and she might need her. Two, Reese may have turned up at prom. She welcomed good news. She plucked her phone from the counter, and the screen showed Ava's name. Amanda answered, "Ava, everything okay?"

No verbal response, just deep breathing and the hiccup of a sob.

Amanda's body tensed, her back ramrod straight. To think, she had dared to give herself over to *reserved* optimism. "What is it?"

Logan moved behind her and put a hand of support on her lower back.

Ava sniffled, then gasped.

"That's it, I'm coming to you. You at home?"

"No, I'm in Manassas at the prom. Rolling Hills Country Club."

Of all the answers Amanda hadn't expected... "You're— What are you doing there?"

"Just hurry, Aunt Amanda. I'm quite sure it's Reese." More sniffles.

The hairs were up on Amanda's neck, her skin as tight as pulled leather. "What's Reese?"

"Someone's been murdered. People are talking, and it's a teenager. But that's all I know."

Ice trickled down Amanda's back. Was this her fault? If she had been there, could she have stopped this from happening? "Are the police there?"

"Yeah, but please, Amanda. Get here."

Amanda was already slipping into a pair of shoes by the front door. Logan was trailing behind with a bewildered expression on his face. "I'm on my way," she said to Ava.

"Okay." Ava ended the call, and Amanda had her hand on the doorknob to leave.

"Where are you going?" Logan asked.

Her entire body was quaking, and her heart was racing. She'd chanced taking one night off. *Just one.* Yet the universe or whatever saw fit to punish her. But this wasn't about her; it was about a young girl who had lost her life. *Because of me? Did I fail her? Is that teen Reese Thompson?*

"Logan, I need to leave. I think Reese may have just been found murdered at the prom."

His mouth opened and shut. "Murdered?" The single word seemed to scratch from his throat. "I'm not sure what to say."

"There's nothing to say." She put a hand on his chest. "I'll make this up to you, I promise. We'll have another date night yet."

"Don't worry about that. Go, and be safe."

She pecked a kiss on his cheek, and ran to her car. As she pulled out of her driveway, she saw his frame silhouetted in the front window. She hoped he was truly as understanding as he was coming across. If he left her now, it would hurt a lot more than it had before.

NINE

Amanda called Trent to meet her at the station and placed a slew of other calls—Sergeant Malone, Crime Scene, and the medical examiner—as she drove to Central. She wasn't there long before Trent pulled up in his Jeep Wrangler about seven, only fifteen minutes after she'd called him.

He got out and headed toward her. "Every time I try and get my hopes up..."

Life had taught her that hard-knock lesson a long time ago. It was always better to prepare for the worst. "Here, you drive." She tossed him the keys and loaded into the passenger side.

He turned to her after they got down the road. "You sure it's her?"

"I have a feeling." She retreated inward, crushed under the weight of guilt. She never should have attempted to settle in at home. What had she been thinking? And even if this teen wasn't Reese, could she have saved her? "I should have been there. I might have been able to prevent this from happening."

"I highly doubt whether you were there or not, it would have changed the outcome." Trent merged onto Highway 294 West to take them to Manassas.

"Guess we'll never know." And they wouldn't until they knew time of death. Had she been killed on location? If so, then Amanda's presence might have been enough to prevent this. The girl might still be alive.

"You always do this… Beat yourself up about things you can't control."

An ache pierced her heart. "Please, just get us there as fast as you can."

The car lunged forward as he pressed harder on the gas. She regretted now that she hadn't driven, as she had a heavier foot than her partner. But they were still on track to hit Manassas within the thirty-minute travel time it normally took.

"So tell me all you know about Reese and her family," he said.

"I'm quite sure I told you everything. Reese was last seen Wednesday night and last heard from on Thursday."

"Right, the friend got a text message. But you aren't sold on it being from Reese?"

"That's right. If this victim is her, we need to get Laurel's phone—that's the friend—and have Digital Forensics look at it. See if they can confirm."

"Good idea."

"Yeah." Amanda's mind was buzzing with nonstop chatter and chastisement.

Trent got off the highway and took them to Rolling Hills Country Club. The place was luxury personified and sat over acres of manicured land—rolling groomed greens, as their name implied, and tended garden beds. Even this early in the year, annual flowers were in full bloom amid evergreens and other hardy winter flora.

Lights were on inside and glowed brightly through the two-story high windows. Where there wasn't glass, landscape spotlights shone onto the brick. Pot lights also accentuated the gardens and steps to the main doors.

All that hinted at darkness were the two police cruisers parked in front of the outside staircase. Officer Wyatt was leaning against one. He pushed off when he saw her and Trent approaching. There was no sign of a vehicle from Crime Scene or one belonging to the medical examiner yet.

"Where is she? Who found her?" She punched this out as she closed the distance. "Do we have an ID? Tell me as much as you can, as fast as you can."

"Unidentified female, late teens. Found on a toilet, in a restroom stall..." Wyatt stopped speaking, as if he hesitated to say more. But how much worse could it get? She'd been discarded in an undesirable place.

"Cause of death?" Trent asked while keeping an eye on Amanda—as if she had the answer. "And was she killed there?"

"We'll need to wait on the ME to know COD, but I've heard it's looking like strangulation. As for whether she was killed this evening, I don't know. Again, the ME would be your best bet."

"But he's not here yet," Amanda said, more statement than question.

"Not yet."

"Again, who found her?" Amanda looked around, trying to spot her niece, but no one was milling outside in the lot. Everyone must be sequestered inside until they were questioned and their information collected.

"Lisa Bradford, part of the janitorial staff. Doors for the club were already open for people, but she was doing a final check on the restroom within a few minutes of six thirty. I pulled her background, and it's clean."

Amanda released a deep breath. "Not a student, then?"

"No. And that's a small mercy. It's not a pretty picture in there."

Pretty or not, Amanda needed to move. "Where is the restroom?"

Wyatt gave them directions, and she and Trent headed for the doors. She immediately felt the cloying pall of death in the air.

"Come to think of it, who called you?" Trent faced her.

There was no point in lying, he'd see right through it. "Ava."

"Ava?"

"Yes. She's gotten in over her head, but her motives were pure." Or at least Amanda imagined they were. "Ava's just being a good friend." As the words spilled out, she realized how much she was defending her niece's actions.

"She should have left this to the police... to you."

Amanda wasn't going to argue that point. For one, he was right. Two, there were other priorities.

As they entered the expansive lobby, no one was within sight, but dulled voices traveled from the west side of the building. Officers must have corralled everyone into the grand ballroom. Just not before the rumor mill gained traction. And along those lines, where was Ava? She was a ninth grader, and wouldn't have been admitted—unless she snuck in. Once Amanda found Ava, they'd have a talk about boundaries and lines that shouldn't be crossed.

Amanda keyed a quick text to Ava telling her she was at the country club, and asked where she was while telling her to stay put until she got to her.

Since Ava's presence was out to Trent, him practically being family, she said to him, "Please keep your eye out for Ava."

"You got it."

Amanda imagined what sort of hell her sister Kristen was going through wondering where Ava was, or had the girl concocted some cover story to explain why she wasn't home? Regardless, when Kristen found out the truth, Ava might be lucky not to be grounded for a year. And Amanda would be lucky to escape her sister's wrath unscorched. Kristen would find some reason to blame her.

She and Trent passed a small gift shop and then came to the restroom. Officer Brandt was posted at the door. He dipped his head before stepping aside to let them enter.

"Any words of caution before we head in?" Trent asked the officer.

"Just that it's not a pretty sight."

Trent nodded. "That we've already heard."

They put on protective booties and gloves, and Amanda led the way inside. Her phone pinged with a response from Ava.

In the ballroom.

At least she was safely tucked away. She pocketed her phone and steeled herself for what she was about to see.

The end stall was open, and Reese Thompson was right there.

There wasn't anything that could have prepared Amanda for this sight.

TEN

Officers had tried to warn them about the crime scene. It was now clear that real life was far more macabre than Amanda's imagination.

Reese Thompson was dressed for prom in a pale-blue puffy dress complete with a tiara. She was seated on the toilet, sunglasses on her face, her arms dangling at her sides, and her head pushed back toward the wall. Around her neck was a bulky chain, the links close to half an inch thick.

"Dear God," Trent muttered from behind.

Amanda wasn't on a friendly basis with a greater being since she'd lost her family, but she doubted *God* had anything to do with this. Reese's text, *I'll show everyone*, popped into Amanda's head. She'd bet money that text came from her killer. Placing Reese here had been planned. They needed to get their hands on Laurel's phone more than ever. Those in the Digital Forensics Unit might be able to sort out exactly who sent it— whether they physically used Reese's phone or spoofed her number—and from where.

As she continued to look at the girl, Amanda realized what else made the posed scene so creepy. Reese's face was made up with cosmetics, but it was the fact her brightly painted red lips were pursed together. When a person died, all muscles relax, including those in the face and jaw. The girl's mouth should be slack and gaped open. She pointed this out to Trent.

"What the...?" Trent said.

"If you're not going to be more talkative than that, I might as well work this by myself." She hadn't intended to sound so snippy, but she was on edge, frustrated, and angry with herself. She shouldn't have been at home with Logan. She should have been here. *But how could I have known?*

He shook his head. "It's just, why are they always kids?"

They were vulnerable, weaker, made for easier targets than adults, but she got the spirit of his question, which leaned toward existential. "Never easy."

"And was she killed here or brought here? She was found just minutes after the doors opened for prom. But what time window are we looking at? You'd think the club would always be crawling with people."

"Which is why I'm leaning toward Reese being killed elsewhere and then dumped here. It would also take more time and finite orchestration to kill her here and stage her without someone walking in."

"They could have locked the door, but still... Either way, it would have taken precise timing to go unseen."

"Let's hope you're right and someone saw something." She paused, battling with guilt again. If Amanda had been here earlier, would that have changed Reese's fate?

The door swung open, and crime scene investigators Emma Blair and Isabelle Donnelly entered, booties over their shoes, gloves on their hands, and holding on to their collection kits.

"You got the short straw too, I see," Trent said.

Blair froze on the sight of Reese. "Seems so— Dear God."

"Poor girl," Donnelly added.

"Well, let's get to it." Blair set down her case and took out a camera.

Amanda and Trent stepped back and let them work. There were people to question, starting with Lisa Bradford, but it was always best to be armed with some information about the crime itself before doing those interviews. They'd stay here until they had a little more to go on.

Blair stepped inside the stall and snapped off a series of photographs.

"We found the fact her lips are together curious," Trent said.

The investigator lowered the camera and looked over a shoulder at him. "They appear to be stuck together."

Stuck...? "Like with glue?" Amanda asked.

Blair held up her hands. "We'll need to wait for Rideout."

Amanda was pleased that Hans Rideout was assigned the case. He'd also be coming from the Chief Medical Examiner's Office right here in Manassas. It was the same building where the crime lab was housed.

But it was standard for CSIs to show first, photograph, collect—process the scene. When they finished, then the ME got the body. Sometimes waiting was painful, but tonight even more so.

Amanda was haunted by all that had been lost. Photos of Reese Thompson showed someone who had a spark and love for life. Her smile was infectious, and Amanda imagined her laugh had been too. She also likely possessed gifts either about to be discovered or being cultivated. The worst was thinking that just three days ago she had been alive and full of fire.

Clarissa Thompson was going to be destroyed, broken. Needing to process a child's death was unnatural on its own, but trying to reconcile the murder of one would be incredibly tough. To make it worse, from all appearances Reese may have suffered greatly at the hands of her killer before the darkness claimed her.

Amanda turned to Trent. "We need to trace her every move from leaving her house. Call on the status of that warrant. We need authorization to request her phone records and tracking history immediately."

"Sure thing. I'll call Judge Anderson." Trent pulled his phone to place the call. Anderson was always available, fair, and reasonable. "Hi, it's Detective..."

Amanda tuned her partner out as she returned her attention to the CSIs. She pointed out the lock on the door and suggested they dust it for prints just in case it ended up mattering.

Trent hung up. "Anderson's going to get it signed and back to us tonight."

"Good. As soon as you get that, forward it to the service provider."

"Will do." He pushed his phone into his back pant pocket. "I heard you mention the lock."

"Yep." She crossed her arms, taking a moment to try and remove herself from the scene. Impossible. "What do you make of all this? First impressions?"

"I'm not the expert that Rideout is, but I'd say she's been dead several hours given the coloring of her flesh."

She'd been so busy blaming herself for this, she hadn't noticed. But he was right. She'd seen enough dead bodies to know they turned an ashen blue as time passed, and Reese's flesh was definitely tinged blue. Trent's observation allowed her to unpack some of the guilt she carried for staying home tonight. "Now you say it, I see it. And my guess is she's been dead at least eight to twelve hours, because her hands appear to be in rigor."

"Huh. That's rather precise."

"You'll feel comfortable making that type of call after you've seen more dead bodies."

His face shadowed, and he turned away. "I've seen enough in this life. Thanks."

She could have smacked herself in the forehead. Trent still had moments when his mind dipped to last October. He'd suffered an ordeal when a suspect decided to shoot himself with his service weapon—while the gun was in Trent's hands. The swift action had left no time for intervention. Reasoning and logic still failed to alleviate his guilt. "I apologize. That was thoughtless of me to say."

He waved a hand. "Don't worry about it. So"—he nudged his head toward the stall—"we need to figure out how the killer got her in here."

"More importantly, who the bastard is. I'm sure she had her enemies, but to hate her this much?"

"Teens can be idiots and susceptible to mob mentality, but do you really think they're capable of this?" He gestured with a full hand toward the stall.

"I learned a long time ago not to misjudge anyone. It often has a way of biting you in the ass. And we are technically talking about adults here." In a way, it was easier to accept a psychopath had stalked and targeted Reese, opposed to it being one of her peers. Possibly more likely. The murder had been meticulously planned—the location, the timing, the presentation. "Well, whoever it was dressed her in a gown that wasn't hers. In fact, it is vastly different. Reese bought a fitted dress in a pale pink."

"That may be a valuable lead right there. Did the killer dress her this way to humiliate her? As a way of saying 'up yours'? If so, that sounds like adolescent thinking. Who did Reese beat out for queen?"

"Makayla Mann."

"And with Reese out of the picture, she'd be prom queen."

"Except the flaw in that theory is the prom will likely be canceled."

"Or postponed, giving this Makayla person the opportunity to wear the crown."

Amanda hadn't met Makayla yet but found it hard to imagine a teenage girl being able to arrange all of this. "We'll talk to everyone, obviously. But you brought up humiliation. Everything about this scene speaks to that. Just look where they placed her."

"No one deserves to die on the can or even be found there."

"Nope. And instead of asking who simply hated Reese, we need to explore who might have had reason to humiliate her."

"And was it one person acting alone or a team? That chain around her neck appears quite heavy. Then again, it might be a prop. Until we get our hands on it, we won't know."

He had a point, but she thought it appeared to be the genuine article. "It sure looks like the real deal."

"If so, it probably involved some muscle. If we are looking at Reese's peers, I'd say it was a group of them. Teens are always eager to rally together in support of a cause."

"We were wondering how one killer would have pulled this off. Now you're suggesting more than one?"

"More questions than answers."

"Blame the investigative process."

"Don't I know it. And they're just getting started."

She nodded and turned her attention to the investigators. Amanda felt like she'd not only failed her flesh and blood but also Reese Thompson.

ELEVEN

Ava had her arm around Nadine. Her friend hadn't stopped shaking since the rumors started circulating about the dead teenager in the women's restroom. It didn't help the latest to hit their ears included mention that the girl was in a prom dress.

"It's her, isn't it?" A fresh wave of tremors barraged her friend.

Ava faced her, putting her hands on Nadine's shoulders. "My aunt's here now, and she'll take care of this."

"Take care of it? How can she *take care of it* if my sister is dead?" Rage and sorrow morphed Nadine's face into an ugly mask.

"She will. Trust me."

"She can't bring her back from the dead," Nadine spat.

"No, but she can find out who did this to that girl. We need to stay strong. It might not even be Reese."

"It is." Nadine's anger dissipated like steam. "I feel it here" —she laid a hand over her stomach—"and here." She placed the other one on her heart.

"We'll know soon. Okay?"

Nadine nodded. Ava wanted to suck all the pain from her

friend. To start with that required verifying the identity of the dead teenager. She'd ask Aunt Amanda, but she'd be busy right now, and the last thing Ava wanted was to distract her. And would she even tell her? That left the options of waiting things out or seeing what she might find out on her own. "I'm going to walk around a bit. Will you be okay?"

Nadine rubbed her arms and nodded.

"I won't be long." Ava walked off. She planned to move through the crowded room at a slow pace, soaking up conversation and murmurings until she had a full picture.

Uniformed officers were standing on the edge of the room, near the doors, blocking the exits. None of them would disclose the name of who was dead. From watching TV and absorbing police procedure from her grandfather and aunt, next of kin was always notified first. These cops would likely take everyone's information and follow up if necessary.

"I've tried reaching her a million times." Adrian was gesturing wildly with his phone.

"Apparently no one's heard from her for, like, days," Ella said, picking at a fingernail. She was a close friend of Reese's, but the entire school knew she had a crush on Adrian. If gossip was to be believed, Ella and Adrian had dated for all of grade eleven. The fact he'd picked up with Reese the next year might have been a sore spot.

Enough to get Reese out of the way? Ava's mind always dipped to tragedy, but she was predisposed. She had an aunt in Homicide and a grandfather who had been police chief. One day, Ava just might follow in their footsteps. They made a difference in this world.

But could Ella really be a killer? She was mousy and so calm, it was tempting to check for a pulse. Though wasn't it always the quiet ones that harbored the most violent tempers?

"Hey, I got a text from her on Thursday." Laurel ran her

fingers through her blond straight hair. It was like a pony's mane. "She said she was going to show everyone."

Ava perked up. *A text on Thursday?*

"Show everyone what?" Hailey, another friend of Reese's, was Plain Jane next to Laurel and Ella. She was wearing a simple black cocktail dress with a cubic zirconia necklace with a teardrop pendant. She was tracing the lip of her glass with a finger.

"Who knows?" Laurel fluttered her eyes.

Ava fought an eye roll. Laurel had a way of making everything about herself. Just drama, drama, drama. Time to move on...

But Laurel's words were burning in Ava's mind. *I got a text from her on Thursday.*

Why would Reese talk with her friend and not her own sister? That didn't make any sense. And Ava wasn't just taking Nadine's word for how close she was to Reese; Ava had witnessed their sibling friendship in action. Reese made Nadine feel seen every day.

Ava shrugged deeper into her jacket, thankful she wasn't wearing something sleeveless like so many of the girls here. She was chilled. Call it a bad feeling. After all, if the dead girl wasn't Reese, who was she? The evidence lined up as far as Ava was concerned—ghosting her sister, her phone in the river, not coming home for her prom dress...

"Rollins?"

Only one guy always addressed Ava by her last name. She turned, and Craig Shepherd was standing in front of her decked out in a tux. He was two grades above her, but she'd had a small crush on him since his family moved down the street a few years ago. "Huh, someone cleans up well." She smiled at him.

"Thanks. You too." He'd offered the compliment, but there was a twitch to his lips that contradicted his words.

"You don't mean that."

At least he had the decency to blush. "I do. It's just..."

"I'm wearing pants and not a flashy gown?"

"Yeah, I guess."

"Welcome to the twenty-first century, when women dress how they like."

He held his hands up. "My apologies, but what are you doing here?"

Run or own it? She chose the latter, sticking out her chin. "Snuck in."

"Impressive, Rollins."

"That's me." She swayed at the hip, then stopped herself. *What am I doing?* But the truth was, he had a way of making her feel uncomfortable. She'd get this pulsating through her entire body. Her breathing became heavier and her head lighter. Butterflies were set free to flutter about as they wished in her stomach. She had this same reaction to Nadine sometimes too, but she wasn't sure what to make of that. "It's crazy what's going on here tonight. A murder...?" She fished for what he might have seen or heard and failed at doing a smooth job of it.

Craig leaned in toward her ear. He smelled of heady cologne and soap. He spoke lowly. "Heard it's a sight..."

Ava would imagine most murder scenes were but gathered he meant it was grotesque. Her stomach tossed. "Yeah? How do you know that?"

He drew back. "Not like I know firsthand. Jeez, Rollins. You should see the way you're looking at me."

"Sorry. I didn't mean to look at you in any way."

"See that woman over there? The one talking to the cop?" Craig butted his head toward the corner of the room.

Ava followed the direction he'd indicated to see a woman about her aunt Amanda's age with curly, frizzy brown hair. "What about her?"

"She's the one who found the body."

Ava kept her gaze on the woman. Her facial mannerisms were expressive, and she gestured wildly as she spoke. She pushed a hand through her hair. Whatever she was relaying to the officer had her uncomfortable in the least. Horrified and in shock, the worst.

"When you say 'a sight', you mean...?"

"Gruesome." He punched that out as if it wasn't connected to a murder.

Ava thought she had sleuth mode down, with a strong handle on her emotions, but actually hearing *gruesome* shook her. She'd been so locked in mission mode that she'd turned the search for Reese into robotic actions—one step after the next. Everything she had done was based on reasoning and logic. But reality, the full impact of murder and its repercussions, was sinking in. Her objectivity often turned her perceptions to black and white, but they filled with vivid color and clarity. Suddenly, she didn't feel too well.

"Are you okay?" Craig reached out for her arm.

She pulled back and pressed on a smile, even as her stomach flip-flopped. The butterflies now felt more like bats, their thick, powerful wings slapping her insides. "I'm fine." She cleared her throat. "Do they know who it is yet?"

"No idea, but it's going around the dead girl is in a gown and tiara. People think it's Reese Thompson."

Ava laid a hand over her gut. "Sorry, I have to... have to..." If she didn't get to a restroom fast, she was going to vomit right here in the ballroom, in front of everyone. She'd never live that down. Grade elevens were here, and they'd be around to make her next year hell. Heck, Craig was here. She certainly couldn't be sick in front of him.

She rushed to a restroom that was located off the ballroom and emptied her stomach in the toilet of the first stall and flushed. Her head was throbbing, and she leaned against the wall.

It was quieter in here than the ballroom itself. Still, muffled voices made it through. She stood there for a few seconds, savoring the stillness, the solitude.

Someone whistling an upbeat tune cut through her reprieve.

It must have been coming from the men's restroom next door. But who could be so cold and callous considering the circumstances?

She washed up and left the restroom.

The men's door swung open, and a giant of a man walked out. She'd noticed him earlier. He'd been sticking to himself in a corner near the table full of hors d'oeuvres. He wasn't a teacher she recognized unless he was a new temp she hadn't had yet. He might be a parent, there to chaperone. Though she hadn't seen any of the students speak to him. Then there was the possibility he worked for the country club. But he wasn't wearing a shirt with the Rolling Hills name and logo. He returned to the food table.

"There you are." Nadine came over to Ava. "I could use some company."

"Of course. Sorry." But Ava was distracted by a tingling that danced over her arms. Call it a feeling, but that man, the Whistler, didn't belong here.

TWELVE

Amanda would have liked some input from the medical examiner, but she was tired of standing around waiting for him to arrive. As they did, the case just got colder. After all, the first twenty-four hours of any case were crucial. She and Trent needed to get out there and start obtaining answers and securing leads.

They'd removed the plastic booties and were on the way to the ballroom now. Once she stepped inside, Amanda was catapulted back in time to her prom, even though this place was decorated to the nines. It didn't seem any expense was spared, which was both surprising and impressive for a small-town high school. Gold bunting draped from the ceiling congratulating the graduating class. White fabric also crisscrossed the beams and drew the eye to the center of the dance floor and a grandiose crystal chandelier overhead. An ice sculpture, in the shape of a hand clutching a diploma, commanded attention on a table spread with a variety of nibbles.

All this beauty mere feet down the hall from the macabre ugliness of murder...

"They went all out," Trent said.

"I was just thinking that."

"Can I help you?" A uniformed officer, new to the PWCPD, came over and was eyeing them with suspicion.

Amanda swept her jacket aside and tapped the badge clipped to the waistband of her pants. "Detective Amanda Steele, and my partner, Detective Trent Stenson."

The officer's shoulders relaxed. "Sorry about that."

"You're just doing your job," she said. "You must be new?"

"Yeah. Officer Cannon." He tapped a finger toward the embroidered name on his uniform. "Actually, just call me Isaac. Is there someone specific you're looking to speak with?"

"For starters, Lisa Bradford," Amanda said. "Do you happen to know where—"

"Right there, ma'am." Isaac pointed out a woman in her mid-thirties with brown shoulder-length hair.

"Thank you," she told him.

"Don't mention it."

Amanda and Trent started toward Lisa, while Amanda kept an eye out for her niece. Ava should be in this room somewhere. Unless she hadn't done as Amanda had asked. Then she spotted her. Ava's back was to her, but it was unmistakably her niece, and Nadine was beside her. Amanda took a deep breath, trying to cool her temper. Ava hadn't said anything about dragging that poor girl out here. "One sec, Trent." Amanda walked up behind the girls and cleared her throat.

Ava pivoted, and her cheeks flushed. "Aunt Amanda."

"Where do your mothers think you are?"

Ava glanced to the floor. Just a flick of her eyes, easy to miss, but Amanda caught it.

"Ava," she prompted.

"Mom thinks I'm at Nadine's for a sleepover, and I am."

"Huh. Seems to me you're in Manassas—a half hour from home—at a prom you're not even supposed to be attending." Amanda didn't care if she sounded like her own mother had when Amanda had gotten herself into trouble as a young person. She had good reason to be upset, and she suspected Kristen would turn this around and somehow blame her too. Her sister didn't handle deceit well, not that Amanda blamed her. The world was too scary a place to let kids roam free doing whatever they wanted. They weren't equipped with the necessary life experience to make wise choices—case in point right now.

"I just... I'm sorry."

"And you should be." Amanda didn't doubt her niece's intentions were in the right place, but that mattered little in this scenario. She looked at Nadine. "Where does your mom think you are?"

Nadine's chin quivered and tears fell.

Ava wrapped an arm around her friend. "We snuck out. But Aunt Amanda, it's not what you think."

"What I think is you're both in a heap of trouble..." Amanda bit back the urge to point out what this would be putting Clarissa Thompson through, assuming she'd realized a second daughter was unaccounted for. And now, Amanda was faced with the knowledge Nadine's sister was dead down the hall.

"Please. I just wanted to help my friend." A spark of aggression rose in her niece's eyes but was quelled with her next breath. "Is it Reese?"

If Amanda answered, it would have her breaking protocol. It festered that Nadine was watching her with hooded eyes, desperate for an end to her mental and emotional anguish. But Clarissa had the right to be the first to know, and Nadine was just a child. She'd need a solid support system once she heard the news.

"If it's her, please just tell me," Nadine said. "I can't stand not knowing."

"I'm sorry, sweetie, but I can't say right now. I need to work for a bit, but I'll be back for both of you. Stay out of trouble," Amanda added, directing that advice specifically to Ava.

"Aunt Amanda, please." Ava's petition housed desperation.

She peacocked her posture. "Parents are to be the first informed. No exceptions."

"Then it is her," Ava pushed out.

"I didn't say that." *When did Ava get so intuitive?* "Just give me some time, and then I'll drive you and Nadine home."

"Fine. But you should know something. See that guy?" Ava nudged her head in the direction of the food table.

Amanda noticed a tall, strongly built man hovering around. He was balding and had a pronounced cleft chin. "What about him?" She was almost afraid to ask.

"I don't know who he is and why he's here."

"He's not a teacher, a parent, someone who works here?"

"Don't think so. I haven't seen him around school before if he's a teacher."

"He could be a new hire," Amanda suggested.

"I'm quite sure he was whistling a happy tune just a moment ago in the restroom."

A stone landed in Amanda's gut. Who would muster joy with news of a murder floating around? The man would certainly be strong enough to wield that chain around Reese's neck. "I'll find out. But you"—she nudged her niece's shoulder and held up a pointed finger—"need to leave the detective work to me. You understand?"

"Yes."

"Promise you'll leave it alone?" Amanda recognized understanding and refraining were distinctly different in the mind of a teenager.

"Yes."

"Good." Amanda walked away, hesitantly. Ava wasn't prone to lying, but this situation with Reese was bringing to light a different side of her. She seemed to justify her actions as being for the greater good.

"Everything all right?" Trent asked when she rejoined him.

"I won't be for a very long time."

Trent's brows lowered in a vee. "You told the girl about her sister?"

"Absolutely not. Mom gets the bad news first, but it pretty near killed me to keep it from her."

"You did the right thing."

Sometimes doing the right thing didn't feel good. "We'll drive the girls home and notify Ms. Thompson when we finish up here." Her gaze drifted to the man that Ava had pointed out. She got the attention of Officer Cannon. "Please make sure his statement is taken." She indicated the man by the food table.

"Will do. Would you like me to send you that when it's finished?"

"Would appreciate it. I'm interested in not just who he is but why he's here."

"You have reason to think he doesn't belong?" Isaac was looking at her like she was some sort of clairvoyant.

She certainly wasn't going to tell him she got the tip from her niece. "He's alone in a room full of people. Stands out to me."

"I'll make sure someone talks to him next."

"Thanks," she said, and gave him her card to forward the information to her. She walked toward Lisa Bradford, Trent next to her.

"So it's against the law to hang out by yourself now? He might be shy, a type of wallflower," Trent said to her.

"Ava doesn't know who he is. She says he's not a teacher or parent, and he doesn't work here. No shirt with the country club's name. Also, she said he was whistling a happy tune."

"Hmm. So we're taking a lead from a fourteen-year-old?"

"An intelligent one. And during a murder investigation we take all we can get. Beggars can't be choosers."

"Well, she probably does have detective DNA running through her blood."

"Not doubting that."

"Just remember, she's your niece and rather close to the whole situation. She could be seeing what she wants."

"It's possible." Let Trent believe she was in agreement. But Ava wasn't easily swayed or convinced of anything. Rather, her niece tended to be cynical, a trait that came with being a Steele. As she had told Trent, though, at this early stage of an investigation, all things needed to be considered.

THIRTEEN

Everything had been a success, and now it was time to sit back and relish the spoils. Beautiful people were all around him, but it was hard to enjoy that aspect. Most of them young, but all were shallow, pathetic creatures longing for approval and acceptance. But they had no idea what it was like to be him, feeling like he lived on the fringes of society, rejected and an outcast. He had stopped searching for belonging because he didn't believe the world was capable of offering that to him.

Those who fit society's confines, those like Reese Thompson, had everything—the looks, the charm, the popularity. Even God had blessed her, endowing her with a stunning smile and a soothing voice like a cherub.

Ah, a cherub. Speaking of, was she up communing with angels now? Or down in hell with Beelzebub?

If he had a say, the man with the horns and pitchfork were the least of what she deserved for her transgressions in this life.

Just like most of them here, who were superficial and accepting as long as you fit the mold. But there was one girl who stood out as somewhat different. Maybe she'd been rejected like him.

She was good-looking, though, with long, straight brown hair. She was comfortable enough with herself that she wore a pantsuit among the many gowns of her peers. Yes, she was probably like him. A loner.

He watched her move through the crowd, her eyes taking in everyone she passed. Her steps would slow, and he was sure she was eavesdropping. A nasty habit, but she sure was a curious little thing.

She stopped and spoke with a young man, and her blushed cheeks transported him to his past. How great it had felt to be in love, like the world was all shiny and new and held no threats. As if he were perched atop a mountain, above and out of reach of harm. Just at the term of affection coming from Staci's lips, he'd go weak. *Moon Pie.* That was until her true self emerged, and she'd not just broken his heart but also his spirit.

The prom had been approaching, and the poll for queen was in her favor. All because of his nomination. But Staci didn't appreciate that. As it turned out, she didn't even care. She'd used him and toyed with his feelings.

He came out of class one day to the word *Freak* spray-painted across his locker and Staci, her boyfriend, and their group were there laughing when he'd discovered it. They had been waiting.

Staci stopped cackling for just long enough to say, "You seriously didn't think I was your friend? Or that I wanted to be your *girl*friend?" She had then turned to her boyfriend and started making out with him.

But the torture didn't stop there. He was walking home from school and was jumped by Staci's clique. With her egging on her friends, they corralled him into a wooded park and shoved him to the ground. They choked him with a chain. He'd lost consciousness to the sounds of hackles and Staci's cries, "It's the least of what you deserve!"

When he regained consciousness, he found that they had

taken off his shirt and pants. He was forced to walk home in his underwear.

He never reported the assault, too embarrassed, even thinking he'd brought it upon himself somehow. Even though the weather was getting warm, he had worn high collar shirts until the bruising disappeared.

After all these years, that memory had bite. And truly, it had affected the course of his future. He never made it to college, and his self-esteem had plummeted. He didn't think he deserved anything good in life. Out of high school, he took deadend jobs and lived in a cheap apartment. It wasn't like he had parents who cared either. They were never the Brady Bunch—happy and carefree with problems being solved by calm discussion. Growing up had been a lot of screaming, fists, and empty whiskey bottles, until one day there was neither. First, Dad left, and then Mom kicked him out after he'd graduated high school. More specifically, after he'd decided to share his soul's truth with her.

He had struggled and scraped together an existence, controlling what he was, within his grasp. He took hormones and supplements and built up his body like a temple. And while he finally got a job he was proud of, he was lonely as he couldn't trust anyone after Staci. People served their own agendas, period. Any interest or concern they showed in others was designed to manipulate for their own advantage.

His mind returned to the present, and he watched as that unique girl slipped into the restroom. *Good a time as any*, he thought, and did the same, going into the men's.

The girl beat him out, and he noticed her eyes darting about as if she were looking for someone. Then he saw Nadine Thompson headed right for her. *Shit, what was she doing here?* Nadine was only in grade nine, if he remembered right.

He moved behind another man who was making his rounds at the food table. Nadine couldn't see him, or she might recognize him and start asking questions. If she did, he'd give her some convincing cover story, but he'd prefer not to chance it.

He helped himself to some crackers and cheese—empty calories, but these last few days had increased his appetite.

As he nibbled, he continued to watch the girls. What were they talking about, and why were they even here?

A redhead in her mid-to-late thirties, dressed in pants with a jacket, caught up with the girls. The trio spoke for a while. Nadine's friend nudged her head in his direction, and the woman looked his way. Thankfully, Nadine didn't. Was their interest in him or someone else?

He tucked behind a man who seemed to have set up camp in front of the puff pastries. By the time he looked over his shoulder, the woman was walking away. Then she turned to say something else. It was then he caught a glimpse of a gold badge on her waistband.

She's a cop!

He nearly choked on a mouthful of dry cracker. But who was that girl—the curious little thing? And why was she talking to the police and pointing him out? Could she be his undoing? She was still looking in his direction.

He'd be keeping an eye on her too. But for now, he was going to find a way out of there.

FOURTEEN

Amanda and Trent guided Lisa Bradford out of the ballroom into the lobby. Amanda preferred that this interview be afforded privacy from the hundreds of prying ears.

"Ms. Bradford, we'll only take a few minutes of your time. If you'd like to sit..." Amanda gestured to a group of leather chairs. They didn't appear to be the most comfortable-looking seats, but they were what was available.

The three of them sat down, and Amanda's assumption had been proved false. The chairs were cozier than they looked.

"My name is Detective Steele, and this is Detective Stenson." She was tempted to provide first names, to ease the woman's discomfort. But it was best to remain at a distance until, or unless, Lisa could be cleared from suspicion. Considering she had found the body, the possibility she was involved needed to be considered.

"I told that officer in there everything." Lisa sniffled and rubbed the side of her nose.

"We appreciate your cooperation thus far, but my partner and I need to speak with you. Some of what we ask may seem repetitive, but it's part of the process." A disclaimer Amanda often put up front to get it out of the way.

"Sure. Whatever you need. If it will help." Lisa's eyes were shadowed by black bags, and her frizzy hair only emphasized her haggard appearance.

First impressions, Lisa Bradford was an unfortunate soul who had stumbled into the macabre scene, but Amanda wouldn't let her guard down for one second. Officer Wyatt had informed them Lisa didn't have a criminal record, but that meant little right now. "Please run us through what happened, Ms. Bradford. What time you showed up for work, what took you into the restroom, what you found there. Start from the beginning."

"I showed up for my shift at eight this morning."

"Long day," Trent inserted, showing empathy.

Lisa's posture softened at Trent's kindness. "An eternity."

"We're sorry to prolong it." Amanda didn't have the heart to point out it might be a while yet before Lisa could go home. Assuming she was released, sleep probably wouldn't come easily. "If you could just tell us..."

"I found her about six thirty-five. Management wanted me to take another look in the restroom, but I didn't get there until after the main doors were unlocked."

"They were locked?" Amanda asked.

"Yes. We had shut down the course at five for the event."

Trent scribbled in his notepad. Amanda found the detail just as interesting as he did.

"And the main doors opened right at six thirty?" Amanda asked.

"That's right."

That potentially left an hour and a half for the killer to get Reese in the restroom. It was fortunate that an early arriver to prom hadn't made the discovery instead of Lisa Bradford. That would have been a surefire way to screw up a teenager's head.

"But the course and club were open earlier in the day?" Amanda asked.

"Uh-huh."

The killer could have smuggled Reese's body into the club during the day, concealing her someplace, and then returning later when there was less traffic. But if the club doors were locked, how had they gained access? Were they looking at an insider? If not, it felt like the killer had pulled off the impossible.

Amanda's mind was certainly whirling. Who was in the clubhouse between five and six thirty? She suspected there might be some straggling customers, club staff, caterers, and decorators. Every one of them was a potential suspect. There was also the possibility of an unknown party. They could have snuck in with Reese's body minutes before the club's doors were locked or had been inside for a while and tucked away. Or did they have access to a key? So many questions. But either way, the killer had found a way to get Reese into the stall before Lisa's final check. "Did you happen to see if anyone used the restroom between five and six thirty?"

Lisa shook her head. "I'd have no way of knowing. A caterer made a horrible mess in the kitchen, and I was sent to help clean up."

Amanda nodded. "It was after that that your boss asked you to check the restroom?"

"That's right." She sniffled. "I wish I hadn't done as he'd asked."

"I'm sure. You mentioned the caterers. I'm assuming ones for the prom? When did they get here?" Trent asked.

"They've been buzzing around since four getting things ready. Decorators for the ballroom were in at eight this morning when I got in, but they left about four."

"Very helpful. Thank you." Scratch decorators off the suspect list. Not a huge stride forward, but being down one group was better than none.

Trent was writing furiously in his notepad. "So anyone with the catering crew could have used the restroom earlier this evening?"

Lisa shook her head. "Staff, including those brought in with events, are directed to use the restrooms in the back."

"You mentioned your boss wanted you to take one more look at the restroom, so I assume it was cleaned prior by someone else?" Trent asked.

"Yes. Vince, that's the manager, wanted everything to be perfect for tonight."

"What time was it cleaned?" Amanda angled her head, squinted, her mind hard at work trying to assemble a puzzle she didn't even have all the pieces for.

"I'd suspect just after the doors locked at five."

That chips away even more at the killer's time window... "I'm guessing you didn't do the cleaning?"

"Nope. Susie Valentine was to handle it."

"Another person on staff?" Amanda asked.

"Yep. You can always consult the restroom cleaning log. It's in a frame just inside the door."

"How long does it take?"

"Fifteen minutes."

That afforded the killer one hour and fifteen minutes to get in and out without being detected.

Trent looked up from his notebook. "And do you know where we might find Ms. Valentine now?"

"Home, I'd suspect. She usually finishes at six."

If Lisa was right, Susie Valentine was the only person in the restroom when the clubhouse doors were locked. She would have had the time and privacy to get Reese into the stall. "Can you describe Susie to us?"

"Ah, she's small. Five feet tall... maybe. Early fifties."

"And is she a strong woman?" Amanda asked.

"Strong enough to do a good job around here, but she's not any type of bodybuilder."

Amanda nodded. She and Trent would want to speak with Susie Valentine. It was hard to reconcile Susie's described age and stature overpowering Reese Thompson, who Amanda would guess was closer to five foot nine and of athletic build. Not to mention Reese had youth on her side. And while Reese may have been incapacitated, someone of Susie's size would have had a tough go of carting a dead body around. Then again, adrenaline could work wonders. "Is there anyone else who had access to the premises besides club staff and caterers during the time of five and six thirty, when the doors were locked?"

"Not that I know of, but you might want to talk with Vince."

"We will. His last name?" Amanda asked.

"Galloway."

Amanda didn't want to dredge up the image she'd seen in the restroom and showed Lisa a picture of Reese that Clarissa had given her. "You ever see the girl before?"

"Oh my god, that's her?" Tears beaded in Lisa's eyes. "She really was beautiful and so young." She sniffled.

"She was," Amanda agreed.

"And, no, I never saw her before tonight."

Amanda gave the woman her card and thanked her for her cooperation.

"Can I go now? I have a huge headache and... What am I saying? That poor girl is dead, and I'm complaining about a headache."

"Don't do that to yourself, Ms. Bradford. You've undergone a lot yourself today, and, yes, you can leave." Amanda really didn't peg Lisa Bradford as the killer they were after.

"Thank you." She pulled a well-used tissue from a pocket and blew her nose.

Amanda walked to the closest uniformed officer, who happened to be Tucker. "See that she gets home all right."

"You got it."

Tucker went over to Lisa, and Trent turned to Amanda.

"We have an hour and fifteen minutes when no one entered that restroom."

"At least when no one was *seen* going in there," she corrected and looked up at the ceiling in search of a security camera. She didn't see one.

"There might be no one else to see because this Susie Valentine is our killer. She could have snuck Reese in. Somehow."

"Yes, somehow. We'd then circle to motive, but short of speaking with Valentine and digging into her, there's no place to even begin theorizing."

"Yeah, I know." With his sagging shoulders, he appeared as frustrated as she was.

FIFTEEN

Amanda and Trent returned to the restroom, putting the booties on once again, and found Hans Rideout and his assistant, Liam Baker, starting to get underway. She'd hoped things would be further along by the time they finished speaking with Lisa Bradford. As it was, the CSIs were still lifting prints and scouring for trace evidence.

"Hey," Amanda said, the greeting meant to encompass everyone, mainly Rideout and Liam.

"Heya, Detectives," Liam said.

Rideout waved a hand overhead and barely glanced over a shoulder. He had his frame wedged in the stall and was facing Reese. "This poor thing," he said. "Every girl dreams of her prom, but not showing up like this."

Rideout made it sound as if he had been a teenage girl at one time.

"You still there?" Rideout looked back at them. "I have a daughter." He must have read her facial expression, a mix of amusement and bewilderment.

She hadn't known that, but she wasn't privy to details of his personal life. "What's it looking like?"

"The chain wound tightly around her neck gives the first impression she was strangled." He was moving his arms, but Amanda couldn't see what he was doing with them. "Oh."

"Dr. Rideout?" Trent prompted.

"Normally petechiae shows in the mouth and gums when asphyxiation is a factor."

Petechiae were small red dots that resulted when a person was starved of oxygen. "What do you mean *normally*?"

"I was going to check, but her lips appear to be glued shut. I'll check other common locations such as her arms, legs, and stomach, once I have her back at the morgue. Although... it can show in the eyelids too. Let me check— Dear God." He walked backward out of the stall and stepped to the side to afford everyone a view.

Amanda's gaze was first on the sunglasses in Rideout's hand —the pair that had been on the girl—then it traveled to Reese's face.

Her eyes had been cut in their sockets. Not removed. Mutilated.

"Whoa." Trent pivoted, turning his back on the grisly sight.

Blair peeked around the stall's doorway to see what the excitement was about. "Whoa is right."

Amanda was at a loss for what to say. She'd been on this job a number of years and had seen a lot, but this scene was shocking in its brutality. Who would go to such lengths to brutalize and mutilate this young woman? First, gluing her lips together. Then, cutting her eyes.

"What kind of person does that?" Donnelly put a gloved hand to her forehead.

Amanda had one idea. "Her killer vehemently hated her, and that..." She paused there, considering her next thought before speaking it out loud. "Hate is a strong emotion, and that typically indicates a personal connection. Even the way she's been posed suggests the killer may have been privy to Reese's personal life."

"Reese's killer very well could have been someone the girl had known and trusted," Trent said.

"I'm wondering if that's the case." She'd best steer herself back to objectivity and professionalism or she'd quickly spiral into an abyss of dismay. "Was she alive when...?"

Rideout shook his head. "I'd say after."

"So she wasn't tortured beforehand." Amanda's voice was a near-whisper, as if she were treading upon consecrated ground.

"I wouldn't go that far, Detective."

"What kind of implement was used to inflict the damage?" Trent asked.

"I'll need more time to figure that one out—if I ever do. But whatever it was"—Rideout returned inside the stall and kept his legs back while leaning over the body—"made a mess of things. It's like her eyes were mashed to pulp."

Her father had told Amanda when she'd signed up for the academy that if she followed through on becoming a cop, she'd see things she wouldn't be able to unsee. He tried to warn her that one day, if she wasn't careful, they might accumulate and steal her sanity. He'd cautioned that he'd seen this firsthand with several good men in law enforcement—those he respected and who had mentored him. Sometimes there were warning signs—alcoholism and narcotics addiction—other times it rushed over a person like a tsunami, instantly wiping them out.

"You all right?" Trent stepped up next to her.

She nodded, though it wasn't the full truth. It was spooky how Trent could read her mind and seemed to always sense when her thoughts drifted into the darkness. Sometimes she felt so close to the edge, as if she were one deep breath from toppling over. Her only saving grace was clinging to what she had to be grateful for.

"Now, there appears to be what are small droplets of blood on the front of the dress," Rideout added. "If that's indeed what it is, then she was wearing it when her eyes were stabbed."

After seeing the aftermath, *stabbed* downplayed reality. Hacked or pulverized seemed a more apt description. She put her focus elsewhere. "Is that chain the real deal or a prop?"

"Oh, it's the real deal and quite heavy."

"Time of death?" Trent asked.

"She's starting to come out of rigor, so in or around twenty-four to twenty-eight hours. I'll run tests at the lab to see if I can narrow that down."

That would place TOD between seven and nine PM Friday. Amanda breathed somewhat easier. Her not being here hadn't resulted in the girl's death. In fact, she was gone before Amanda even had a chance to save her. But her relief was a fine line, as it revealed another horror. She turned to Trent. "Reese left home Wednesday night and was killed yesterday, that being Friday. So was she with her killer for a couple of days?" They'd worked a case last October where the killer held his victims for days, and she didn't even want to contemplate what Reese might have suffered during that time. Sexual assault? *No!* She'd stop her wild thoughts before they galloped ahead of her, sweeping her up in horror.

"Hard to know yet. Remember, there was that message she sent on Thursday," Trent pointed out.

"That's true, but also assuming she sent it."

"We'll get that phone from her friend."

Amanda nodded. "When will you be doing the autopsy?" The actual work landed on Rideout, but she directed the question to Liam. He kept Rideout's calendar.

"Tomorrow morning." Liam didn't even take out his tablet, which he normally did to consult Rideout's schedule.

"Time?" she pushed.

"I'd like to do it first thing and have the rest of my day,"

Rideout told Liam.

"Then eight o'clock." Liam pulled the device from a bag now and tapped on the screen, presumably adding the "event."

"We'll be around when we can," she said, not wanting to commit to a set time.

"See you when you get there. Liam, help me get this girl bagged and loaded." Rideout shimmied out of the stall, and Liam put the tablet away and rushed to attend to his boss's request.

The CSIs stood by, breaking from their collection work. They'd wait until Rideout and Liam left and do another thorough sweep of the stall.

"Guess that's it for us, for now. Here, anyway." Next stop was breaking some hearts. She turned to leave, standing beside the frame on the wall posted by the door. It was the cleaning log Lisa Bradford had mentioned. A fresh sheet with one entry. She pointed it out to Trent.

He angled his head. "Messy handwriting, and so is the signature. I'd say it could be Susie Valentine. Looks like she finished at five fourteen PM tonight."

"Around the time Bradford figured."

"Yep, sealing up our window of opportunity for the killer from five fifteen until six thirty."

"We'll question Valentine. If she's guilty, she might go down as the dumbest criminal of all time. She's placed herself here—in writing. Then she presumably leaves at six, which affords forty-five minutes for someone to find Reese before she heads home. Ask me, and I'd say someone else came in with Reese after that."

Trent shrugged. "Do we know if she clocked out at six? She could have left earlier or later even."

"We will find out." She'd try not to think about the next steps in too much detail or she'd become overwhelmed. "And I know we haven't really looked into her yet, but I strongly believe Reese knew her attacker or in the least was known by them. Her abduction and murder may have been opportunistic, but they must have known about her being prom queen and where the event was being held."

"It could have been a stalker who took things a step further."

"Way further. I say we ferret out everyone in Reese's immediate world and on the fringes of it. We also talk to neighbors, see if any saw her leave on Wednesday night and, if so, in what direction."

"We need the friend's phone," Trent interjected.

"Yes, that too. And there's Prince William Forest Park where Ava pulled Reese's phone out of the river. One thing with this case, there are no shortage of starting points."

"Now if only we could be cloned."

"I know how you feel. It's going to be impossible to take care of everything tonight. But there is one thing we can't put off—notifying the Thompsons about their daughter."

"Agreed. She's been living in hell long enough."

"Sadly, her stay is going to be extended."

They left the restroom, and Amanda stopped to talk to Officer Brandt.

"Detective Stenson and I will be leaving for a moment to inform next of kin, but we'll return as soon as possible. Make sure the club's manager sticks around. That's if he's still in the building."

"I'll make sure that happens."

"And since there's no way Trent and I can question everyone of interest tonight, make sure officers take everyone's statement, no matter how brief, along with their name and contact information for us to follow up."

"That's been underway since the body was found."

She nodded. "When that's done, unless an officer deems it necessary for a person to remain here for us, people can start to leave. Just wait until the ME's van is gone with the body."

"Yes, ma'am." Brandt spoke into his radio, likely to the uniformed officers' sergeant.

"I'm going to get Ava and Nadine." Amanda found her niece and her friend just inside the ballroom door. "Come on. I'm taking you both home."

Nadine wasn't meeting Amanda's eye, but Ava's look was one of disappointment, as if Amanda were holding back the victim's identity out of spite.

They walked into the lobby area, and Sergeant Malone was coming through the main doors. At the same time the restroom door opened, and Rideout and Liam were wheeling out the body. They passed, going in opposite directions.

Nadine gasped, and Ava hugged her.

Shit! "I'm sorry you had to see that." Amanda should have waited to get the girls until the body was loaded in the ME's van. How would Nadine handle this thinking back, that it had been her sister in the bag? How would she scrub that memory from her mind?

Malone headed straight for her and Trent. For a brief second, his mouth set in a straight line at the sight of Ava but then bounced back. "Hi, Ava."

"Hi, Mr. Malone," Ava said, and the girls seemed to shrink together, morphing into one. Both seeking comfort.

"Detective Steele, a minute?" Malone nudged his head, inferring that she step aside from the teens, out of earshot.

"Ah, sure." She joined him about twenty feet away.

He spoke in hushed tones, but his message got across loud and clear. "What is Ava doing here? Isn't she a freshman... fresh*woman*?"

"Think it's just freshman, and yes, she is." Amanda hesitated to answer his real point of interest—an explanation for Ava's presence. The full truth was incredibly loaded. Even though Malone had proven himself rather understanding of personal connections in the past, that was before his sick leave. Was he the same man? "You know how kids are. Wishing they were older than they are."

"You're trying to convince me she was here to crash prom? Who is that with her?"

"Ava's friend."

"Steele," he seethed. Use of her surname didn't bode well for what was to come.

"Nadine Thompson."

He lowered his voice and said, "The victim's sister? What the— Steele, we can't have teens running around investigating murder. You should know that."

"They aren't investigating murder. The girls don't even know the vic's ID." Amanda would cling to that defense and go down with the ship if necessary.

Malone was shaking his head. He scratched his beard, dropped his arm. "I'm thinking that you may be too close to this one."

She'd expect that sort of statement from the previous sergeant. Katherine Graves had a sensitivity for any investigation that smacked close to personal. But she had her reasons, having been kicked out of the NYPD when the chief played favorites and brought in a relative for her replacement. "I didn't even know the Thompson family before today." Amanda squared her shoulders, prepared to stand her ground.

"I don't know..."

"Sarge, I can handle this, and I am motivated." She stopped short of providing her reasons. One, young victims touched a certain spot inside her and molested her moral code, rousing her redhead temper. Two, she wanted to investigate for Ava.

After the passing of painful seconds, Malone spoke. "Fine. Run with it."

"Will do." She laid out her and Trent's next steps.

"All sounds good to me. Keep me posted."

She nodded and gathered the teens and Trent, and they left the country club. Trent drove, and as the golf course disappeared in the rearview, a pit grew in her stomach. The next hour was going to be hell.

SIXTEEN

Aunt Amanda wasn't talking to her, but she didn't need to. The message was loud and clear—the dead teenager was Reese. And whenever her aunt came out with that, Ava would be there for her friend. After all, Ava wasn't a stranger to loss. She'd lost her cousin Lindsey and her uncle in a car accident. They had been on the way home from Ava's seventh birthday party. Ava hadn't fully been able to process it then, but that experience had become part of who she was.

Death was a black void. Cold, bitter, ever present.

But it was also a motivator. A reminder to live to the fullest while you had the chance.

Trent turned down Ava's street.

"What are you doing?" Ava squeaked. "I'm not leaving Nadine right now."

"You are, Ava," Amanda said firmly.

"But Mom thinks I'm at Nadine's. Take me there. Please."

"Not negotiable."

Her aunt set the bar high for stubbornness, but Ava wasn't without a dose of her own. "No. Take me to Nadine's." She crossed her arms and punched her back into the seat.

Amanda turned to face Ava. "You need to come clean with your mom and dad about tonight. I'll be by your side while you do it."

No wiggle room for debate. It was in her aunt's eyes, the set of her mouth, her tone of voice.

Trent parked behind her dad's SUV. Amanda got out and stood beside Ava's door.

Ava turned to her friend. "Nadine, you know I'd go with you if I could—"

Amanda knocked on the window. Ava rolled her eyes at being summoned like a puppy.

"I think she's dead." Nadine's chin quivered, and Ava hugged her friend, pulled back.

"Call me or text, whenever you want. I'll keep my phone on me."

Nadine nodded, and Ava got out of the car.

"You didn't need to knock on the window," Ava grumbled, leaving Amanda to follow.

Ava would have loved to slam the door in her aunt's face. But she didn't. She'd just had time to shove off her shoes when her mother came prancing down the stairs. It was ten thirty at night, and she looked amazing and had a bounce to her step. Talk about high standards to live up to.

Her mother's eyes danced over her outfit, then to Amanda. "What's going on?"

"Ava has something she needs to tell you, but so do I." Amanda's voice was soft, and it tugged on Ava's heart. "It's best we have this conversation at the kitchen table, but I can't stay long."

"Okay," her mother dragged out.

Ava walked down the hall to the kitchen—a short trip usually. Tonight it felt like anchors weighed her every step. She and Amanda sat. Her mother headed for the kettle.

"Should I make tea? I get the feeling this conversation might be easier with one."

"No time for that. Ava," Amanda prompted.

"Fine. I wasn't entirely honest with you about tonight."

Her mother pulled out a chair and dropped into it. "I did notice your outfit change. So you lied to me?"

"I never *lied*." God, Ava detested that word, even if she was guilty of it for a few things she'd told her mother earlier. The loophole here was that she had intended to sleep over. "I was going to spend the night at Nadine's. We just weren't there all evening." She looked at her aunt, hoping she'd intervene. She gestured for Ava to continue. "Nadine's sister has been missing for a few days and—"

"Missing?" Her mother looked at her sister. "Amanda? Would you step in here?"

Amanda leaned forward, clasped her hands on the table. "Ava's been concerned about her friend's sister and doing what she can to be there for her and help look—"

"Investigating, in other words? Like a cop?" Her voice took on a high octave as she leveled her gaze at Ava. "Am I putting this together correctly?"

"Not like a cop," Amanda corrected. "Like a concerned friend. Tonight, she and Nadine found their way to the prom."

Ava had been bracing herself for how her mother would react when she heard Manassas. Thankfully, Amanda had left that tidbit out. But it likely wouldn't remain secret for long. It might be better to just fess up. "It was in Manassas, Mom. And before you flip out, we are fine. We're not kids."

"Yet you were sneaking around like one." Her mother's eyes dulled, and her body tensed. She didn't say it in so many words, possibly due to empathy for her friend's predicament, but she was disappointed. That hurt Ava more than any amount of yelling or grounding was capable of.

"I'm sorry, Mom."

"We'll talk about your punishment in the morning. For now, hand over your phone." Her mother held out her hand.

"You can't take my phone!" *What if Nadine needs to reach me?* Frustration built in her chest, and tears burned in her eyes.

"Phone."

Ava pulled it from a pocket and handed it over. "I hate you." The words flew out, propelled on wings of hurt, but the way her mother's face pinched, she wished to take them back.

"Well, I'm not a fan of you right now either."

"I will call you if there are any updates, Ava," Aunt Amanda told her.

"Please just tell me… is Reese dead?"

Her mother paled.

Amanda sat back in her chair, her arms going to her sides. "I wish I could tell you, but the family needs to be notified first."

"You suck too. I can't believe this. You get on us teens about not being straightforward. Adults are worse." Ava got up and pushed her chair into the table with a whoosh. It fell back and landed on the floor. She left it there. To hell with it. To hell with everything.

She stormed up the stairs and kept going despite her mother's yells for her to get back there. No way. She was done. She'd get into bed, stare at the ceiling until morning when she'd leave her room to find out she was grounded for eternity.

Beneath her room, she heard the raised voices of her mother and aunt talking for a few more minutes, then the front door opened and slammed shut.

Tears squeezed from her eyes, their warmth pelting her cheeks.

Ava dropped onto her bed after grabbing her stuffed bear from a bookshelf. Rocky had been her best friend when she was a child and had a way of making things better. She hugged him to her chest, needing him to come through for her tonight.

SEVENTEEN

Amanda felt like shit. Ava was mad at her, and Kristen blamed her for Ava's deviant streak, accusing Amanda of enabling her and keeping the situation about Reese quiet. Still, Kristen didn't need to go *fireball* on her. As for Ava, if Amanda could have told her about Reese, she would have—in a heartbeat—to save her some pain. But she had to follow protocol. And now she was about to execute said protocol and destroy the Thompson family.

Nadine got out and stood next to the department car. "Mom's going to kill me."

"She'll just be happy you're okay," Amanda said, speaking as a mother herself. Once Clarissa knew about Reese, Nadine's excursion would be forgotten. When Trent joined them, Nadine drew in a deep breath and led the way into the house.

Amanda and Trent followed but stayed back, letting the girl have some space.

"Mom?" Nadine called out as she walked down the main hallway.

Muffled sobs traveled to Amanda's ears, and Nadine stopped outside Reese's bedroom and pointed inside. Amanda peeked through the doorway. Clarissa was on the floor at the end of Reese's bed, her back against it, crying into her hands. Amanda's heart fractured at the sight. "Trent, could you...?" Amanda said.

He nodded, receiving the rest of Amanda's unspoken request.

"Let's go in the front room and wait for them," Trent told Nadine.

After they left, Amanda entered the room. "Ms. Thompson?"

Clarissa sniffled and pawed at her wet cheeks. She looked up at Amanda, her eyes slits. "Detective?"

"Let me help you up." Amanda held out a hand.

Clarissa took the proffered assistance and stood. She put a hand to her forehead. "It's spinning."

"You might have gotten up too fast." That's what Amanda said, though she was quite certain Clarissa was drunk. She clung to Amanda's arm for stability.

"Is she... *is she*...?" Fresh tears fell as Clarissa gasped for air.

"I'm going to make you some coffee, but let's go sit down and talk." Amanda held eye contact with the woman. This wasn't how she wanted to tell Clarissa that her daughter was dead—with her wavering on her feet in the girl's bedroom, inebriated.

Clarissa barely nodded, and Amanda started down the hall with her.

The fragrance of fresh coffee reached her nose and the gurgling machine hit her ears, as she and Clarissa entered the living room. Trent must have already had a feeling. But even numbed by alcohol this was about to become the most painful night of Clarissa's life.

Amanda saw her to the couch, sitting her next to Nadine.

"You're home, baby," Clarissa said to her daughter and wrapped an arm around her.

Nadine flinched and withdrew against the side of the couch. As Amanda suspected, in light of her and Trent's presence, Clarissa wasn't concerned about where her daughter might have been anymore.

Trent returned to the room. "Coffee's on," he said, taking a seat.

Amanda followed his lead. "Ms. Thompson, this is my partner, Detective Trent Stenson."

Clarissa nodded at him, but said nothing.

It was time to tell her... "Unfortunately, we have bad news about Reese—"

"I knew it!" Nadine wailed and leveled a glare at Amanda. "Why didn't you just tell me?"

Clarissa looked at her daughter. "Nadine, what are you talking—"

"Ms. Thompson, Reese's body was found tonight at the Rolling Hills Country Club in Manassas. Murder is suspected." Amanda would sidestep Clarissa's curiosity about the meaning behind Nadine's statement.

"She... she was...?" Clarissa's eyes blanked over, and she appeared stoic.

"I'm deeply sorry for your loss," Amanda said.

Nadine continued shooting daggers at Amanda.

"I needed to tell your mother first, Nadine." Amanda spoke softly, hoping the girl would understand one day.

"I just knew it was her." Nadine got up and stomped off in the direction of her bedroom.

Clarissa's mouth was gaping open and shut, open and shut. Her eyes were blinking slowly, her lashes wet. "What happened to my baby girl?"

Amanda's heart sank. No mother should have to hear the grisly details.

"Please, tell me. And do you know who did this to her?" In this moment, Clarissa appeared stark sober, accepting and allowing the news to enter in, but Amanda knew from experience it was surface level. It took much longer for true acceptance to set in.

"It's uncertain yet, but it appears that she was strangled." Amanda stuck with the basics. "It's still early in the investigation, but I assure you we will do all we can to find out who did this."

"I can't believe this... We just had a fight, she stormed out. I figured I'd see her again." She was speaking robotically as her mind and heart tried to process the news.

"We're both very sorry for your loss." Amanda repeated the sentiment, hating how those words, even spoken with genuine compassion, fell flat and shallow for the good they accomplished.

"I don't know how I'm ever going to get through this." Clarissa crossed her arms and rubbed them.

"It will take time," Amanda offered softly. She didn't want to warn her this moment would come to define the rest of her life. That the best she could hope for was it would eventually hurt a *little* less.

"You've lost a child?" Clarissa snapped, eyes narrowed, her tone skeptical and biting.

"Yes. My six-year-old daughter, Lindsey."

"Oh." Clarissa's mouth twitched. "Sorry for your loss too."

"Thank you." Amanda could have pointed out Lindsey had died years ago but to what end?

"I should have known something happened. She was gone for days. I just wanted to keep positive. Little good that did." Clarissa hugged herself and rocked back and forth.

Amanda joined her on the couch.

"How would you like your coffee, Ms. Thompson?" Trent asked.

"Two sugars, a splash of cream."

Trent left the room, and Amanda turned to Clarissa, her heart pounding.

Clarissa met her gaze, her pain so fresh and raw, and a tear fell down her cheek. "Please find who did this to her."

"Here you go." Trent handed Clarissa her coffee.

"Thanks." Clarissa took the steaming mug and blew on it before taking a sip.

Trent bobbed his head at Amanda. "I'll go get Nadine."

Amanda stayed next to Clarissa, soaking up what she could of the woman's grief. Though at the same time she erected a barrier to protect her own heart and emotions. She hated how her past possessed the power to come back with scolding potency, but feared what it might mean if it ever stopped.

Trent returned with Nadine, and the poor girl was a mess. She was still in a dress, but her makeup had dissolved with tears, her eyes puffy and cheeks red.

"Here you go, sweetheart." Amanda relinquished her spot on the couch next to Clarissa so mother and daughter could be together.

Nadine dropped down, and mother and daughter hugged.

Amanda and Trent took to the chairs they'd been seated in before. She allowed a few minutes to pass before she spoke. "Trent and I need to ask a few questions before we leave. You going to be all right for that?" She posed it as a question, but the answer wasn't exactly multiple choice. This investigation got moving in earnest the second Reese was discovered in that restroom.

"We'll push through... For Reese." Clarissa snatched a tissue from the table next to the couch and blew her nose. She then reached for Nadine's hand and held it.

"I need you to run us through the last time you saw Reese. What was the fight about, what led up to it?" It would be a painful journey for Clarissa to take, but it was necessary.

"Uh, sure. Reese's prom dress came in, but she was angry at

me for leaving it to the last minute." Clarissa clamped her mouth shut, her face contorting as if fending off a bout of tears. "But I work full-time to keep a roof over her head. It's not always set hours."

"Where do you work?" Trent inserted, his notepad and pen at the ready.

"McDougall's. It's an auto insurance company. I cover the front desk. It's a reliable paycheck, and a decent wage, but they expect their employees to drop everything in their personal lives if there's an overload."

"And that made it so you couldn't pick up her dress earlier than Wednesday?" Amanda asked.

Clarissa nodded.

Amanda found it hard to believe that was the argument that triggered Reese storming out of the house, but teenagers were stereotypically volatile. "And that's all?"

A deep breath. "She gave me the spiel about being eighteen now, 'a legal adult', she said. I, of course, kicked back that as long as she lives under my roof, I make the rules."

"What was she wanting permission for?" Amanda had done her share of pushing her mother at that age too. It was like as soon as the calendar flipped to her eighteenth birthday any existing independent streak took on a life force of its own.

"She wanted to stay at a hotel with Adrian and threw it in my face that she wasn't a virgin anyway. But I said no. Put my foot down." She bit her bottom lip and more tears fell.

It would seem, despite her fight with Adrian and freezing him out, Reese had planned to forgive him.

"And that's when she stormed out?" Trent angled his head.

Bless his ignorance for not knowing the plights of a teenage girl, though he should have had a front-row seat with his two sisters. Then again, boys were preoccupied with themselves at a young age too. Some never pushed past it.

"Yeah. She said she never wanted to see me again." Clarissa

collapsed onto herself, and Nadine put a hand on her mother's back and rubbed it soothingly.

Amanda turned her attention to Nadine, who was crying silently. To think all this had started because of a boy and a teenager asserting her independence. If only Reese had been accepting of her mother's decision. "Nadine, did your sister usually react this strongly when it came to Adrian?"

"She usually did whatever she wanted."

"I put a curfew in place for the prom," Clarissa clarified. "That's what really got the ball rolling."

"Okay, but we understand that Reese has run away before. Is that right?" Amanda briefly glanced at Nadine but settled her gaze on Clarissa.

"She was always back by nightfall."

"Then this type of behavior was different for her?" Trent asked.

"Yes."

It might not mean anything more than a teen demanding freedom, but it could indicate other possible issues. "Did Reese change in any other ways? Did she become withdrawn or more outspoken?"

Nadine shook her head. "My sister always let me in. She was my best friend." The girl's voice cracked on that admission, and a spike of grief stabbed Amanda's heart.

"Ms. Thompson, do you agree?" Trent prompted.

"Yes. And she was no more outspoken or rebellious than usual."

Reese could have gotten into drugs or in with a bad crowd. "Did Reese recently make new friends, start hanging out with different people than she used to?"

Nadine shook her head. "Not that I know of."

"Me either," Clarissa agreed.

Amanda would still make a mental note to ask about this when speaking with Reese's friends, classmates, and teachers.

With that thought, the mystery man Ava had pointed out came flooding back. They needed to find out who he was and why he was at the prom. "Do you know where Reese would typically go after one of your arguments?"

"I assumed to one of her friends. You have their information, I believe."

"Yes. Laurel, Hailey, and Ella?" Amanda prattled off, and the woman nodded. "We know about Prince William Forest Park. Anywhere else she liked to go and hang out?"

"She liked to rollerblade and rock climb."

Amanda didn't know of any facilities offering that in Dumfries. "Where did she do those activities?"

"Rock n Rollerblade and Summit Climb, both in Manassas. I'd let her take my car," Clarissa responded.

"And she'd blade around the neighborhood too," Nadine added.

Trent looked up from his notepad. "Did she follow a regular route?"

"I guess." Nadine told them she'd go a few blocks north and then west and around back home.

Amanda would get officers out to canvass the area. "When she left here Wednesday night, did she have her Rollerblades?"

Nadine shook her head.

That still didn't mean that Reese hadn't followed her rollerblading route.

"Just to clarify, Nadine," Trent started, "did your sister have a set time of day she'd skate around the neighborhood?"

"Don't think so. Just when it struck her."

"And what about going up to Manassas to the rink or for climbing, any regularity there?" If so, the killer could have caught on to Reese's routine.

"Uh-huh. They'd go up Friday nights for skating, and Saturday afternoons for climbing," Clarissa said, and then added Fridays about seven to ten, and Saturdays about two until four.

"And who are *they*?" Amanda asked.

"Her group of friends. The three you mentioned, plus Adrian, probably a few of his friends," Clarissa said.

"And after the climbing, did the group do something else?" It seemed apparent they must have, as they only climbed until four in the afternoon.

Clarissa's gaze dipped to her lap, guilt oozing from her. "I should have made her account for how she spent more of her time."

"As a mother we do the best we can," Amanda offered. "And no matter how hard we try, there's no way we can know our children's every step. What happened to her isn't your fault; it lies with the person who killed her. No one else." She felt the need to stress that point as Clarissa shook with a heaving sob.

"Thank you for saying that. I hope to believe you one day." She let go with a fresh round of sobbing.

"Forgive me for saying this, but your daughter was in good shape, and it seems like she was active with the rock climbing and blading. Was she a member of any gym or fitness center?" Trent asked.

"No. Nothing so rigid. She was eighteen. Weight's easy to keep off then."

Amanda shrunk a bit as the woman leveled a gaze at her, which had her feeling a touch self-conscious. Even though she knew she had nothing to worry about in the weight department. She was only fifteen pounds heavier than when she'd married Kevin, and she could have stood to gain that weight anyhow. But she was blessed with her father's fast metabolism. "Did Reese have any enemies or people who didn't like her?"

"Haters?" Nadine said and nodded. "Everyone wanted to be her. Those who couldn't live up to her were jealous."

When Amanda had first asked, Nadine had clung to

Reese's popularity. To protect herself from the implication or the result of how Amanda had phrased the question?

"Do you have any names for us?" Trent countered.

"Makayla Mann for starters."

"The runner-up queen," Amanda said, recalling the name.

"Uh-huh, and then there's..." Nadine prattled off about ten names, and Trent vigorously scribbled in his notepad.

For an investigation that was just getting started, they already had a lot of potential suspects.

EIGHTEEN

Amanda and Trent left Clarissa and Nadine and headed for the other Thompson—Melvin, Reese's father. They'd asked that mother and daughter refrain from calling ahead to inform him about Reese. Given the man's pale complexion when she and Trent delivered the news, Amanda would say they'd honored that request.

"She's really dead?" Melvin's voice strained with every word, and his eyes were bloodshot. When he'd answered the door, he'd had a rocks glass in hand, amber liquid up a finger's width, and a stagger to his walk. It wasn't his first drink of the night. Amanda wondered if he was drinking because he'd been worried about his daughter too or for another reason. Then again, some people didn't even need an excuse.

Amanda and Trent had corralled him to his living room and informed him once they got him seated.

"I'm afraid so, Mr. Thompson," Amanda said. "My partner and I are very sorry for your loss."

A subtle nod, nothing more than a mere acknowledgment. Though Amanda appreciated the words were powerless to right anything.

"And she was murdered? Who does that to a kid? She..." He clamped his mouth shut, his emotions obviously warring between hurt and rage.

"We will do our best to find who is responsible and hold them accountable," she said.

"You better," he snapped. "Sorry, I just... Wow, all this is quite a shock." He rubbed his forehead.

"I can imagine," she empathized. "We have a few questions for you before we leave."

"Whatever I can do to help." He shook his head as if to fend off a headache.

"We're trying to figure out your daughter's last moves," Amanda began. "We know she left home at five in the evening on Wednesday after an argument with her mother."

Melvin's face tightened and shadowed, as the devil danced in his eyes. "Clarissa," he hissed.

"The fact your daughter is dead is no one's fault but the person who did this," Amanda said, coming to Clarissa's defense. "When did you last see Reese?"

"I usually see the girls about once a month. But don't mention this to Clarissa, please. I know she already badmouths me to my girls enough."

"Unless it becomes relevant to the investigation, there's no need to tell her," Amanda said.

"Thank you. And don't think I don't have regrets. I should have fought harder to remain full-time in their lives. I pretty much just let Clarissa take custody—it was easier that way."

For you maybe... After a few beats, Amanda asked, "We know about the rink and rock-climbing venue in Manassas, as well as Prince William Forest Park, but do you know of anywhere else she liked to hang out?"

"No."

"What about any place you took Reese when she was a

young girl?" She might have retreated to a spot where she had been happy in the past.

"Just that park you mentioned. She loved the spinner... you know that thing that..." He circled a finger.

"The carousel?" Trent wagered a guess.

"That's it. I'd push her on that thing for hours when she was a girl."

Reese hadn't just loved the park, but had an emotional tie to it. Also impossible to dismiss was her phone had been found along the river there—but who had tossed it and when?

"Do you have any idea who might have done this to her?" Melvin asked.

"We are exploring several avenues, but the investigation is still young," Amanda told him. "A few more questions, and we'll be out of your way. Did anyone have issues with Reese that you were aware of?"

"I don't, but as I said, my girls are practically strangers to me."

"Even though you see them every month," Trent interjected.

"It's not like we gabbed for hours on end, but I did know about Reese being voted prom queen. She was so excited about it that she made a special trip here just to tell me."

"Can you see her tossing her phone away?" Amanda asked.

"No way. The girl lived on that thing."

Which seems to be the consensus... It seemed more likely the killer had discarded it in the Potomac. But for what purpose? To muddy the investigation? And had Reese's excitement about being crowned prom queen have her telling anyone who would listen? It was obvious that whoever had killed her, posing her how and where they did, had that knowledge. "When did she tell you?"

"Earlier this month. A Friday afternoon. I remember

because I'd just come home from the job ready to put my feet up."

"Was that the last time your daughter was here?" Amanda asked.

Melvin nodded, pinched the tip of his nose.

"Could she have come over when you weren't here?" Amanda was thinking Reese might have come here after storming out on her mother.

"I suppose."

"Did she try calling you?"

"No."

"Was it common for Reese to run here after fights with her mother?" Trent asked.

"I guess she did a couple of times when she was younger."

It was frustrating sitting here, hoping that Melvin would give them one strong lead. The list of potential suspects was long. If they were going to find justice for Reese it needed to be narrowed down. It might help if Amanda could settle on a motive, but she was curious what Melvin might have to say about the boyfriend. "Reese was seeing a boy from her school—"

"Adrian..." He snapped his fingers. "I can't remember his last name."

"Savage," Amanda provided. "So you know him?"

"He's been here before with Reese. Seems like a nice enough kid."

"Do you think he'd have any reason to hurt Reese?" Trent asked, stepping in.

"I wouldn't think so. They seemed happy together. And besides, I can't see him even hitting her, let alone..."

As for the *happy together* bit, Amanda knew otherwise. "I spoke with Adrian yesterday when I was asking around, trying to find Reese. He made it sound like he planned to break things off with her." She presented it with an air of uncertainty to soften the blow.

"Then I really don't see why he'd have reason to kill her."

"Reese might have held something over him. Not saying that's the case, simply a possibility." She and Trent might revisit the teen and get a better feel for whether he fit as a suspect or not. Amanda stood and took out her business card. "Again, we're very sorry for your loss. This has my information. Call me anytime."

"Sure thing."

At the door, Amanda turned back to say to Melvin, "You have time to fix things with Nadine... that practically strangers thing."

Melvin blew out a breath, letting his cheeks inflate as he did so, and nodded.

Back in the department car, Trent was the first to speak.

"Do you really think it's the boyfriend?"

"Probably not, but he's one of many possibilities."

"There was a lot of evident hate—the glued lips, the stabbed eyes..."

"Seemingly dramatic and over the top? That's not at all how most teenagers could be described." Despite the ugliness of this case hanging over her, she smiled at the sarcasm of her statement.

Trent smiled too. "True enough, but I didn't think we seriously pegged teens for the murder."

"I didn't think we completely ruled them out."

It was one fifteen Sunday morning as Trent set the car in the direction of Manassas. At least their efforts couldn't help but get them closer to Reese's killer—and that was all the fuel Amanda needed to keep going.

NINETEEN

The lot at Rolling Hills Country Club was empty save a few vehicles. The officers must have finished taking everyone's information and statements. Amanda was curious why she hadn't received a message from Officer Cannon about that man by the food table. She had specifically asked that after he was questioned his information be sent directly to her.

Cannon was coming out of the club as she and Trent were headed in. "I never received the info on that man," she said to him, wishing she'd just taken the time to question him herself. Not that she had any second to spare. She'd been in a hurry to consult with Rideout and then had to serve notification to the Thompsons. She hoped she hadn't made a grave error in judgment by demoting the importance of speaking to him.

"Oh, yes. I apologize." Officer Cannon pulled out his notebook and flipped pages until he landed on what he was after. "Here it is. Name's Clifford McIntosh. He's a substitute teacher at the high school."

Ava hadn't recognized the man, but Amanda supposed she wouldn't know all the substitute teachers. "Did he say what grades?"

"Grades eleven and twelve."

"And why was he at the prom?" Trent asked.

"Said he had volunteered as a chaperone."

Amanda turned to Trent. "We'll need to talk to the guy and get a feel for him."

"The guy seemed on the up-and-up to me. I really don't think he's anyone to concern yourself with," Cannon said.

"Thanks." She bit back saying, *Let us be the judge of that.*

"Okay, good night." Cannon carried on his way toward the lot.

"A substitute teacher," Amanda said. "He'd have presumably known Reese was voted prom queen."

"True enough."

"We'll talk to him, along with the cleaner Susie Valentine. Right now, I want to speak with the club's manager."

"Figured that was our next stop." Trent got the door and held it for Amanda.

The clubhouse felt dark and cold, with the tangible silence and heaviness that accompanied death. When they had left it had been masked by the chaos and everyone's energies.

Officer Wyatt stepped through the ballroom doors into the lobby and approached them. "You've probably figured it out, but mostly everyone's been sent home. The manager's still here, though, for you to speak with."

"Wonderful. Thank you," Amanda told him. "Could you take us to the manager? Vince Galloway, correct?"

"That's right. And sure. This way." Wyatt tucked back into the ballroom with Amanda and Trent following. The room had been cleared out except for clean-up staff and a good-looking man in his fifties. Oval face, gray eyes, with a trimmed beard and mustache. "Mr. Galloway," Wyatt said, getting the man's attention, "this is Detective Steele and her partner, Detective Stenson. They have some questions for you."

Vince danced his gaze over the two of them. "I answered a lot already."

"And your cooperation is greatly appreciated, but we need to speak with you. Some of what we ask might seem repetitive," Amanda started. "But I'm sure you'll agree that's of little consequence considering the situation."

"I suppose. I just can't believe this happened here."

It was sad to think Vince's comment didn't refer to the act itself, rather the location of where it had taken place—on his turf. Amanda motioned to Wyatt that she and Trent would take it from here. "We were told that the club's doors were locked to the public from five until six thirty tonight," she said. "Is that correct?"

"Correct. That allows time for the cleaning staff to give the place a once-over."

"Is that standard when the club is hosting evening events?" Trent asked.

"It is."

Predictability left cracks for evil to slip through. Amanda made a note of the procedure in her phone's memo app. "Is it always the same staff on duty for big events?"

He shook his head. "The staff is on rotation."

"Any other repeatable patterns that were followed?" she asked.

"Not that I can think of."

"What about security protocols?" Trent inserted. "Do club staff have keys for the club?"

"Some do. Yes."

"We'll need the names of those who do." Riddle one was figuring out how the killer had gotten Reese into that restroom. Two, was ascertaining when.

Vince prattled off a few names, including Susie Valentine. He'd inadvertently teed up Amanda's desired course for the conversation. "How long has Ms. Valentine been an employee here?"

"Ten years, thereabouts."

"Always as a cleaner?" Not to imply there was anything wrong with that vocation. It was just that so many clambered to climb the ladder to earn a fancy title and receive the fat paycheck that went along with it. Though Amanda suspected advancement within the janitorial field might not be so illustrious.

"That's right. She's a valued employee and a diligent worker."

Given the cleaning log, it placed Susie Valentine in the restroom before the discovery. Of course that didn't mean someone else—the real killer—hadn't slipped in with Reese's body. Circumstantial evidence placed Susie Valentine in the frame, but she didn't feel like the ideal fit. Her size as described by Lisa Bradford, but also what was the personal tie? How would Susie know about Reese being prom queen and, from there, decide on this elaborate display? And now, Vince described Susie as a reliable, long-term employee. That made it hard to reconcile that she'd drop the body off where she worked. Still Susie deserved a closer look. "Do you have surveillance video inside and outside the premises?"

"We do."

"Directed toward the restrooms?"

"No, outside—front and back—and inside the pro shop directed toward the counter."

The shop was located several feet from the restrooms, but the camera may have caught something. Better to have the footage and not need it, than the other way around. "Okay, we'll need everything you have."

"From all of the cameras?"

"If that's not going to be a problem," she countered.

"For when?"

The most logical would be anywhere from four until six thirty. This would allow time for the killer to get Reese inside the building, then into the restroom. But it was possible Reese had been hidden on the premises for hours before being taken out and posed. Not a new thought but a complication, nonetheless. "The last twenty-four hours should be more than enough. But could we watch the video from the shop from earlier this evening between four and six thirty right now?"

"Unfortunately that's not possible."

"Why not?" Trent asked.

"Security is handled by a third-party company off premises. The feeds transmit there where they are also monitored."

Technological advances were good and bad when security personnel didn't need to be on site. "Their name?"

"Protect It."

"Out of Washington." Amanda knew the company as she and Trent had crossed paths with them during the investigation into the murder of Zoe's parents. Protect It had covered their family home.

"That's them. I take it you've heard of them?"

"We have." She was disappointed that their viewing of the footage would be delayed. Surely one of the feeds would show something useful—unless they were searching for a poltergeist. "Were you here between five and six thirty?"

"I had slipped out for a personal errand and returned just after six. I was here when they found..." He rolled his hand in obvious avoidance of saying something like *the dead girl*. "I was kind of responsible for it."

Amanda stiffened.

"Oh, not for the death. I just mean I had Lisa check the restroom, and that's when she found the girl."

"Did you notice anything or anyone that stood out to you?" The question was a long shot.

"The officer asked me that too. I can't think of a thing."

"Did you know Reese Thompson?" Amanda asked for due diligence.

"Never heard her name before."

Amanda fished out her phone and brought up Reese's photograph. She held her screen for Vince.

He shook his head.

"If something in your memory jogs after we leave, call me." She handed him her card.

"I will. Am I cleared to go home now?"

"You are," she told him.

"I hope you find who did this to that girl... Reese."

Makes two of us. Amanda didn't say the words out loud.

"I can call Protect It right now." Trent had his phone out as they headed back to the lobby.

"Go ahead and give it a try, but don't be surprised if they request a warrant."

He pushed on his phone's screen and then held it to his ear. As he spoke to the security company, her mind processed what little they knew. Self-chastisement often crept up at some point, but she always managed to bat it away with logic. The murders they investigated were no fault of hers. Typically by the time she and Trent were brought in, it was too late to save anyone. Their job became sorting through the aftermath to find justice and bring closure to loved ones. Same applied to Reese. Amanda didn't have a chance to save the girl. As Rideout had said, she was dead at least twenty-four hours ago —long before Amanda had even heard of her. In fact, she'd just been going about her life. And that might be what stung the most—while she was oblivious, Reese was suffering. But that was a cruel mind game that would claim her sanity if she let it.

"They want a signed warrant before they'll part with the footage," Trent said, still holding his phone.

"Wish that surprised me."

"And I quickly checked my email. The signed warrant for Reese's phone records is there from Anderson."

"Okay, good. We'll get it forwarded to the service provider. And another warrant request to Anderson. Before we go to Central though, I want to speak with Clifford McIntosh and Susie Valentine."

"Not a problem, but it is three fifteen in the morning now."

"I know, but it can't be helped. Both are possible suspects, no matter how thin the evidence against them."

He met her gaze but didn't say anything. She surmised he was thinking that their running themselves off their feet wouldn't bring justice any faster. And there was a point to that. Science proved an exhausted mind wasn't good at reasoning and solving puzzles. But how could she go home knowing that Clarissa and Nadine Thompson were currently in a living hell? To add more pressure, she knew they were relying on her to bring in Reese's killer.

She threw up a hand. "What are we supposed to do, Trent? Go home, get some sleep? Because right now I'm not sure I'd even get any." The image of Reese sitting on the toilet, the thick chain around her neck, her stabbed eyes and glued lips... She pinched her eyes shut hoping to eradicate the recollection, but it clung on tight.

"I know."

"All right. Let's get moving then. One of us goes back to Central and handles the paperwork. The other goes to speak with Susie Valentine and Mr. McIntosh."

"Huh, why don't I like the sound of that? Oh, because one of them might be the killer we're looking for?"

"See the importance of speaking with them?" she volleyed back.

"Yes."

"And I'm not going home until at least these four things are knocked off." She ran through them in her tired mind again, the paperwork submitted for a warrant, the approved one forwarded to the cell phone service provider, and visits to McIntosh and Valentine.

"All right then. Neither am I."

"Good to hear it." That was one thing she'd learned a long time ago about Trent; he was reliable. He had her back and was eager to follow any lead through to its conclusion, whether it netted a reward or not.

A quick look in the department vehicle's onboard computer told them Valentine lived in Manassas and McIntosh was in Woodbridge.

Trent got them on the road, and as they left Rolling Hills Country Club, Amanda's mind was a tangle of thoughts. Ones not just of Reese, but of Amanda's niece and Kristen, of Clarissa, Nadine, and Melvin Thompson, and of little Zoe.

My little Zoe.

She'd text the friend's mother to check in if it wasn't so late, but no news was typically good news. Besides, Zoe would be home in less than twelve hours, and Amanda would be there to welcome her—come hell or high water. This was Zoe's first sleepover at a friend's—a huge deal—and Amanda wanted to hear all about her daughter's adventures. She desired to follow the example her own father had set. He'd been police all of Amanda's life, but he'd never used his badge as an excuse to be absent from his children's celebrations and graduations or sporting events, such as her brother's football games.

"Here's the deal. We'll take care of this and see where it takes us, but regardless of the outcome, I'll need to at least pop home at noon tomorrow." Just the thought of hugging her daughter gave her fuel to keep going.

"You mean today?"

"Yeah." *Where does the time go?*

Trent looked over at her, confusion briefly dulling his eyes before they lit. "Right, this was Zoe's first sleepover weekend, wasn't it?"

"It was." She mentioned it to Trent every day this past week but was still touched that he remembered. Honestly, she was more worked up and anxious about it than Zoe had been. She'd never gotten this far with Lindsey, having lost her before she was old enough for sleepovers. And while Zoe had spent a night here or there with Libby DeWinter, her "aunt", this was the first for back-to-back nights at a friend's place. Amanda was finding it a little hard letting go.

"Yeah, you'll need to get the scoop. We'll work around it." He smiled at her before putting his focus straight ahead again.

As she watched the headlights dance on the pavement, her vision blurred, and again her mind wandered.

Who did this to you, Reese Thompson?

TWENTY

According to the background they pulled on Susie Valentine, Amanda was expecting a woman in her early fifties with dark hair to answer the door. All the lights were out—not a surprise given the hour. But the vehicle in the driveway was registered to her, so presumably she was home, but she must sleep like the dead.

Amanda pounded on the door again.

"I'll try her number." Trent took out his phone and did that.

Amanda heard Susie's voicemail answer. "*Leave a message...*"

Trent hung up without leaving one. "She might have her ringer off for bedtime."

"She could." Amanda didn't like the timing of Susie's seeming disappearance though. After all, she was the last on record in the restroom where Reese's body had been found. "We'll come back in the morning."

"Not sure what other option we have. We can't force our way inside, and she might not even be home. She might have been picked up by a friend and went out, stayed over..."

"*Or* Susie Valentine was involved with Reese's murder. She

left before the discovery, taking off before police had a chance to talk to her."

"Except her car is here." Trent gestured to the dark blue sedan.

"Yet, it doesn't seem she is."

"Right, but as you said, she'd have to be pretty stupid as her name is on record for us to see when she was in that restroom."

"Yeah, dumbest criminal ever. But still." She didn't relish leaving and coming back, but they didn't have any other recourse. "Let's hit our next stop."

They got back into the department car and headed to Clifford McIntosh's residence in Woodbridge. His background didn't show a criminal record—neither had Valentine's. All that meant was neither had gotten caught for anything illegal.

The teacher answered the door to his apartment after the second knock. He was wearing a cotton robe and slippers.

"What is it?" His brow was scrunched up, his eyes slits.

Amanda held up her badge, as did Trent next to her.

"We're Detectives Steele and Stenson. We'd like to come in and ask you a few questions."

"Ah, sure." He opened the door wider and stepped back. "Something to drink? Coffee or water?" His eyes were growing more alert with each passing second, and while coffee sounded heavenly to Amanda it wasn't practical. Once the paperwork was taken care of, they'd need to salvage a few hours' sleep. Caffeine wouldn't help with that endeavor.

"No, thank you," she told him. "And we won't be long."

"Sure." He took them to his living room, which was beside the entrance.

Once they were all seated, Amanda spoke first, starting from the beginning. "Why were you at the prom tonight?"

"I did give a statement to Officer Cannon. Did he not pass this along to you?"

"He did, and I was remiss not to let you know that some of

our questions might seem repetitive to you," she started, "but if you'd indulge us..."

"All right. Well, I was there in the capacity of chaperone. I sub for teachers who call in sick or who are out on maternity leave for the senior grades at Potomac High."

"Do you know a Reese Thompson?" Amanda asked.

"Do I?" He shook his head and was obviously aggravated at the mention of the name. "That girl was a thorn in my side. Popular kids usually are."

Trent's facial features sharpened, and his mouth curved downward. "So you didn't have a good relationship with her?"

"Relationship? That's stretching things. She was a student, in a class, I'd sometimes teach. That's all. Please don't imply anything improper." A crease formed between his eyebrows, insulted.

Amanda doubted that Trent had meant his words to carry that accusation, but she understood why Clifford might be sensitive and made that leap. "I don't believe that was the intention. My partner was simply building off what you said about her being a thorn in your side. How was that exactly?"

"She and her friends would pass notes and chuckle every time I turned my back."

"Do you think they were making fun of you?" Trent asked.

"Quite certain of it."

The substitute teacher was a large man, not exactly muscular, but not entirely flab. He had a definite pear shape though, a balding head, and a bit of a limp to his walk. Teens would find his appearance something worth picking on. But had their murmurings been enough to push Clifford McIntosh to murder? She had no doubt he'd have the strength required to subdue Reese, wield that thick chain, and strangle her. To go to the other extremes—the stabbed eyes, the glued mouth—for some teenage jabs seemed a stretch. Still, she asked, "How did that make you feel when she and her friends poked at you?"

Clifford tugged on his robe, pulling it even more securely across his legs. "Why are you asking about Reese Thompson?"

She'd have assumed anyone would have put that answer together given the circumstances, so either Clifford was playing dumb, or he was... a little slow. Most of all she didn't care for his avoidance of her question. "How did it make you feel?" she repeated in a firm tone.

"Like crap. I know I'm not the most handsome man on the planet, but I'm not the homeliest either. And at the end of the day, they were just teens. They're wired to pick on anyone who's different."

"So it was just harmless fun they were having at your expense," Trent said.

"How I saw it."

"You really were all right with it?" Amanda asked.

"I never said I was all right with it, but I put it into perspective. You need a thick skin to be a high-school teacher—especially a substitute. And it's not like I had to deal with them on a regular basis."

Amanda considered that, balancing it with the evidence. Reese's crime scene had spoken to a lot of pent-up hatred—but that might have been sparked from past experience spilling over, not even necessarily directly relating to Reese herself. Why would Clifford risk lifetime imprisonment when walking away from the teens was an option? Though she did have another matter to discuss before she and Trent left. "After the girl's body was found, you were heard whistling a happy tune... In the men's restroom off the ballroom."

"Not me. I can't whistle." Clifford puckered his lips together and blew. His cheeks puffed out, but that's about it. His technique was all wrong. "And even if I could, why would I whistle a happy tune? A teenage girl was dead, murdered violently, if the rumors going around were to be believed." He peered into her eyes as if expecting her to confirm what he'd heard.

With the reminder that the rumors circulating were of a violent murder, she was thinking that a person whistling a happy tune was more suspect than she first gave it credit for. Only a psychopath or the killer—one and the same?—would be cheery at a time like that.

"Detectives, why are you really asking me these things? I'd wager a guess, but it's probably best if you just tell me."

Trent looked at Amanda, and she blinked consent for him to field this one.

"Reese Thompson was the girl who was found in the restroom at the Rolling Hills Country Club," he said.

"It was... *She* was... ah...?" He rubbed his throat, running his hand repeatedly over his Adam's apple.

"Where were you Friday, Mr. McIntosh?" Trent asked, his notepad cradled in one hand, his pen dangling in the other.

"I spent the day with my mother."

"All day, including seven until nine in the evening?" That would specifically cover the time-of-death window.

"Yes. She's in a home and suffers from Alzheimer's. She doesn't know who I am more than half the time, but I'm all she has. I try to spend as much time with her as I can... Dinner and a movie on Friday nights." He paused, his bottom lip trembling. "Truth is we never know how long any of us have."

Sad, sad, truth. But it made every minute count even more. "We'll need her name and the name of the home she's in."

Clifford gave them both, and Trent scribbled away in his notepad.

They'd firm up his alibi and ask around more about him, get a true feel for Clifford McIntosh, but Amanda didn't think he killed Reese. She certainly believed his little performance a moment ago. He couldn't whistle. And he had a valid reason to be at the prom. They'd talk to the principal at Potomac High just to confirm though. But his telling them about Reese being problematic seemed genuine. Amanda would push just a little more, feel out his sincerity. "When you stepped in for Reese's class, did you ever witness anyone who had an obvious dislike for her?"

"I actually stood in for her class this past week. And I hate to point a finger at any kid, but Makayla Mann was shooting her daggers from across the room."

"Makayla, the runner-up prom queen?" Not the first time her name came up, but the logistics were hard to assemble. It may just be they didn't have all the pieces yet. But would she possess the power to strangle Reese with the thick chain, assuming it was the murder weapon? Where would she have killed her? And how could she have carted Reese's dead body around?

"I'm not saying Makayla had anything to do with this, but I'd start with her."

"She was just shooting daggers at her, though?" Trent started. "Anything else?"

"Not that I saw. Though I got the sense there were a lot of pranks being pulled back and forth between Makayla's clique and Reese's."

Amanda nodded and stood, pulling out a card for him, and running through the regular spiel.

Back in the department car, Trent yawned and made no attempt to muffle it. Amanda smiled at the dramatics, thinking of her brother, Kyle, and how he'd often do the same thing as a kid. It used to piss her off, but that's what brothers were for—driving you crazy. As it sank in that she'd lined up her partner and brother on par, an easiness settled over her. Last year, she and Trent had shared one awkward moment. They'd crossed the professional line and kissed. But they'd decided to put it behind them and forget it even happened. There were times that hadn't been easy, but now it was evident Trent had returned to being her friend and partner—completely off limits. Such a very good breakthrough.

"It's almost time for bed," she said to offer some encouragement.

"If that's meant to be a pep talk, it stinks."

"Think of Reese's family, Trent. Let it push you through."

"I have been. That's how I got this far." He tapped the dash drawing attention to the time. 5:35 AM.

"Actually, you know what? Go home and catch some sleep. I'll get the paperwork together for the security video warrant. If you can forward the signed one for Reese's phone records, I'll get it to the service provider too."

"You sure?"

"Yes. I've got your back, partner." He'd always required more sleep than her. After losing her family, for a number of years she'd only reach dreamland with the aid of pills, but she'd also conditioned herself to need very little rest. Her mother often told her she ran on fumes—not far from the truth.

"I appreciate it. I'm starting to see double and—"

"Maybe I should drive us back to Central."

"I'll be fine."

She nodded, trusting that he'd get them to their destination safely. She might kick up more fuss if they weren't just a few blocks away.

As he drove, she spoke. "We'll verify his alibi and talk to the principal, but I don't think Clifford McIntosh is our killer."

"I didn't get that either."

"Though, it still leaves us with the happy whistler."

"Happy whistler?" He cocked an eyebrow and looked over at her.

She nudged her head toward the windshield. "Eyes stay on the road, please. Well, you saw him back there. Clifford doesn't know how to whistle. And who whistles a happy diddly—"

"Diddly?" He laughed.

"Just back off, would ya? It's going on six in the morning, and I've been up nearing twenty-four hours."

He lifted his hands.

"Back on..." She pointed at the steering wheel. "But in all seriousness, to be whistling a happy tune with all those rumors flying around about a murder...? It seems..." She searched for the right word and was blank.

"Macabre."

"That works."

Trent pulled into the lot for Central and turned the car off. "If we need to give this unknown person a moniker, let's just trim it down to the Whistler."

"Whatever works. Night, Trent."

"Night."

He headed to his Jeep Wrangler, and she entered the station. She checked her phone as she walked and saw a message from Logan. Sent around midnight.

Just going to tuck in. Hope you're safe out there. Xoxo

She smiled at the brevity of the message, not just the words. It didn't embed any pressure to get home or check in. There was just acceptance and support. Her job being responsible for him breaking things off with her in the past was a distant memory. And really, she could hardly blame him. A serial killer had targeted him because of her. But she and Logan were in a great spot now. Right where they were. She hated to think that things rarely stayed the same.

TWENTY-ONE

He hadn't slept this peacefully in years, and the morning's sun was blasting through the bay window. Its warmth kissed his skin as if he were being blessed by the universe for taking action. Finally, he'd stood in his full power and took control of his life. It was as if the clock had been reset and all wrongs reconciled and healed. He'd done it for his present and his future, but even more importantly, for his younger self. There was nothing to regret, but he wasn't stupid enough to think that he didn't have to look over his shoulder. He would need to watch his steps and play his next moves ever so carefully.

Today was his day off. It was to be one of rest that he had planned to spend in quiet reflection, savoring the last few days of sheer exhilaration. But he could still smell Reese with her coconut hair spray and lavender soap. At first the sensory memory disgusted him. To realize though that was all that was left of the teen settled his stomach again.

The only thing hanging in the air, inching toward him as an incoming storm was that nosy girl at the prom, the friend of Nadine Thompson's. He had followed her home last night, appreciating that despite the pants at prom, showcasing her independent streak, she was beautiful. She'd be accepted by her peers and was undoubtedly a breaker of hearts. And if she hadn't yet, it was simply a matter of time. The good-looking people always got their way and didn't think twice about trampling on those who fell short—perceived or real.

And while he had turned his story around and met with some financial successes, including buying a house, he hadn't reached his fullest potential. He certainly lived a lonely existence being unable to trust another human being. And all because of Staci—from high school. Her hatred and betrayal drove home that he was "less than" just for being true to himself. He hadn't even realized how much he was scarred until he heard Reese prattling on about being voted prom queen and how she'd beaten out "some loser" for the crown.

Maybe he'd look up Staci and set the past right.

But Staci's betrayal had taught him he would need to defend himself without relying on other people. Due to this, he'd focused inward and wielded what was within his power. He built his physical strength and even won several bodybuilding competitions. The awards were building up in pride of place in his home office. And he had a practical outlet for his brawn too, working now in construction and renovation.

It was because of taking employment with Gray's Building Projects that he knew his way around Rolling Hills Country Club. How interesting and amusing to look back and see how different parts of his life had aligned, laying out before him like a cosmic staircase of sorts. He just had to take the first step. And then the next would form ahead of him. And the next...

He flexed the battle ropes, lifting his arms up, down, up, down, up, down and sweat poured off him.

The resultant cardio high was like no other—or so he had thought. In the last few days he had discovered that killing was even more satisfying. Unmistakably therapeutic.

To think that he even had his next target...

He let go of the ropes and breathed in deeply, extending his arms overhead, as absolute bliss filled him. He whistled a nameless tune while thinking, *Little girl, little girl, I'm coming for you...*

TWENTY-TWO

Amanda's time with Logan was the only thing pure and good about the last twenty-four hours. She'd cling to that as she and Trent followed leads in the Reese Thompson case today. Her mind had her out of bed at eight thirty, after only two hours of sleep. She was careful not to wake Logan and left a note for him in the kitchen, telling him she'd be back before noon.

She pulled into the lot for Hannah's Diner, craving a fix. They had the best coffee Amanda had ever tasted. Just like remembering her time with Logan, it would also buoy her in the hours ahead.

The door chimed as she walked in, and former police sergeant Katherine Graves smiled at her from behind the counter. Even after a few months of Graves working at the diner, Amanda was still adjusting to seeing her there. The establishment was owned by May Byrd, and as it had turned out, Katherine was her estranged niece. When Malone had returned to work, Katherine left law enforcement to help her aunt at the diner. She seemed happy about her choice, even for working on a Sunday morning. It was a good arrangement for

May, who was in her sixties and could benefit from some time off.

"Hey, Amanda," Katherine said. "What can I get ya?"

Amanda was still adjusting to that aspect too—not just seeing her former sergeant behind the counter but to being the one giving her orders. "Extra-large black. Actually, make it two." She'd give one to Trent.

"Coming up right away." Katherine smiled, the expression touching her eyes. She certainly seemed happier working here than Amanda had known her to be while at the PWCPD.

Then again, Katherine was serving up coffee and breakfast, not trying to find who brutally murdered a teenage girl. Amanda imagined that she had to miss some aspects of the job though, specifically the happy endings when the bad guy wound up behind bars.

Amanda pulled her phone out and checked her messages. No approved warrant for the surveillance videos yet, in response to the paperwork she'd filed in the wee hours before heading home at six fifteen that morning. Nothing from the service provider this soon, but she hadn't expected a response yet. They usually took days. There was a text from Sergeant Malone saying he'd meet her at the station by nine, to which she replied, *I'm on the way now.*

Trent hadn't responded to the text she'd sent before leaving her house. It wasn't even showing as read. She fired off another one. *Heading into Central. Will I see you there?*

"Here you go." Katherine set the cups on the counter.

Amanda handed over some cash and shoved her phone back into a pocket.

"Working a case?" She pointed to Amanda's now empty hand.

"What gave me away?" Though it wouldn't be hard to piece together. It was 9 AM on a Sunday. If that wasn't enough, the request for two coffees would have been the tip-off.

"Well, good luck on catching the bad guy."

"Thanks." Amanda collected both cups from the counter and raised one in a toasting gesture.

The ten-minute drive to Central passed in a blur, and she was at her desk by nine fifteen. No sign of Trent, and he hadn't responded to her texts either. If he didn't show up soon, she'd get a start without him. She certainly wasn't going to sit around when there were things to do—speaking with Reese's classmates, starting with Makayla Mann, and Susie Valentine from the country club. Though she didn't think a single teen was behind the murder. It could be a few working together, even if that was somewhat inconceivable. But as the saying goes, all things are possible. There might also be a chance one of Reese's peers witnessed someone watching her from a distance.

Trent breezed into her cubicle. "Sorry I'm late."

"You lose your phone too?" She raised her brows. "I messaged you a few times."

"Oh, don't go there."

She remained quiet, but the silence screamed she *was* going there.

He sighed. "I was so tired when I got home, and I thought I'd plugged my phone in, but it turns out that the charger cable didn't actually get inserted so..."

"I can see how that's possible."

"Why thank you ever so much for your understanding," he replied sarcastically. "Did the warrant come through or the phone records?"

"I'm sure you can guess the answer, but I got you a coffee."

"You're a lifesaver," he said reaching for it. "Thank you."

"You got it. Malone should be here soon, and we'll brief him before we head out. I'd like to start with Makayla Mann. Her name's come up a couple of times now. She and Reese obviously had a rivalry going." She laid out her thinking to him.

"Works for me."

"I'm ready for that briefing." Malone swept by the opening to Amanda's cubicle, gesturing for them to follow.

Neither hesitated.

Malone dropped into the chair behind his desk, and she and Trent sat in the two that faced him.

They ran through the case thus far, telling him about the part-time teacher and Makayla Mann. They also said they had tried reaching Susie Valentine but hadn't met with success.

"Do you think a teenage girl is behind this brutality?" Malone scratched at his neatly groomed beard. "Possible, I guess, if she had help. And don't get on me for what I'm about to say, Amanda. But there are lots of hormones floating around at that age that can make a girl off-balanced, irrational."

She should be offended, but she remembered what it was like being a teenager. She'd certainly reacted stronger to situations than she would now. "You had two sons, so what would you know of— Oh." He was referring to what he'd witnessed with her and her sisters when they were teens.

"Right. So..." Malone pressed his lips.

"We're best to focus on possible motives to determine the strongest one," she said, returning to business. "Makayla didn't get the votes to make prom queen, whereas Reese did."

"Possible motive for the girl. Though we could be looking at something else entirely."

"I realize that. It's far too early in the investigation to pigeonhole it," she countered. "I would like to get officers out canvassing in the Thompson neighborhood."

"Around her home? Or her father's place?"

Amanda gave Malone's question some thought. "Both. Reese was at her father's at least once a month."

"It's not like I have a myriad of available officers, Steele. Manpower is rather limited."

"Start in the neighborhood where she lives."

"And what exactly are you hoping to accomplish with this?"

"Reese stormed from her home Wednesday. We need to know if anyone saw her. Possibly the direction she went or if she met up with anyone," Amanda said.

"All right. Makes sense."

"We also found out that Reese rollerblades around her neighborhood," Trent started. "She follows a particular route. It might be a good idea to have officers extend their canvassing to cover that area as well."

Malone rubbed the top of his head, over his thinning hair. "We'll do what we can."

"As we should. Reese was only eighteen with her entire life ahead of her." Amanda grieved for the young woman. There was so much she'd never get to experience, learn, see, become...

"As I'm well aware." Malone's tone held a touch of nip.

"Once they finish with those locations, they can ask around Melvin Thompson's place, even if just a few of the neighboring houses. He doesn't think that Reese showed up there Wednesday, but he was also working late. She could have showed and left. A neighbor might have seen something... *someone*."

"Fine, I'll send them over there too."

"Great."

Malone pointed a finger at her. "Hide that smirk, Steele. I only gave you your way because it all makes sense for the case."

"Of course. Why else?" Being the sergeant's friend had its perks, and intended or not, she was extended more liberties than her fellow detectives.

"And the autopsy? When is that taking place?" Malone asked.

"This morning. Trent and I are going to pop by at some point, probably this afternoon to discuss the ME's findings. And while we're in Manassas we'll follow other leads."

"The roller rink and the climbing wall place?"

She and Trent had told him about Reese's regular haunts when summarizing the case thus far. "That's right."

"All sounds good. Keep me posted if there are any more developments. But call my cell phone. After I get things worked out with the uniformed officer division, I'm heading home."

"There's actually something else you might be able to help with," Amanda said.

"And that would be?"

"Apply pressure on a judge to sign the warrant for video surveillance. I submitted the paperwork last night," she said.

"Don't you mean this morning?" Trent interjected.

Traitor. She nudged her elbow against his.

"Ah. Give people some time to read the request."

"So that's a yes you'll follow up?" She grinned, wishing in this moment she had dimples to really sell the ask.

"Yes."

She acknowledged with a dip of her head and led the way out of Malone's office.

Trent turned to her. "You know if I pushed the sarge like that, he'd eat me for breakfast."

"I know." There was nothing wrong with taking advantage of what a person had at their disposal. With that her mind slipped to Reese Thompson. The girl had a lot in her favor—good looks and popularity—but she also had a broken home. Her mother and father on opposite sides with her and Nadine in the middle. Amanda would see to getting that poor girl justice.

TWENTY-THREE

Amanda was at the address on file for Makayla Mann. She knocked, and a woman in her late thirties answered. Fine lines fanned out around her eyes, and she had a haggard look to her. Amanda held up her badge. "Detectives Steele and Stenson," she added, gesturing to Trent. "Mrs. Mann?"

"That's me."

They had pulled a brief background on the parents—Gloria and Rex Mann—both thirty-eight. "We'd like to speak with your daughter, Makayla."

"What about?"

"Pertaining to an open investigation, ma'am," Trent intercepted.

Gloria danced her gaze to Trent. "This have to do with that dead girl at the prom?"

Amanda swallowed back her irritation at Gloria's tone and for her downplaying the situation. She resisted the inclination to snap back with it had to do with the *murdered* girl, but there was no benefit in being snide. "It does."

"Come in." Gloria opened the door wide, stepping back and gesturing with a sweeping arm for them to enter. "Living room is the first door on the right. I'll get Makayla." The woman pivoted at her hip and yelled out her daughter's name.

Amanda and Trent wiped their shoes and slipped into the living room. It was painted with a minimalist's brush and presented a rather sterile environment for a home with a teenager. The couch, chairs, and walls were cream, and the room was accented with metal and splotches of red.

"Makayla!" Another roar by Gloria.

"I'm coming. Jeez, Mom, what the hell—"

"Watch your mouth." Gloria pointed a finger in her daughter's face.

Amanda saw this because she'd chosen a seat that gave her a line of sight to the doorway.

"What is it?" The question carrying on a sigh of exasperation.

"The police are here and want to talk to you."

"Why?"

"Let's go find out, shall we?"

The girl mumbled incoherently, but she entered the living room ahead of her mother.

"Makayla, we're detectives with the Prince William County PD. My name is Amanda Steele, and this is Trent Stenson." Amanda figured going with first names would help set the girl at ease. "We need to ask a few questions, if you'd like to take a seat."

"Sure...?" The girl looked at her mother as if for approval, and Gloria leveled her gaze at Amanda.

"Ask whatever you need to, but I'll be staying in the room."

Mother and daughter sat on the couch, each tucking tight against the arms. "We're not sure how much you know, Makayla," Amanda began, "but you likely heard there was a body found at the country club last night." She let that sit out there and read the girl's expression. It was no question that the rumor had reached her ears. But Amanda let the silence grow hoping it would encourage the girl to speak.

"I heard. Why are you here though?" The girl's complexion paled.

"Reese Thompson was the victim, strangled from what we can tell so far," Amanda said.

"Reese?" This from Gloria, mouth gaped open.

"Yes, ma'am," Amanda confirmed. "And from what my partner and I have been told, Reese and your daughter didn't get along very well. Is that correct?" She looked at Makayla.

"Well, I didn't kill her."

"The girls were best of friends," Gloria said as if struggling to grasp the news of Reese's murder.

"The best of friends?" Trent volleyed back.

Makayla scowled. "That was a *long* time ago."

A month was an eternity to a teenager. "How long ago?"

"In elementary school, but not since Potomac High."

"Was there a falling out between you?" Trent asked.

Gloria stiffened. "Are you here to accuse my daughter of murder?"

Trent held up a hand. "We're just asking some questions, Mrs. Mann."

"I ought to call in Rex's brother. He's a lawyer."

"Mom, please." Makayla rubbed her arms. "Reese thought she was too good for me after grade-eight graduation. Oh well. She changed into a complete—" She snapped her mouth shut, censoring what she really thought, but it was communicated without saying it. *Bitch*.

There certainly didn't seem to be any love lost when it came to Makayla's feelings toward Reese.

"Listen, I didn't like her, but I didn't hurt her."

"Sadly someone did more than that." Amanda thought it best to point that out.

"Well, it wasn't me!" Makayla spat. "She ruined prom for all of us."

Amanda bristled. As if Reese's fate had been of her choosing. But Makayla's strong outburst had revealed a nugget of truth—whoever had killed Reese not only hated her, but was smiting the prom itself. In the least the event had been postponed, that's if it wasn't being canceled altogether. She let the girl cool off, then asked, "When was the last time you saw Reese?"

"Wednesday at school. We got into it during class and were sent to detention. Which, of course, she lied her way out of."

"How so?" Amanda suspected they were about to be enlightened to another side of Reese.

"She said her younger sister was ill and her mother was working late, so she had to take her home from school. All a lie. Besides, Nadine's old enough to be alone."

Amanda and Trent may follow up with that, but it was unclear how that tidbit would get them closer to their killer. Then again, it was important to account for all of Reese's last moves. She noted that Trent was scribbling away in his notebook, possibly also seeing the relevance. They'd need to ask Clarissa Thompson when Reese got in from school on Wednesday. "How did you know it was a lie?"

"I saw Reese with Adrian through the window."

"What window?"

"The one where detention was held. She was on the school grounds, hanging all over him." Makayla rolled her eyes and shook her head. "She acted like he was awesome, but he's not that great of a guy."

Jealousy might be warping Makayla's view, but for now Amanda would play along. "What makes you say that?"

"He's a cheater. He was totally stepping out on Reese with Ella."

"And she is?" Trent angled his head.

"Supposed *friend* of Reese's." Makayla added finger quotes.

Amanda framed some questions in her mind, still unsure how the pieces fit together. Had Ella killed Reese to have Adrian for herself? People had murdered for less. But where would she have held Reese? That was an integral part of the riddle that needed an answer. It applied to any suspect, teenage or adult. But one theory that was just briefly considered was that Reese might have something she held over her boyfriend, Adrian. Could it have been she knew about the cheating but was able to blackmail him somehow, guilt him into staying with her? And if so, why? Just to avoid possible humiliation? "Do you know if Reese knew her boyfriend was cheating on her?"

"*Pft.* No way. She'd never put up with that crap. But she did deserve what she got."

Amanda bristled, at first taking that to mean Reese deserved to be murdered. Makayla at least realized how her words could be interpreted, and added, "Being cheated on, I mean," in a quiet voice.

"Why do you say that?" Trent asked, sounding leery as if he were stepping on a potential landmine.

"Ella had been with Adrian in grade eleven, but then Reese set her sights on him."

Most of the time Reese was cast in a favorable light—a popular teenager who was good to her younger sister. But there were smudges against that image. Amanda recalled the darker elements that Clifford McIntosh had mentioned of Reese's personality, specifically the pranking. "We heard that Reese and her friends and you and your friends would prank each other."

"Really? That's the best you have." Gloria was red-faced, and her forehead glistened with sweat. "My girl didn't do anything. Can't you leave now?" She started to tuck a strand of her daughter's hair behind an ear, but the girl pulled away and gave her mother a glare.

"We'll leave shortly. After all our questions are answered," Amanda said firmly. "Is it true that you pranked each other?"

"Sure, but Reese was an absolute witch." Makayla's eyes narrowed, full of rage.

Gloria turned to her daughter. "What did she do to you, baby?"

Makayla flinched at being called *baby* and pushed out her chin. "Earlier last week... on Monday, she slipped a box of apple juice under me just as I was taking a seat in the lunchroom. The thing burst open and... well, I looked like I'd pissed my pants." The girl's jaw tightened even more. "She and her friends laughed and pointed and called me a baby."

And her mother had just called her that... No wonder the strong reaction. The scene Reese had caused would have been humiliating. Then Reese beating Makayla for the title of prom queen would have added insult to injury.

"That's not even the worst of it." Her face scrunched up. "Can you believe that bitch broke into my locker and filled it with boxes of adult diapers? Yeah, I hated Reese, but I didn't kill her."

Amanda believed half of Makayla's claims—her hatred for Reese. "Where were you Friday evening between five and nine?" Amanda stretched the estimated time-of-death window.

Makayla remained silent, her eyes darting about the room.

"Answer her," Gloria prompted her daughter.

"I bowed out of class on Friday."

"You what?" Gloria gasped.

"Mom, don't get up in my face. It's not like you didn't skip class a million years ago."

Gloria's mouth tightened.

"And where did you go?" Amanda asked.

"Just hung out at friend's and went for ice cream. Nothing really exciting. Then popped home."

"You lied to my face when I asked about your day," Gloria seethed.

Makayla rolled her eyes again.

"And did you do anything Friday night?" Amanda asked again. She was most interested in five o'clock on.

"I met up with friends again. We grabbed a pizza and ate it down by the river in the park."

"Which one?"

"Prince William Forest. What does it matter? It's not like it was exciting. We skipped some stones." She whirled her fingers to imply a sarcastic whoop-de-do.

Amanda got up and gave Makayla her card and one to the mother. "Thank you for your time and honesty, Makayla. If you think of anyone who might have killed Reese, call me."

"Who wouldn't have wanted to? Unless she accepted you into her circle, you might as well have had a hex on your head."

"A hex?" Trent asked, latching on to that.

"Not, like, a real one. Just meant that you didn't amount to anything." Makayla got up and left the room.

"Thank you for your cooperation too, Mrs. Mann, in letting us speak with your daughter." A half-ass expression of gratitude given Gloria's attitude.

"Not like I had much choice." She shut the door behind them, a little heavily.

And there it was...

"Quite an interesting family," Trent said, loading into the department car.

"Yeah, you could say that. And I wonder where Mr. Mann was."

"You think we should come back and question him?"

The adage *to leave no stone unturned* was a good one to follow with investigations. Some parents would do anything to spare their child pain—even go so far as murder. Even she and Trent had seen that before. "Gloria didn't even know the extent to which Reese had bullied Makayla. I doubted the teen came clean to her dad about it. We'll leave him for now, but I do want to find out Reese's last moves. She skipped detention, so where did she go?"

Trent turned on the car, and cool air blew from the vents. She sighed a welcome relief. The day was a hot one, and it was just getting started.

"Last seen with Adrian," Trent said. "Want to go there or to the Thompson house to look around Reese's room?"

"The latter. Hopefully we'll discover something useful, but one quick stop on the way... I'd like to see if Laurel Wilkinson will hand over her phone."

"Oh, good luck to us trying to pry that from a teenager's fingers. We're going to need it." Trent smiled, put the car into gear, and hit the gas.

TWENTY-FOUR

Amanda was grateful the stop by the Wilkinson house had met with success. Laurel had handed over her phone, due in part to her mother talking reason to her. Though, what closed the deal was her mother's promise to buy Laurel an upgraded model. It said something about the girl when she needed to be bribed to do the right thing.

Trent raised his hand to knock on Clarissa Thompson's door for the third time, but footsteps were padding toward them. The interior door whooshed in, and the screen door was pushed open. Clarissa was standing there with bloodshot eyes, her hair wrapped in a towel and wearing a cotton robe.

"Did you find who did this?" Clarissa's mouth and chin quivered as she spoke.

"I'm sorry, but not yet." Amanda wished she had better news, realizing how hope was as fragile as thin glass.

A single tear fell from Clarissa's left eye, and she swiped it from her cheek. "Thought I'd ask."

Amanda put a hand on Clarissa's forearm. "That's completely understandable, but I promise that as soon as we have news, we'll pass it along to you."

The woman nodded, her eyes glistening. "Sorry it took so long to get to the door." She adjusted the towel on her head. "I was in the shower... obviously, and Nadine's out cold. Poor girl just fell asleep an hour ago. Come in, but please, be quiet."

Amanda stepped inside, Trent at her heels.

Clarissa took them to the sitting room and sat on a chair, crossed her legs, with a mindful tug on her robe. "If you're not here to tell me you caught Reese's killer, what is it? Can I help you with something?"

Amanda nodded. "We have some questions, and we'd like to look around in Reese's room."

"Whatever you need, but please don't mess things up in there."

"We won't," Amanda said. She appreciated from real-life experience that the room belonging to a dead child quickly morphed into a shrine. "We'd just like to fill in her Wednesday a bit more. Did she go to school that day?"

"Yes."

"What time did she get home?"

"Was about five."

"Was that the normal time for her?" Amanda asked.

"That's right."

"School's out about three thirty," Trent started. "How does she fill the time?"

"She often goes to a friend's place or goes out with them... somewhere." Clarissa bit down on her bottom lip and briefly closed her eyes. "I wish I knew more about how she spent her time. I'm starting to wonder if I knew her at all."

"You sound like a mother who did all she could, the best she knows how. We can't be on top of our children's every movement." Amanda would tuck away this speech to give herself in moments when she thought of herself as a bad mother.

"You're right. And you ask them too many questions, especially at Reese's age, and they'll clam up and not say a thing."

"It's apparent that you deeply love your daughters," Amanda said. "That's not under suspicion. We only ask these questions because we're trying to get a complete picture of Reese's life."

"I wish I had more to tell you."

"It's fine." Amanda gave Clarissa a pressed-lip smile. They'd have to ask Reese's friends to see how they used their time from when school let out until five. "Do you know if Reese kept a diary or journal?"

"She had a sketchbook and was doodling away in it any chance she got."

"She was an artist?" Trent asked.

Clarissa nodded. "You could say that. She had big aspirations. She was quite good too."

The loss of a young person was devastating enough on its own. When the victim possessed a unique gift in its relative infancy, it was felt even more. "If it's not a problem, may we look in Reese's room now?"

"Yes. Oh, please keep the noise down for Nadine." Clarissa's eyes glazed over.

"We'll do our best." Amanda stood and toed quietly down the hall with Trent.

"You doing all right?" Trent asked, coming in the bedroom and speaking softly toward Amanda's ear as he passed her.

He snapped on gloves, and so did she.

"I'm good." She smiled and bobbed her head, an action to reassure him, but she wasn't sure he bought her response. Still, he headed for Reese's dresser, while she stayed put looking at the gown the girl would never wear to prom. Just for a second. Maybe two. Again, the contrast between it and what the killer put her in struck. Was there another message in that? As they'd considered before, had it been to humiliate Reese? To shame her? Or was it simply what the killer had at their disposal?

She opened the closet's bifold doors and staggered back.

The Thompson house was modest, a definite fit for middle income, but Reese's clothes were brand-name and relatively new. "Look at this, Trent."

He left the drawer he'd been looking in and joined her. "Oh, nice clothes."

"Maybe a little more than nice." Amanda pointed out some tags.

"Reese might have had a part-time job after school or on the weekends."

"Surely Clarissa would have mentioned it if that was the case."

"Unless Reese hid it from her mother."

"Suppose."

"Not to judge Clarissa, but she doesn't seem to know a lot about how Reese spent her time. Well, aside from hanging out with her friends in Manassas on Friday nights and Saturdays."

"We'll find out if she had a job. If she didn't, clothes like these raise red flags for me."

His features darkened. "You suggesting she was being groomed by some pervert?"

"Precisely that." Amanda knew how they worked from bringing down the sex-trafficking ring in Prince William County. A friend she'd made in Sex Crimes, Patty Glover, had been very insightful on the topic. One thing these people did was lure girls in with expensive gifts. But Amanda refused to sink into that line of thought too deeply. They had far more to unravel about Reese before venturing down that nightmarish path—including whether she had been sexually assaulted. Rideout should be able to give them that answer this afternoon.

Trent returned to the dresser drawer, and Amanda pushed some of the clothing aside, the hangers dragging noisily against the metal rod. She winced and stopped, thinking about Nadine in the next room. She quietly parted the articles of clothing instead, and at the base of the closet, she found a well-worn pair of Rollerblades and a few pairs of running shoes.

On the top shelf, there were a couple of small totes and a shoebox. Amanda pulled that down and cracked the lid. Inside was a glittery pair of high heels, obviously brand new. They were the likely accompaniment to the prom dress.

Amanda then took out one of the totes, and there were small trinkets and cards from birthdays and holidays past from her parents, sister, and friends. These mementos told Amanda that Reese had valued the small things in life.

Amanda exchanged that tote for the other one, which was heavier and larger. She set it on the bed and opened it up. There was a stack of sketchbooks. She peeked inside the top one. Doing so made her feel like she was violating the girl's privacy. Art was a personal, creative expression, and to look upon it was an admission into the artist's soul. After all, whenever brush was put to canvas or drawing implement to paper, emotions had a way of spilling out through the medium.

Reese's drawings were in charcoal pencil, the black in places intentionally smeared for effect. Amanda turned the pages, and a pattern emerged. Reese's main subject wasn't landscapes, people or animals—with none in sight. Rather her passion appeared to be fashion. She sketched dresses and pant suits. Some were colored in pencil crayon while others were just a raw outline. Reese initialed the bottom of each page and dated them.

This book contained pictures from January to April of this year.

Amanda gently worked her way through each sketchbook in search of the most recent one. Didn't find it and glanced over at Trent. He was down to the bottom drawer and apparently hadn't had any luck or he'd have said something. "Hey, Trent. Look at these."

He came over, and she showed him a few of the sketches.

"They look professional."

"I think so too. Reese had real talent, a good eye, and a brilliant imagination."

"She did."

"Looks like she's been at this a while, but the most recent book I came across only goes until April of this year. Most look to hold about three to four months' worth of drawings."

"Huh, so where is the latest one?"

"That's my question. Given how often she contributes a sketch to the book, there should be one. What about you? Guessing nothing noteworthy in her dresser?"

He shook his head. "Not really. There are some more nice clothes, but most are department store brands."

"Which makes these stand out even more." Amanda gestured toward the closet full of high-end names.

"I'd say so."

Amanda looked around, trying to sink into the mindset of a teenage girl. There weren't many obvious places to hide things, but she had one idea. She set the sketchbooks back inside the tote. "Put this back on the top shelf of the closet, if you don't mind?"

"Sure." He closed it up and did just that.

She lifted the edge of the mattress.

"Hold up. I'll help." Trent rushed over and assumed half the weight.

With the mattress on its edge against the side of the bed, the box spring was exposed—along with a stack of bills. They looked at each other, and she grabbed the cash and counted.

"Five hundred dollars," she told him.

"That's a lot for a teen to have lying around."

"We definitely need to talk to Clarissa again and find out—"

"What are you doing?" It was Nadine, and she was standing in the doorway. Her gaze was jumping from them to the disturbed room.

"Hi, Nadine," Amanda said. "We're just—"

"Snooping in Reese's room?" The question was entirely accusatory.

Amanda left the bed and walked over to Nadine. "We're trying to find out as much as we can about your sister, hoping that whatever we discover will help in finding her killer."

Nadine knotted her arms. "You aren't going to find the killer under her mattress, in her closet, or her dresser." Her voice rose in pitch as she rattled off each location.

"Do you know where your sister would get this kind of money?" Amanda held up the cash not about to continue pacifying the teen.

"I have no idea."

"Did Reese have a part-time job?" Trent asked, stepping up behind Amanda, and she moved aside to give him more room in the doorway.

"Don't think so."

Amanda's earlier thought about Reese being groomed had the hairs rising on the back of her neck. *Please no.* While those types didn't normally kill their girls—or merchandise, a term that sickened Amanda—they wouldn't tolerate any who rebelled or posed a threat either. And to kill Reese in such an elaborate manner didn't really fit either. She tried to think of another reasonable explanation for the money and landed on one. She vaguely recalled Clarissa saying Melvin gave them money when they were married to compensate for working long hours. "Does your father give you money?"

Cheek to shoulder. "Sometimes."

"Nadine Thompson. I can't believe you." Clarissa manifested in view of the doorway. "You kept that from me... you and Reese?"

"I'm sorry, Mom. We didn't know how to tell you. We didn't want you to feel bad."

"Too late for that. Has your father been giving you money all this time?"

Nadine toed the carpet, looking down at her foot, then, "Even more since he moved out."

"I'm going to kill that man."

Amanda bristled. It wasn't exactly the best thing to say in front of cops. "Is that how Reese afforded those clothes?" Amanda nudged her head toward the closet, and Nadine nodded. "And where she got this cash?"

"Probably."

Amanda pounced on the weakness in the girl's statement. "You're not sure though?"

Nadine shook her head.

"It's okay. We'll figure it out," Amanda said.

Clarissa held a hand over her chest. "She told me that she found those nice clothes at a vintage store here in town. It prides itself on gently used... I'm such an idiot."

"We want to believe our daughters," Amanda said.

Clarissa let out a puff of air. "You find anything helpful to the investigation? A clue to lead you to my girl's killer?"

"Amanda found her box of sketchbooks," Trent started. "Looks like the most recent is missing. Any idea where she might have kept it?"

Nadine sniffled and said, "She always kept the one she was working on with her."

"When she left here Wednesday night, did she have it?" Amanda asked.

"She did. And I figured she'd just go draw in the park. I gave her a couple of hours to cool down, and slipped out there..."

"But she wasn't there," Amanda finished, and the girl nodded. They had found Reese's cell phone in the river at the park. Was her sketchbook there too? If so, that might be where Reese had crossed paths with her killer. Regardless, the park was a real possibility for ground zero. It was feasible Reese had gone there and encountered her would-be killer before Nadine arrived at the park. If so, it seemed even more likely the text sent to Laurel from Reese's phone had been sent by the killer. A grand announcement to their planned display? The thought instantly sickened Amanda. They needed Laurel Wilkinson's phone looked at—and the sooner the better.

"All right, Clarissa and Nadine," Amanda began, "please don't contact your ex or your father, as we need to ask him about the money."

Clarissa bunched up her face and curled a hand into a fist. "Let me know once you have because I want to wring his neck."

Amanda nodded, ready to go.

But she and Trent were leaving the Thompson house with more questions. Where was Reese's recent sketchbook? Was her father the source of all her money? Had her killer taken her from the park Wednesday night?

Amanda clicked her seat belt into place. "Maybe it's best you take us over to Melvin Thompson's. It would be nice to get the money thing sorted and out of the way."

"You got it."

Amanda hoped that Melvin would confirm what Nadine had told them—he was the source of Reese's nice things and the cash. To consider the alternative that Reese was groomed wouldn't end with her murder. It would mean another sex-trafficking ring had set up in Prince William County.

TWENTY-FIVE

Amanda was keeping a close eye on the time. Zoe would be dropped off at home in forty minutes. "I'll need to make this a quick visit." She tapped the dash, indicating the clock.

"This shouldn't take long." Trent was the first out of the car and to the front door.

She'd like to believe him, but she'd seen short visits take a turn before. Making her uneasy was the presence of a second vehicle in Melvin Thompson's driveway. It hadn't been there on their first visit.

She joined her partner on the front step. Smells from inside the home wafted outside. Something good was cooking. She'd guess pancakes or waffles. Certainly food of the sweet variety. And bacon. Her stomach grumbled, wishing she'd grabbed more than a piece of toast with a thin smear of peanut butter before leaving home.

Trent knocked. The door was answered before a second time was necessary.

A woman was standing there and eyeing them curiously. "Yes?" she said, dragging out the word.

Amanda flashed her badge. "Detectives Steele and Stenson. Would Mr. Thompson be in?"

"Absolutely." The woman pivoted and called behind her, "Mel!"

A few seconds later, Mel joined the party at the front door. "Detectives, come in." He stepped back and told the woman, "These are the detectives investigating Reese's murder."

The woman nodded grimly. "I'm Roxanne Burgess, a friend of Mel's."

"Roxie lives a few blocks over, but we've been seeing each other casually for a few months," Melvin amended.

"Nice to meet you," Amanda said cordially. "Mr. Thompson, we have a question for you, if you have a minute?"

In response, some appliance beeped in the kitchen.

"Oh, that's the waffle maker. I better get in there." Roxanne disappeared, leaving the three of them in the entryway.

"Where is my mind?" Melvin said. "Let's go to the living room and sit down."

Amanda imagined his mind should be a tangled mess having been informed within the last twenty-four hours that his teenage daughter had been murdered. Though she wasn't sure he was giving that impression. Rather things between him and his friend seemed rather cozy. Melvin was dressed in loungewear—Puma jogging pants and an Adidas T-shirt—and he was certainly branded. It brought Amanda to her and Trent's primary reason for being here. "Did you give Reese an allowance?"

Melvin pinched the bridge of his nose. Silence stretched out. Then he nodded. "Clarissa doesn't know anything about it, though, so please don't mention it to her. She won't be too happy about it."

"Too late for that," Trent said drily.

"Just wonderful." His inflection saying the exact opposite.

"Why hide this from your wife?" Amanda asked.

"*Ex*-wife."

Trent shrugged. "Detective Steele's question still applies."

"After the divorce, even before that, we lived separate lives. Anyway, I know she hates me giving the girls money. The fact I make a bigger salary than her has always been a bone of contention between us."

"How much did you give them?" Amanda asked.

"I gave both girls a thousand a month, around the first."

Amanda settled back into her chair. She hadn't expected that much. "And that's why you saw them every month?"

"Yeah."

"What do you do for work?" she asked.

"I'm a pharmaceutical rep." He listed off the name of the company, but it didn't mean anything to Amanda.

"They must pay good money?" Trent said.

"You'd be surprised, but the reason I can give the girls so much is I started investing in stocks. I've made some good choices and netted sizable dividends."

"You could have put money aside for their college funds." Far more logical than handing a chunk of cash over to teenagers.

"They are both taken care of that way. One day, I'll find a way to break that news to Clarissa. And, yes, a grand a month is a lot for kids, but they're young and should be having fun. I also know what it's like growing up with little and getting teased for no-name running shoes and frumpy clothes."

Amanda wondered if he'd shared his story with Reese and whether it had fueled her love for fashion. "Reese had a lot of nice clothes," she said.

"She had an eye for what looked good." With the statement directly relating to his late daughter, Melvin's voice turned gravelly.

Amanda thought of that pale-pink gown hanging in Reese's room. "Did she buy her own prom dress or was that something you got for her?"

"That was all Clarissa. Some mother–daughter thing. I was told in no uncertain terms to keep my nose—and my wallet—out of it."

"Were you aware if Reese had a part-time job?" Amanda asked.

He made a funny face. "That would be news to me. And she could have come to me if she needed money."

Throwing cash at the girl wasn't the solution. Reese would have benefited from earning her own paycheck. Though that didn't seem to be the case. If it was, Reese had kept her job from her parents and sister. "Okay. Thank you for your time, Mr. Thompson." Amanda got up and headed toward the door, Trent with her.

"Wait."

They both stopped walking and turned to face Melvin.

"Are you any closer to knowing who killed my girl?" he asked them.

"We're following every possible lead, and trust me when I say we're doing all we can." It sounded like a well-practiced brush-off, but it was all she had right now.

"Okay. Thank you."

She and Trent left the house with Melvin softly shutting the door behind them.

"His generous allowance probably explains the girl's wardrobe and the money under her mattress," Amanda concluded. It was a bittersweet realization. A part-time job would have given her and Trent a lead to follow, but it was better than the alternative that Reese had been groomed by a predator.

"Sounds like it to me."

"Now I thought about this when we were at Clarissa Thompson's, but we should get officers on Prince William Forest Park. Reese made a habit of going there, and the fact her phone was pulled from the river, it very well might be where she encountered her killer." She'd dismiss the possibility it entered the river at another point and rode currents to where it was found.

Trent nodded. "They could also search for her sketchbook. Or anything else to prove she was there on Wednesday night."

"Hopefully her phone records can tell us more once we get them—whenever we get them. But I hear you." She took out her phone and texted Malone, not eager to hear his complaints about limited manpower again. *Need officers in the park, looking for any sign Reese was recently there. Her sketchbook is missing and may be there too.*

"We'll see how long he takes to—" Her phone bleeped. "And there he is." She read the message out loud. "'Will take care of it.'"

Brief, and to the point. She'd definitely made the right call in skirting a verbal request. "We should see if we can get video surveillance from the park. Though I'd suspect a judge will want solid proof Reese was last seen alive there. Which we don't have."

Trent tapped the dash, pointing out the time. "I'm to assume before we do anything else, I'm to take you to the station for your car so you can pop by home?"

Faced with the question, guilt twisted through her like a vine, sucking life from her conscience. But getting home for Zoe wasn't negotiable. Amanda wanted to share in reliving her daughter's experience. That was the least she could do. As it was, Zoe would be expecting to spend the rest of the day with her and Logan, and that she couldn't follow through on. Not with all the boxes to check off with the investigation—including a trip to Manassas. "You know what... why don't you just come home with me? Take a little break yourself?"

"Yeah, I don't know about that... Won't Logan be there?"

On second thought, Trent being there would make things awkward. Not that Logan knew about her kissing Trent—even though that had been before she and Logan had officially gotten back together. Still some things were better left as secrets. Less hurt that way. "Suppose you have a life you might want to pop into for an hour or two." She smiled at him.

"I do, but..." He winced.

"What is it?"

"I'd rather keep goin', ya know? But I completely understand why you want to drop by home."

"What are you going to do then?"

"I was thinking I'd ask you for Jacob Briggs' phone number, for starters. I know from before he usually works nights, but if I could get Laurel's phone to him, he might get started on it sooner. Better still, I can give him a heads up and take it to his office."

Amanda admired Trent's initiative. Briggs was her go-to in the Digital Forensics Unit and had been a tremendous asset on previous cases. If he'd been working when she dropped off Reese's phone, she would have placed it directly in his hands. "Sounds like a great idea. Also, I haven't heard a thing about Reese's phone yet. Maybe Briggs could help that get rushed through. Sending his contact card by text right now..." She forwarded it from her phone, and Trent's chimed a second later.

"All right, and I was also thinking I'd go to Central and brainstorm a list of possible suspects for us to run down."

"Very organized. I like it." Amanda was so used to juggling names in her head, but to have one coherent reference point—especially with this case that had a number of possible culprits—would prove invaluable.

"I'll also be getting something to eat because after smelling the waffles and bacon..." He patted his flat stomach, and hers growled.

"I hear you there."

"And I hear you." He laughed.

. . .

Amanda slipped out of her shoes and hugged Logan just as Sheila Marsh was pulling into the driveway. She was Maria's mother, and that girl had been a friend of Zoe's since she'd started Dumfries Elementary. It made Amanda think a lot of her own friendship with Becky Tulson, her bestie since kindergarten.

Amanda stepped outside the front door and waved at Sheila after she'd unloaded Zoe's bag from the trunk and handed it over to the girl.

"Beautiful day," Sheila called out.

"It is." She'd keep to herself that it wasn't entirely, not through the lens from which Amanda was looking anyhow.

Zoe was trudging up the driveway like she was climbing a mountain.

Amanda helped close the distance. "Want me to take your bag?"

"No." Zoe drew back. "I'm a big girl and can carry it."

"I was just trying to be nice, Zoe."

Zoe didn't say anything as she walked past Amanda into the house. *Huh.* That wasn't exactly the reception she'd expected. She tailed the girl and shut the door behind them.

"Logan is here?" Zoe dropped her bag on the entry floor.

She would have seen and recognized his truck in the driveway. "He is."

"There's my girl." Logan came out from the side hallway, all open arms and smiles for Zoe. She crashed into him.

If Amanda hadn't felt snubbed before, this did it. After they hugged, Amanda said, "Where's mine?"

Zoe walked over as if approaching her execution and wrapped limp arms around Amanda.

Amanda pulled her in tight and mussed her hair. "Glad you're home, kiddo."

Zoe mumbled something and gathered her bag from the floor and started to cart it to her room.

"I'd love to hear everything about your adventure," Amanda called out cheerfully behind Zoe, her petition meeting with an energetic thud—the girl's bedroom door being shut. "What the...?" Amanda said lowly to Logan.

He put a hand on her shoulder. "Don't take it personally."

"Hard not to." The hurt part of her wanted to set off to lecture Zoe. After all, she'd left an active investigation to be here. But she reeled herself back. Encumbering Zoe with guilt wasn't the mark of a good mother. She *should* use her maturity to see that Zoe's acting out wasn't personal, as Logan had suggested.

Logan traced strands of Amanda's hair across her forehead, down the side of her face, then tucked them behind her ear. He kissed her exposed brow and lowered his to meet hers.

"Thanks for trying to make me feel better," she said.

"Hopefully I'm succeeding, if only a little."

"You are." And he was, but sadness remained in the pit of her gut. Zoe usually greeted her with such exuberance, smiles, hugs. If anything, Amanda had to typically pry Zoe off her.

Logan pulled back. "Good. So are you home for the day now or...?" His blue eyes took on a moody intensity, disclosing he figured what her answer would be and didn't like it.

"I've got to go back. But if she's just going to be broody, then it might be best if I left now." The words came out, and she felt instant shame; her wounded pride had bit back. "Actually, I should talk with her. It's obvious something happened to upset her."

"Probably a good bet."

"When I do leave later though, I can't say when I'll get back. Could I ask a favor of you?"

"Anything."

"Will you take Zoe to my parents tonight for the weekly dinner?"

"And stay myself or..."

She nudged his shoulder. "Yes, of course." Her family had met him before and he'd attended in the past, but she was always by his side. "Everyone likes you."

"If you say so. Kyle glares at me when you're not looking."

She laughed. "That's a big brother for you." Hearing that Kyle was giving Logan a bit of a hard time actually made Amanda quite happy. She'd always been close with her brother, but she'd hurt him a lot when she withdrew from her family after Kevin's and Lindsey's deaths. The fact he was looking out for her sealed the fact he still cared about his sis.

"Well, he needs to get the message I'm not going anywhere."

He peered into her eyes as he said this, and it had her heart hammering and her chest feeling tight. She attempted a smile, any visual suggestion for that matter, that she'd heard him, acknowledged his words, felt the same way... But her throat was dry. "I, ah, better go check on Zoe."

He nodded, but she witnessed the subtle flicker of hurt dance in his eyes as she stepped around him.

She rapped her knuckles on Zoe's door and slowly opened it at the same time. Zoe was sitting on the floor on the other side of the bed. Just the top of her head showed over the mattress.

Amanda didn't wait for an invite and joined her. Zoe was clutching onto Sir Lucky, a stuffed dog that had been her favorite toy until she'd turned seven last August and declared herself too grown up for the doll.

Amanda dropped onto the carpet next to Zoe. "Everything all right? Did you have fun?"

Zoe didn't answer but petted the dog's head with both hands.

"You can talk to me, you know. When I was your age, I was terrified of the dark. I swore I saw shadows walking around the room." She stopped there, thinking that in her effort to share a story that could bond them, she might have given the girl's imagination fodder. *Oops.*

"I'm not afraid of the dark." Spoken through gritted teeth as she continued to pet the toy. She was applying so much pressure, the dog's head was bending backward at an unnatural angle—skull meeting spine.

"I never said you were."

She looked at Amanda. "Then why tell me that?"

Amanda thought if she shared one of her younger self's fears, Zoe might open up. But forget that. It was time to nip this girl's attitude before it got any worse. "I was really excited you were coming home, Zoe. I looked forward to hearing all about your time at Maria's." She was saying everything wrong. The last thing she wanted was to burden Zoe with unmet expectations. As if Amanda were one to make demands with her intrusive, unpredictable job that didn't afford set hours.

Zoe tossed Lucky across the room. "Maria's not my friend anymore." Her eyes pooled with tears, and all Amanda wanted to do was pull the girl into her arms and suck out her hurt. But the girl's energy told her that gesture of affection wouldn't be welcome. This also wasn't the first time Maria had wounded Zoe's feelings.

"Sorry to hear that, sweetie. If you want to talk to me about—"

"No. I just want to be alone." Her chin was quivering, and a few tears fell.

Amanda debated what to do. Would leaving make her a bad mother or a good one? She thought back to when she was young and desired to be alone. Any pushing her mother did netted the opposite of her intention. "All right, I'm leaving, but I was going to make pancakes for lunch. What do you say to that?"

"Okay."

The limp response had Amanda's heart squeezing. Pancakes were the girl's favorite. "I'll call you when they're ready." The gist of her earlier encouragement to Clarissa, came back to Amanda now. *I'm doing the best I can!*

Zoe didn't say a word as Amanda left the room. To further support Zoe's request to be alone, Amanda closed the door behind her.

In the hallway, she tried calling Maria's mother, but Sheila's phone rang to voicemail. Amanda hung up without leaving a message. A text might work better anyway. She could ask about the sleepover without the possibility of Zoe overhearing.

After hitting send, she tucked her phone back in her pocket and set off for the kitchen to make pancakes. Bacon too.

TWENTY-SIX

Making the batter and flipping the flapjacks was meditative and let Amanda's mind wander. Not that it took a long trip. It felt like she was poised on the edge of a precipice as she waited on a response from Sheila Marsh. An hour had passed since she'd sent the text, and she was now heading out to meet up with Trent.

It had taken all of her and Logan's efforts to coax Zoe from her room. And this from a girl who usually wore more pancakes than made it into her mouth. It was a feel-good meal, but it was obvious the girl wanted to stay stuck in her bad mood. Even so, leaving Zoe had been torture.

Logan was there for both of them, but Zoe was her daughter, her responsibility. Though, she supposed, in a way he'd accepted it too. He knew Zoe was part of the package when they got back together. And he'd never complained about the obligations that came with being a father figure—ever. Amanda was quite sure he loved Zoe and that the feeling was mutual.

As she thought about all this, breathing became harder.

I'm not going anywhere... That's what Logan had told her.

What did he mean by that? She swallowed hard. She should have seen the signs—how he was at her house more often, how close they'd become, how he was with Zoe. But taking it one day at a time was working for her. The future was just too—*too, too*—much to think about. She rubbed her throat, feeling as if invisible hands had a tight grip on her neck.

She parked in the lot at Central and steamed through the station's halls and found Trent at his desk.

"There she is," he said, smiling. "Zoe have a lot of fun?"

"Going to guess no."

"Going to guess?" His brows tightened, and he angled his head.

"Well, she's not exactly being talkative, so I can't know for sure but..."

"Oh, something must have happened on the sleepover."

She steepled her hands together and half-bowed. "Why thank you, Sherlock."

"No need to get sassy." Though he only took mock offense and started laughing.

"You get Laurel's phone to Digital Forensics?"

"I did and got ahold of Briggs. He'll work on it when he gets in tonight. He'll also follow up on the status of Reese's phone."

"Great. How did you come along with the list of potential suspects?"

"Look for yourself." Trent handed her a piece of paper.

It was a printout with names and generalized suspects set out in bullet-point fashion. She read down the page.

- *Susie Valentine*
- *Other staff at the country club (those with key access and on duty)*
- *Catering staff*
- *Any high-school faculty or staff there early*

- *Makayla Mann and/or her friends*
- *Ella, Reese's friend (jealous of relationship with Adrian)*
- *Adrian Savage, boyfriend*
- *Unknown party*

"Wow. This isn't overwhelming at all. Especially the enigma surrounding the last one." She sat on the edge of his desk. "Suppose we could narrow it some by thinking more about means, motive, and opportunity. Who has all three?"

"Motive is a tricky one until we dig deeper."

"If we're looking beyond teen rivalries. Then means and opportunity... club and catering staff, unknown party."

"Yes. And we need to figure out if any of the club and catering staff had a connection to Reese or knowledge she was voted prom queen."

"And any reason to be bothered by it."

"I did go ahead and get a list of names for the club and catering people. We can see if any of them mean anything to Clarissa, Nadine, or Melvin Thompson."

"You work fast. I was only gone an hour and a half."

"I'm motivated."

"You and me both. To save some time, we could email the names to the Thompsons, see if they recognize any. Actually, I'll do that while you drive us to Susie Valentine's."

"Sounds good." Trent pushed his chair back and got up. "And she's in Manassas, so we can see Rideout while we're up there."

"Makes perfect sense to me." Amanda pulled out her phone. Still no message from Maria's mom. "Where the heck is Sheila?"

"Who's Sheila?"

She hadn't realized she'd said that out loud. "Sheila is

Maria's mother. Maria is Zoe's friend, though I'm not sure if that's still the case." *Since when did everything become so complicated?*

"All right, then."

"Sorry you stepped in it? But, yeah, Zoe said something about Maria not being her friend anymore. Why is still a mystery to me." She left out the flourish with which Zoe had emphasized her point, though Amanda vividly recalled the fervor with which the stuffed dog flew across the room. "You know what? I'm going to try calling her again."

"Sure. I'll go on ahead and get the car. Your valet will pick you up at the door."

Amanda shook her head but was smiling. She selected Sheila from her contacts. The line rang to voicemail again. "What the hell?" She no longer cared that she was talking to herself. There was a beep in her ear, and she left a message. "It's Amanda. Please give me a call back when you get this. I have questions about the sleepover." She left her number and ended the call. Guilt set in. Maybe she should have given Zoe more time to open up. Had she crossed a line, or had she handled this situation like a good mother would? Whatever the case, she didn't have time to figure it out now. Also what was done, was done. She joined Trent in the department car.

"So?" He glanced over at her as he put the vehicle into gear.

"Had to leave a message."

"I hope you get it sorted sooner than later. It must be driving you nuts not knowing."

"Understatement."

He smiled at her, then put his attention on driving. She was left to rip apart his words. What made him assume she'd be going *nuts*? Was she that predictable? That much of a control freak? And since when did she break down every spoken word to this extent? She must be going nuts. Was this how it began—

by talking to oneself in riddles? But it wasn't just her personal drama nattering away at her, her mind was also processing that extensive list of suspects that Trent had pulled together. Did Reese really have that many people who wanted to kill her?

TWENTY-SEVEN

Ava considered herself a smart kid, possessing more than an average intelligence, and she would go insane stuck at home all day. Her mother had barely uttered three words to her since she woke up that morning. She had been clear when she said Ava's only outing for the foreseeable future was dinner at Grandma and Grandpa's tonight.

Goody.

Not that she didn't love them. She did. And any other week she'd happily sit at the dinner table as her cousins and aunts and uncles chatted about the minutiae of their lives. Ava valued the closeness of her family. So many people didn't have that. But there were times being that tight-knit was a curse. It was impossible to make a move without everyone finding out about it.

She had no doubt her grandma would have heard about her exploits last night, and she probably had a lecture prepared. Another curse was Ava's ability to see things from other people's perspectives. She appreciated that those who cared about her would be alarmed by her recent actions. After all, she wasn't a cop with a badge. *Yet.* One day she would be. She had every intention of following in her aunt's footsteps with the

Prince William County PD. She'd climb the ranks, and one day make her grandfather proud by claiming his previous post as police chief. Yes, Ava had plans for her future. But none of that did her any good when she was a prisoner in her own bedroom.

Somehow, she had to break free. It was sad enough that she couldn't reach Nadine with her phone confiscated. And just when her friend needed her most, having lost her older sister. That was a level of grief Ava was left to imagine as she didn't have any siblings. But her familiarity with death from a young age had never left her. It was all too easy to recall the darkness, the hopelessness, and the abandon of reason. She'd quickly learned trying to cling to logic only brought more pain. There would never be satisfying answers to justify the death of loved ones. But still Ava found herself wanting to try and find them for Nadine and her mother.

Ava flopped back on her bed, laying out, staring at the ceiling. It was the position in which she often did her best thinking.

The whistling man... the happy tune...

She sure hoped that Aunt Amanda had taken her seriously when she told her to look into him. Ava had never seen him before, she'd swear to it, so why was he at the prom?

He had haunted her nightmares last night. Or more so, his whistling had. It had been so cheerful, almost celebratory. Who but a killer would feel happy in the wake of a murdered teenager?

She shut her eyes, letting her mind run through the evening. She rewound, playing it from her and Nadine's arrival at the country club.

We beat most of the crowd, but there are early arrivals. We watch as seniors climb out of limos and others from their own cars. Couples are holding hands, and everyone is smiling or laughing. Some are obviously already drunk .

A few stay outside the front doors smoking cigarettes. Others are slowly filing inside.

But Nadine and I can't just enter through the front like the rest of the students. I may be more mature than most my age, but I don't look old enough to be in grade eleven. Neither does Nadine. If anyone is checking at the door—and there most likely will be—Nadine and I will be turned away.

The idea hits that we should slip around the rear of the club. "We'll use the back door, sneak in that way," *I say.*

Nadine nods, as if it was some genius move rather than an obvious plan.

We go to the back of the clubhouse. It is a wall of windows, but there is a door. I try it and find it locked.

Then another door opens, and a man steps out into the night air wearing pressed pants and a uniform shirt with STAFF *on the back. He's built and quite muscular.*

He turns to look over his shoulder, and Nadine and I move tight against the building and hide behind a storage unit.

We only pop up again when we hear his footsteps fading away.

Ava sighed and opened her eyes. *And so what?* Thinking wasn't going to get her anywhere!

She stared at the ceiling of her bedroom for a few seconds, wallowing in defeat. Then she decided to surrender and closed her eyes again. Not like she had anything better to do anyway.

Nadine and I head toward another door and find it pried open. I peek in and see it goes into the kitchen. People are bustling around, and there is no way they'd even notice us.

I lean in toward Nadine and say, "This is our way in."

Nadine enters while I hang back, looking over the greens.

Ava shakes her head, comes back to her bedroom again. Frustrated. Is any of this actually helping? But why was she interested in the golf course? *Think, Ava!*

Then it hit! *Whistling!*

Ava bolted upright. Someone on the greens had been

whistling! Could it be the same man she saw coming out of the restroom?

But the man she remembered seeing outside had been wearing a club T-shirt. How did that fit with the other man inside? He wasn't wearing a shirt from the club—but he was the right size. Had he ditched his shirt, possibly somewhere out on the greens, and then came back into the clubhouse? If so, why, and what was Ava supposed to do with that theory? Maybe if she found the shirt... Though surely it wouldn't just be sitting around.

She got up and paced. Sitting still was impossible. Staying in her room now was less of an option than before. She had to check it out. Try, at least.

But how was she going to get to Manassas?

She should probably call Aunt Amanda and pass along the tip, but she wasn't exactly happy with her at the moment.

No, Ava would take power into her own hands and find out if there was any merit to her brainstorming. Just how to break out of jail? As her predicament landed again, the solution came quickly.

She smiled, pleased that her big brains weren't going to let her down.

TWENTY-EIGHT

Amanda had sent the list of employee names from the club and catering staff to the Thompsons. Now it was a waiting game. She knocked three times on Susie Valentine's door, but the place was silent just like last night. It didn't look or feel any different either with Susie's car still in the driveway. "I don't like this," she said to Trent.

"We considered innocent explanations for her car being here and her not. If you are seriously suspecting she might have killed Reese, her place isn't exactly isolated. We do think it's possible Reese was held for a few days. And there's no garage."

"Now, you've lost me."

"A garage would make concealment easy."

"I see what you mean." And she did. Once the door was down, those inside had privacy. It just took her a second to latch on to his thinking. It's not like she had the luxury of a functioning garage—yet. After this case was closed, she'd finish what she'd started. "If we're really going to put Susie Valentine in the frame for murder, what was her connection to Reese Thompson?" Amanda tossed out the question, which might as well have been rhetorical. "Can we connect them?"

"We'll need to dig. If we're seriously looking at her or another adult, for that matter, is there something in their past that set them against prom queens? I doubt it was the girl herself, rather something she triggered in the killer."

"Sticking to the topic of Valentine..." She'd hoped for some revelation, but no insight was bursting to light yet. But that didn't mean nothing was niggling her about this. She put her finger on the number one thing... "Valentine's background was clean and yet for her first crime she violently murders a teenage girl?"

"And puts her name on it—the cleaning log."

"Which we thought was rather stupid..."

He raised his brows plainly not getting where she was heading with this conversation, and she wasn't certain either, so fair enough. She was just brainstorming out loud.

"Her vehicle's here, there's no answer... We know that Valentine was entrusted with a key to the club and—"

"Are you trying to say what I think?"

"Did anyone actually lay eyes on Valentine at the club on Saturday?"

"Are you suggesting that the killer took Susie out of the way to get her key to the club?"

"Why not?"

"Oy vey."

Amanda felt cold run over her shoulders. "And maybe they knew the club's protocols for evening events—the doors being locked at five, opening back up at six thirty. And how do we know for sure Valentine cleaned that restroom? I want to take another look at that cleaning log. The killer could have forged her signature."

"We'll see if we can get a sampling for comparison."

"Yep. We'll make sure the lab tests the sheet for prints too, see if that gets us anywhere."

're right about all this, Susie Valentine might be unable to answer."

"...call Malone to advise of our suspicions, but I already know what he's going to say. He'll want us to talk to people at Rolling Hills to see if anyone saw her there yesterday before he'll give us the green light to request a warrant."

"While she might be dead in there."

"If she is, cold as this sounds, we're too late to help anyway." She sure hoped that Susie wasn't inside clinging to life while they jumped through procedural hoops.

"Huh. Guess that's one way of looking at it."

"Before we head out, let's speak with Valentine's neighbors to see if they saw her or anything, anyone, suspicious hanging around." She led the way to the two-story sided house to the east of Susie Valentine's.

No one was home. Same to be said for a few more houses. They got an answer at the door across the street. A woman in her sixties, who told Amanda and Trent her name was Beverly Robin.

"We're curious to know when you last saw your neighbor Susie Valentine?" Amanda indicated the gray house across the street.

"Oh, I think it was Saturday morning, though I could be wrong. And it's not that I saw her, but her curtains were opened not long after I woke up. She opens them every morning, closes them at night. Suppose she's home now, though. Maybe she just isn't fit to answer the door."

Exactly what we're afraid of... Sometimes it was unsettling having a mind that leaped right to the macabre. This woman wasn't exactly a reliable spy either. The curtains were closed when they stopped by early that morning. "Did you see her close them last night?"

"Huh. You know what? I'm not sure come to think of it."

"Did you happen to notice if she had any company yesterday?" Amanda wasn't about to hold her breath for an affirmative answer.

"Actually, yes. A man came over."

Amanda glanced at Trent and found him looking at her. "What time was this?" she asked.

"Say about eight thirty in the morning. Does that help you?"

"It may be helpful." When she and Trent got an audience with the golf club's manager, she'd confirm Valentine's working hours yesterday. Also whether employees used a machine to punch in and out. "Did you see this man at her house before? Possibly he was her boyfriend?"

"No, can't say I have, and I'm not sure if he was there for work or pleasure."

"Why is that?" Trent asked.

"He got out of a white van."

"Did it have lettering on it? Perhaps a company's logo?" Adrenaline was pumping through her system, giving her a touch of euphoria.

"I didn't see a logo, but he was wearing gray coveralls and carrying a black duffel. I just figured it was the cable company there to fix something. Could have been a new vehicle to the fleet, not lettered up yet." Beverly shrugged.

"Then the van appeared to be a new model?" Amanda asked.

"I'd say so."

"Do you know the make or model?" Amanda said.

"It was a GMC. Don't know the model, but rather boxy, big..."

"Probably the Savana." Amanda knew this because her brother's love for cars made her more observant of vehicles than most people.

"Could have been."

"Did you happen to see the license plate?" Trent had his notepad out with his pen.

"No. Afraid not." Beverly's voice had lowered, and she spoke slowly. A flicker passed across her eyes, and Amanda guessed the woman was battling with curiosity and apprehension.

"You mentioned gray coveralls, but can you tell us what he looked like? Hair color, build? That type of thing?" Amanda asked.

"Brown hair, came to about here." Beverly indicated just above the shoulders. "Huge build. Mid-forties."

"Thank you for your help, Ms. Robin," Amanda said.

"Don't mention it. Say, is something wrong? Is Susie all right? Should I be worried? I live here alone." A slight tremor disclosed her apprehension.

"I'm sure you're fine," Amanda assured her and pressed her card into Beverly's palm. "But you can call me if you don't feel safe. Also, please reach out if you remember any more about that man or if he returns."

Beverly nodded, and Amanda and Trent went to the department car.

He'd just hit the driver's seat when he spoke. "A man was seen at her house... Holy shit. Susie Valentine really might be dead inside her house right now."

"Okay, first of all, breathe. Let's not make any leaps."

"Kind of hard not to."

She agreed, but as the senior detective she had to keep her head. "We'll swing by Rolling Hills, ask if anyone laid eyes on Susie yesterday. We'll also verify she clocked in for her shift, and when that might have been. Then, if it warrants, I'll go to Malone."

"All right... and the morgue? As you said, even if Valentine is dead, she's not going anywhere."

Wow, that sounded even colder served back...

"Vince Galloway might not even be at the club," he said.

"And I'm assuming we'd want to speak directly to the manager. Do you want me to call ahead?"

"I'll do it. You get us to Rideout." Amanda justified the next step, even though it might be callous. But if Susie Valentine was dead, she wasn't going anywhere. What they might learn from the ME could have everything clicking into place. And finding the killer trumped all.

TWENTY-NINE

Amanda and Trent signed in at the Office of the Chief Medical Examiner and headed toward the morgue. As she walked, she checked her phone. The Thompsons had emailed to say the names she'd forwarded meant nothing to them. She shared that with Trent and looked at the text she'd sent Sheila. It wasn't even marked as read yet. *Unbelievable!*

"Still no word from the girl's mom?" Trent asked, either reading her mind or picking up on her aggravated huffing.

"Nope." She pushed her phone back into a pocket and swung open the morgue doors.

No other medical examiners were working, and they headed straight through to Rideout's office located at the rear of the morgue. He was at his desk and looked up with a grim expression, but he waved a hand welcoming them inside.

She and Trent sat in chairs facing him.

He lifted a folder from a tray on the corner of his desk and opened it. "Deceased is Reese Thompson, eighteen, daughter of Clarissa and Melvin Thompson."

The cold summation tallied up that a teenage girl was killed just as her adult life was starting.

Rideout went on. "Cause of death was ligature strangulation."

"The chain?" Trent asked, and Rideout nodded.

"It seems so."

"What can you tell us about the chain? Its intended purpose?" Amanda asked. "We might be able to narrow down where it was sold."

"As you saw, it's a rather heavyweight chain. Three eighths link, galvanized. And grade thirty from what I can figure."

Her mind was still curious why their killer had used it as the murder weapon. "Which means?"

"It's used for general purpose applications. Not for overhead lifting. Think pulling stumps from the ground, securing cargo, that type of thing. But it's rather generic and would be available at any home improvement or hardware store."

The needle in the haystack...

"Our killer may be in construction," Trent said.

"I think you're grasping," Rideout said.

"I agree," Amanda chimed in. "Without knowing when or where it was bought, it's a shot in the dark. Also was it acquired with the intention of using it as a murder weapon or was it simply convenient and within reach?"

"Which would imply the killer already had it on hand," Trent volleyed back.

Amanda nodded. "Not saying we'll rule out anyone in construction." She turned to Rideout. "What was its condition—new or has it seen previous use?"

"That's a tricky question. It's metal. Etches are present right from the factory."

She had a bad feeling he might say that.

Rideout continued. "Moving on... There are contusions present on the vic's neck that were not caused by the chain, rather with repetitive squeezing. This was done by hand."

"Any chance at determining hand size?" This had proven helpful in a previous investigation.

"Not this time."

"You put it as repetitive squeezing. Was Reese choked out?" Amanda blanched at what that might mean. "Specifically thinking erotic asphyxia? Was she sexually violated?" This is where Amanda held her breath, counting the passing seconds until the answer came.

"There is no evidence of sexual assault."

She let out a sigh. At least for all this girl had suffered, she hadn't been raped as well.

"How do you know the choking didn't kill her?" Trent asked.

"Ah, good question, Detective." Rideout smiled at Trent. "Because of the coloring of the bruising."

Amanda was familiar with how bruises changed hues. "How long ago was it caused?"

"A couple days before death."

"She was last seen on Wednesday," Amanda said.

"And time of death was definitely Friday. Specifically, between seven and nine, as I originally suspected."

"Two days later," Trent lamented.

"That seems consistent with the contusions."

Amanda sank into her chair. "She was choked as soon as Wednesday?"

"Based on the coloration, yes. Do you have anything to suggest otherwise?"

"Not exactly." Getting that message to Laurel analyzed just moved up in importance. If Reese had drifted out of consciousness at the hands of her captor, it was highly unlikely she'd have a lucid opportunity to text. Add to that, the killer wouldn't put a phone in her hands when there was the risk of it being used to call for help. "She was taken after leaving home and killed two days later." Saying the obvious just reinforced that there was a window of time in which she could have been saved. If only they had known she was even in trouble then…

Rideout set his lips in a straight line. "I wish I had better news. And, unfortunately, it doesn't get any better from here."

"Fair warning." Though she never expected good news from Rideout. She only ever hoped for tidbits that led to a killer.

"You may remember that I mentioned at the scene that there were blood droplets on the front of the dress she was wearing."

Amanda noted the ME's precise phrasing. *The dress she was wearing* versus *her dress*. The implication and understanding being that the killer had dressed the poor girl. Not a revelation. "Yes, I remember that."

"Well, I have confirmed the blood was hers, but included was aqueous humor, or in layman's terms, eye fluid."

"Oh, don't say it." Amanda laid a hand on her stomach.

"I do need to tell you—"

"Please don't tell me now that she was alive when the killer butchered her eyes?" Amanda wasn't sure she wanted the answer.

"She wasn't, and that wasn't what I was going to say."

Amanda let out a breath.

"I was simply going to point out the killer stabbed her eyes after they had dressed her *and* after they had killed her."

"How do you know that?" This from Trent.

"There would have been more blood. Also some of the fluid landed on the chain as well."

Another small mercy, in addition to not being raped—Reese had been dead prior to having her eyes gouged. What did this say about Amanda's life when these things were considered highlights? "Do you know what the killer used to inflict the damage?"

"I still don't. Just that the tool used would have been sharp with jagged edges."

"I'm trying to understand why the killer jabbed her eyes out after he'd already killed her," Trent summarized, not so delicately. "What kind of monster does that?"

"A sick one, angry one," Amanda said. "Possibly one that wasn't satisfied enough by the fact they took Reese's life."

"Agreed," Rideout told her.

"Given the violence of this act, it might have been a decision in the moment. If so, that might mean he used something close at hand to inflict the damage," Amanda reasoned.

"Bingo."

"So what's commonly within reach that's sharp with jagged edges?" Trent posed the question and netted silence in response.

"Let's hope once we narrow in on a suspect, we'll figure out that piece of the puzzle," she said.

Rideout went on. "I swabbed her lips and took a sampling of the tissue. These were forwarded to the lab. They should be able to determine the makeup of the adhesive used to paste her lips together."

"Was that done before or after death?" Amanda was feeling cocky, hoping that the girl hadn't lived through that horror either.

Rideout's face shadowed. "She was alive. There was indication that she'd tried pulling her lips apart. There were tears and missing dermal layers, the latter only visible under a microscope and after removing her cosmetics. Which leads me to another point. The killer would have put the cosmetics on her."

Amanda shook her head. "I just can't believe the lengths this killer went to in order to set the scene."

"Effort, yes. Homework, no," Rideout said. "The foundation was a couple of shades darker than the vic's skin tone."

"The brand of cosmetics?" Trent asked.

A reptilian smile, if on anyone else but Rideout might have

sent shivers trailing down her back. "I have sent swabs to the lab for processing. They might be able to tell you."

"Great." She tried to tag on a smile. It may prove to be a valuable lead, but sometimes more just felt like more. "And the dress, the tiara?"

"I was getting to those. Both are vintage. I uploaded some photographs into Google and ran an image search. Closest I found tells me the design of the dress dates to the nineties. The tiara is rather ageless in design, but some patina on the back tells me it's older too."

"So either our killer had the dress and tiara sitting around since the nineties or they picked it up at a secondhand shop," Amanda said.

"Yes, either or," Rideout responded. "There was a very subtle smell to the fabric, though distinct. Mothballs."

Just the mention of them had Amanda curling her lips in disgust. She hated their stench. It must have been faint or she would have picked up on it immediately. "Which still doesn't narrow it down."

Rideout pressed his lips and bulged his eyes as if to say this wasn't his puzzle to solve.

"Anything else we should know before we leave?" she asked.

"I've filled you in on everything I found. The lab has the samples and clothing with them. I've sent away for toxicology. We'll see if she was drugged. That can take a week or longer, as you know. Other than that, I think we're done here." Rideout smiled kindly, but his eyes dipped toward the door.

We are dismissed... She got up. "Thanks."

"Don't mention it."

She and Trent stepped into the hall.

"The girl's eyes," he said. "What makes someone do that to a victim who is already dead?"

He was obviously stuck on that point, trying too hard to

rationalize something that didn't stand up to reason. "As we said, someone with a lot of rage and hate to begin with."

"Yeah, I don't think we're looking at a teenager. Call it a gut feeling if you want."

"I'm not leaning that way at all either," she admitted. "That does leave us with another question to answer."

"Of course it does."

"What adult would have this much hatred for a teenage girl?"

"Here's another. Was it Reese specifically or what she represented?"

Amanda would love to refuse that Trent had a point, but it was one they'd considered before. The killer could be some screwed-up adult who took out their past on Reese Thompson. That beautiful teenager could have simply been collateral damage.

THIRTY

Amanda would have headed straight from the morgue to the crime lab if it wasn't a Sunday afternoon. It was unlikely that CSI Blair or Donnelly would be in, even with the case coming to them last night. Her questions would need to wait until tomorrow. And in all fairness, any samples Rideout had collected would have just been forwarded today. They'd need time to process them.

It's just she wanted all the answers yesterday. More importantly, whatever ones would put Reese Thompson's killer behind bars.

Trent was driving them to the Rolling Hills Country Club, and it had been a good thing Amanda called Vince Galloway before meeting up with Rideout. The manager had been at home and asked for an hour, saying that's the soonest he could get there.

Trent glanced at her from the driver's seat. "The man seen at Susie Valentine's, the white van, dressed in coveralls... Is the getup because he's in construction?"

"We will drive ourselves crazy fast if we speculate too

much. As we said, the chain could be explained a million ways. Just like where it was bought and when."

"Again, you're right. But we shouldn't dismiss the possibility the killer may work in construction."

"We can put it in the back pocket, sure, but I don't suggest we fixate on it."

Trent parked in the lot for the golf club, and once they were inside, they were directed up the staircase for Vince's office. His door was cracked open, and his voice traveled into the hall. From the sound of the one-sided conversation, he was wrapping up a phone call.

Amanda moved into the doorway as he replaced the receiver to its cradle.

"Detectives," he said in a broad greeting, gesturing for them to sit in the two chairs across from his desk. Amanda and Trent sat down. Vince said, "I got here faster than the hour and got to work. You had mentioned on the phone, you were curious if anyone saw Susie Valentine yesterday. Well, I've spoken to everyone who was working, and none of them saw Susie."

"And you're sure of this?" Amanda asked. "Even Lisa Bradford?"

"Even her. And I'm just passing along what I was told. I hadn't seen her either. A few minutes ago, I tried calling her, but her phone rings straight to voicemail." He sat back in his chair and rubbed his forehead, narrowed his eyes. "Should I be worried about any of this?"

"Do employees actually clock in here?" she countered, letting his question go untouched for now.

"No, they don't."

"And when was Ms. Valentine scheduled to start yesterday?" They already knew that her quitting time was six o'clock.

"She should have been here for ten in the morning."

Amanda nodded. The neighbor woman saw the man in Susie Valentine's driveway at eight thirty. If he was the killer, that afforded him plenty of time to murder her and even show up at Rolling Hills for 10 AM, assuming her identity. But without a need to punch in that wasn't necessary. It did confirm though, if the killer got to Susie, he must have known he'd need to kill her before her shift yesterday morning.

"Detective, you never answered my question. Should I be concerned about her?"

Amanda's immediate reaction was yes, but there was no sense getting the manager worked up when there was nothing he could do. "We've just been trying to reach her. Would you, by chance, have an emergency contact for her on file?"

"Should have. Let me see." Vince dug into the drawer of a filing cabinet. A few seconds later, he was cracking open a folder, flipping through the pages. "Here it is. Margie Hudson. Relation is sister."

"May I see?" Amanda reached out and took the page. It was a standard form that likely all employees had on file. She looked to the bottom where Susie Valentine had signed off. She pressed a finger to it, pointing it out to Trent. "Would you mind if we took this with us?"

"Ah, I guess that's fine. Let me make a copy though." Vince got up and did just that. He handed Amanda the duplicate.

"Thank you." Amanda stood. "I believe you still have my card. Call me immediately if you see or hear from Susie Valentine."

"Will do."

"Just before we leave, when is she due in for her next shift?" she asked.

"Tomorrow."

Amanda nodded and left his office. Her insides were quaking as adrenaline and suspicion filled her with nerves. She managed to keep quiet until she got into the department car with Trent. "I have a horrible feeling..."

"You're not the only one."

As Trent drove back to Susie Valentine's, Amanda called Malone on speaker. He answered on the second ring, and she filled him in on the situation.

"Huh. Sounds fishy all right. Call the sister, see if she has a way of getting into Valentine's house. Keep me posted on what you find."

"Will do." Amanda grabbed the number for Margie Hudson from the emergency contact form and pecked it into her phone.

"Hello?" The woman who answered sounded hesitant and ready to disconnect if given any reason. Thankfully she'd answered as Amanda's number would have shown Unknown on Margie's caller ID.

"This is Detective Amanda Steele with the Prince William County Police Department," she said. "Are you Margie Hudson?"

"I am."

"I'm calling about your sister, Susie Valentine."

"Is she okay?"

"We are doing a welfare check." Not far from the truth, and it sounded less menacing. "Would you happen to have another number for her? We have her cell phone but haven't been able to get through."

"That's all she has. She had her landline disconnected a while ago."

"You wouldn't by chance have a key to her place?" The sisters were obviously close enough for Susie to provide Margie as her emergency contact.

"I do."

"Would you be able to meet us at Susie's house within the next hour?" Amanda was being generous, not knowing where Margie was coming from.

"I'll be there in less than five minutes. I live the next block over."

Amanda gestured with a pointed finger toward the windshield, hoping Trent would get the enclosed message to press harder on the gas. And he must have deciphered the meaning as they bolted ahead. "We'll be right there. If you beat us, please wait before going inside."

"Okay," Margie dragged out.

Amanda hoped her suspicion about Valentine was wrong, but in case she wasn't, she didn't want her sister walking in to find her dead body.

They arrived at Valentine's and found a woman in her fifties pacing the driveway, looking left and right down the street. She stood still when the department car came to a stop.

Amanda approached, holding up her badge. "Detective Steele. I assume you're Margie Hudson."

"I am." Her gaze drifted to Trent.

"I'm Detective Stenson, ma'am."

She nodded, but given the faraway look in her eyes, her mind was elsewhere. Amanda understood how being called by the police as she had would have been jolting.

"I knocked and tried calling. She's not answering, but her car is here. This makes no sense." Margie raked her hands through her hair, and her complexion blanched.

"As I mentioned on the phone, we're doing a welfare check on your sister," Amanda began, talking calmly. "Could I get the key to the house?"

Margie dug into her pants pocket and pulled out a lone key on a ring and handed it over to Amanda.

"Thank you. Please wait out here with Detective Stenson while I check on her."

"Okay." Margie rubbed her arms.

Amanda left Trent with Margie and went to the front door. She slipped the key into the lock and turned. The click let her know she was good to go inside. She hesitated briefly, then she entered. Her gut already sensed, *knew*, what she would find.

Still, she called out from the entryway, "Ms. Valentine, this is Prince William County PD. Please respond if you're here."

Amanda's voice rang back to her ears as if the home were empty and hollow. The lack of a response was only deepening her conclusion that Susie Valentine was dead. There was also that cloying feeling creeping over her.

She walked down the hall toward the back of the house, letting instinct guide her. She peeked in each room she passed. When she came to a staircase, she headed up.

The smell of decomp reached her nostrils—putrid and slightly sweet.

With each step, the stench was getting stronger. A peek into the second room, on the right, had her drawing back. She blew out the smell and recentered herself.

Susie Valentine was lying supine on her bed, the sheets and comforter pushed down and bunched at the end of the mattress. A chain was wound tightly around her neck.

Amanda retreated from the home, careful not to touch anything. She met Trent's gaze once she stepped outside and shook her head.

Margie's legs buckled, and Amanda and Trent rushed to keep her upright.

"She's, she's... ah...?" Margie said.

"I'm sorry to inform you, but your sister is dead." Amanda would leave the sordid details until later and once they had the poor woman seated.

"No!" Margie wailed out as she lowered to her haunches and covered her face with her hands.

Trent pulled his phone and made the calls to get everyone there, while Amanda comforted Margie, helping her back up and coaxing her to the department car. She opened the back door for her and said, "Take a seat, Ms. Hudson." Not a request but a kind recommendation, which Margie didn't protest.

"I can't believe this. How did she, ah, die?" Margie palmed her wet cheeks, her eyes still glistening with unshed tears.

"We'll need to wait for the medical examiner to arrive, but it is apparent that she was murdered." Amanda didn't feel she'd spoken out of turn. The scene told her all she needed to know about the manner of death. It was most likely the work of the person who had killed Reese Thompson. Otherwise what were the chances that Susie Valentine would wind up with a chain around her neck too?

"What? Why? Who would do such a thing?"

"Is your sister a social person, Ms. Hudson? With lots of friends?"

"She is. Ah, *was*." Her voice cracked on her correction.

"Did she have a new person in her life? A boyfriend or girlfriend?" Without knowing the killer's identity, it wasn't possible to pin down if or for how long he'd been planning the murders.

"No. She would have told me. We spoke often."

"Did she live alone?"

"Uh-huh."

It would seem the killer may have seen Susie Valentine as a means to an end—to get a key to the club. The fact she was single and lived alone made her a soft target.

Two police cruisers pulled up, and three officers got out of them. They talked among themselves, and from what Amanda overheard they were discussing the setting up of the perimeter around the property. It would keep traffic and pedestrians at bay, along with the media.

She excused herself from Margie when Officer Cochran headed her way.

"Busy couple of days for you," Traci Cochran said. "I heard about that poor girl."

"Yeah." There were no more words, and Traci was likely feeling this one more because she'd filed the missing person report on Reese Thompson.

"Do you believe this is connected somehow?" She nudged her head toward the house.

"No doubt in my mind."

"Want me to take over collecting her statement and information?"

"Yes, please."

"On it." Traci tapped Amanda on the shoulder as she walked past to join Margie Hudson.

Amanda headed over to Trent, who had just pocketed his phone.

"Everyone should be here soon," he said.

"You get a hold of Malone?"

"Yep. He's on his way too."

"The killer used a chain, Trent. He doesn't even care that it will connect him to Reese's murder. What the heck are we looking at here?" She meant the question as rhetorical. Her mind tried to see the larger picture and what it told them about their killer.

"It's like killing is a game to him."

"Oh, please don't say that."

"What should I say? I think we can both agree that this killer isn't going to let anything stand in his way."

"Right. It also suggests he wanted Reese Thompson to be found at her prom, no matter the cost or the risk."

"Strongly motivated, check."

"And organized. Reese's abduction was unlikely premeditated as there was no way for the killer to have anticipated the argument she had with her mother."

"Except if she was taken from Prince William Forest Park, a place she frequented, the killer may have taken advantage of the situation. Whether it was an opportunistic killing or planned is hard to say when it comes to Reese." Amanda flicked a finger toward Valentine's house. "With Valentine, it's a different story. It was calculated."

"Agreed," Trent echoed back.

Amanda diverted down another path. "Now the killer could have disposed of Reese anywhere. Why stage her as prom queen and leave her at the venue? Was it important to them?"

"Beats me at this point."

"Me too." But how she wished she had more answers.

THIRTY-ONE

Ava's conscience was nagging at her from the second she'd hatched her escape plan. Compounding her guilt was that she hadn't simply snuck out of the house. She'd lied, right to her mother's face. And she'd taken her word and trusted the readout on the thermometer. She was given a pass to miss family dinner at her grandparents' place. If she got caught, she was dead. Her mother would kill her.

Five minutes after her parents left, Ava got moving. She found her phone in the cupboard where she'd seen her mother put it—an upper one above the fridge—and ordered a ride with a car service to Manassas.

She had wasted no time climbing into the back of the sedan the moment it arrived and promised the driver a nice tip if he made good time getting to the Rolling Hills Country Club.

As he drove, she kept looking out the back window. Not just due to the burden of regrets. Her skin was crawling like she was being watched. But they were on the move, and her many glances over a shoulder didn't show anyone following them. It had to be her vivid imagination in overdrive.

Instead of giving into her paranoia, she would best set her

mind to something productive. Like what she was going to do once she got to the golf club. She was armed with intent only—to find something tangible that would lead to Reese's killer.

The driver dropped her off close to five thirty, and she settled the fare with some of the cash she had. The man took it but wasn't thrilled she hadn't paid electronically. She put her hand on the door handle and stopped. Once she got out, she'd be on her own. Silly to feel that way though. The golf club was doing a healthy business given the full parking lot. Still, she said to the driver, "Is there any way you'd wait for me?"

The driver looked at her through the rearview mirror, his eyes a dull shade of brown. "For how long?"

"Not long."

"More specifically?"

"Say fifteen minutes?"

"That's a little long for me to be sitting around."

"I'll add some money to the return trip to cover your time."

He didn't say anything, simply held eye contact. Eventually, he dipped his head, and she got out of the car.

She took a deep breath, feeling relieved that she had her ride home squared away. She walked up to the country club, and a couple heading out held the door for her. Besides acknowledging her presence, they paid her no further attention. Though she wasn't exactly suspicious looking, no matter how much she felt out of place. And it might be common practice for teens of paying members to show up on the grounds.

Inside, she stopped near the doors, her gaze on the restroom where Reese had been found. Chills ran through her and had her stomach fluttering. A dead body had been mere feet away. And not just any body. That of Reese Thompson—Ava's best friend's sister and also someone Ava had known. She thought she was mentally prepared to return here, but her jitters confirmed how her mind had fictionalized everything, softening the edges of the darkness. But she understood why. It made it easier to deal with tragedy. It allowed her brain to dissect and approach situations with logic. But standing this close to the restroom, this soon after, was almost too much to digest.

"Can I help you?" A man in a club shirt, about her dad's age, was watching her with an eager expression.

"I'm fine. Thank you." She moved to step past him, but he shuffled over to block her path.

"The club is for paying members and their families. I've never seen you before. Who are you here to see?" He narrowed his eyes and slightly tilted his head—both tells she didn't care for. He was suspicious of her presence. "Miss," he prompted.

"I..." She hemmed a second too long.

"Yes, as I thought. You can't come in here to gawk after what happened last night. Please leave." He gestured toward the door, making his entire hand an arrow. It might as well have been neon lit.

Her mind was blank for a reason to stay, but then she caught sight of a woman at the back of the lobby. She wore a collared T-shirt. "I'm here to see my mom." Ava gestured toward her, and the man's eyes followed the direction she'd indicated. Ava didn't wait for him to say anything or react but took off in the woman's direction.

"Really?" the man huffed behind her, and she waved back at him and smiled. He shook his head and flailed his arms in the air.

At least he wasn't coming after her. And the interaction with him had reset her mind and got her legs moving. Not that she had a clue where she should go.

She'd follow her instinct, and it led her toward a door with a card reader and plaque that read *Employees Only*. The room behind here was probably where the man had exited from last night. She tried the handle, stubbornly refusing to accept this barricade, but it was locked.

Most times she was patient and would have stood around

thinking her way through. But she didn't have that luxury right now. The man was watching her from the front doors. She had to move on. She passed through a public door to outside where she and Nadine had been last night. A small lot with golf carts was to the side, and straight back were the greens. Golfers dotted the course. *Unbelievable! Business as usual. Like Reese never mattered.*

She walked along the building, much as she and Nadine had done last night. She glanced over a shoulder at the sound of the door opening. It was that nosy man; he was following her.

Is he the killer?

Her heart paused, and her chest froze on an exhale. Probably just paranoia, but she wasn't going to let him catch up with her to confirm it. Besides, she hadn't even accomplished anything yet.

Thankfully, with all the activity around, she'd blend in with the crowd. She weaved through the small lot and ducked behind a shed next to a garbage bin. As she did so, last night came flashing back—how she and Nadine had done the same thing then too. Different bin, but same aversion method.

Silly thought of no consequence, but it came anyhow.

She overheard the man asking someone if they saw a teenage girl with brown hair walk by, but whoever he'd asked told him no. His asking gave her comfort, because if he was the killer, he wouldn't want to draw attention to himself. Would he?

She gulped.

Either way, his steps were getting closer. If she stayed put, she'd get caught, and that wasn't an option. She had every intention of doing her snooping and making it home without her parents being any the wiser. This man would insist on calling them.

Ava tried the door on the shed—it was unlocked, and she slipped inside. There was little light that fought its way through dirty windows—outlines of riding lawnmowers and weed whippers, and also other machines she didn't recognize. Possibly they were geared more toward maintaining a pristine golf course.

The man's voice repeatedly struck her ears. He must be repeating his question to everyone he passed. Thankfully, she was rather invisible as people kept telling him they hadn't seen a teenage girl.

She tucked against the wall under the window, where she found the most space, and waited until she didn't hear him anymore. She popped her head up and saw no sign of him. He must have given up on finding her and returned inside. She hoped anyway.

After five minutes, she left the shed and walked toward the club and the door the man had come out of last night. If she could get inside there, she might get some answers—who he was, where he came from. All Ava knew was something within her was compelling her forward.

But why she'd bother to check was beyond her. It was probably secured like the one inside. As she got closer she saw the door was propped open. *Finally a break!*

Looking left and right, with a quick shot backward, she confirmed the coast was clear and slipped inside.

It was hot as if the air conditioning didn't even touch this space. Sweat ran down Ava's back as she took everything in. No one was in here, small mercy, and this left her free to poke around. It was a janitorial room with an industrial washer and dryer. Folded towels and table linens—for members and the onsite restaurant—filled several shelves along with cleaning products. There were also large, wheeled bins which could have been used for the laundry or collecting garbage around the grounds.

Ava walked toward a plastic garbage bin in the corner. Its lid was propped up and tilted to the side.

Ava recalled hearing from her grandfather or aunt—or TV

for that matter—that garbage could tell investigators a lot. And it would seem this one hadn't been emptied in a while.

There was no smell coming from it, for which Ava was grateful, and a quick peek inside showed a lot of lint and some empty containers from used-up cleaning products. She wasn't willing to dig down and took this one at face value. She returned the lid and realized how she'd passed up the opportunity to look in the other garbage bins she'd been near on the property. If the crime scene investigators didn't check this one, the likelihood was they hadn't looked in them either.

Ava went back outside and peeked into the bins as she passed them. She stopped when her eye caught on beige fabric. She backtracked and looked closer. It had the club's logo on the sleeve.

Shivers danced over her shoulders. She felt like someone was watching her. But looking around, she didn't see anyone paying her any attention. She pulled out her find. A T-shirt. Aside from being in the garbage, she saw nothing wrong with it. No holes or rips. Why would anyone throw away a perfectly good shirt?

Ava turned it around in her hands. *STAFF* was emblazoned on the back, up near the neck like the shirts employees of the club wore, but this one was an iron-on appliqué. She only knew that from doing crafts with her mother when she was younger. The project had been bedazzling a shirt, and Ava had wanted to put a large cartoon daisy on the front. Her mother had found one at the fabric store and showed Ava how it worked.

But an iron-on appliqué for a uniform shirt? She doubted the legitimate staff shirts had that. It struck Ava as cheap-looking, and not an image Rolling Hills would want to present.

"Hey, kid!" It was that man from the club, and he was bolting toward her.

She pulled off her backpack and tucked the shirt inside,

cringing as a pungent and assaulting odor hit her nose. Mothballs. *Yuck!*

Then she ran as fast as her legs would carry her—around the building to the lot and the waiting driver. She got into the back seat, panting. "Go. Please."

The driver didn't question why a man was chasing her, just hit the gas. His tip would be bigger than the one she'd given him to drive here. As he started down the road, Ava got those chills again, the feeling of being watched. She passed a look through the back window and saw a white GMC van. Didn't she see one on the way here? But, again, she dismissed her fear as paranoia. There had to be a million white vans on the road.

THIRTY-TWO

The street outside Susie Valentine's house was buzzing with police presence. Amanda and Trent were still there, and the investigators had shown up, followed shortly after by Hans Rideout. It was a full-fledged "party." Malone had called to say he would be a bit longer but that had been thirty minutes ago. He should be there soon.

Amanda stood with Trent near the door. Investigators hadn't found any evidence of forced entry. That didn't mean the killer hadn't lifted a window and slipped inside. But it was also possible Susie Valentine had admitted the killer into her home. He could have sold himself as working with the cable company or some other business and wormed his way inside.

For that matter, Susie Valentine may have been murdered elsewhere in the house and then put in her bed. Their killer showed a penchant for staging things. Whatever the case, they'd need to wait to find out what the evidence told them. All she and Trent really had was a man showing up in Valentine's drive around eight thirty Saturday morning. Well, that and the fact the CSIs hadn't recovered Valentine's keys, including one for Rolling Hills.

Officer Cochran had taken Margie Hudson's full statement, then delivered her home and had asked she stay there. She told Amanda afterward that Margie was adamant her sister didn't have a man in her life and had kept repeating, "Who would do this?"

Amanda's phone rang, and she answered upon seeing *Sheila Marsh*. So much had happened since noon that concerns about the sleepover had left her mind.

"Oh my goodness, Amanda, I'm so sorry. I just saw your text. Somehow my volume got muted."

"It happens. Is there anything I should know about? Did something happen when Zoe was sleeping over? She's not herself."

There was a pause for a few seconds, then, "I'm guessing Zoe never told you. I didn't want to make a big deal of it."

"Of what?"

"Zoe peed the bed last night. My fault, really, I should have stopped the girls from drinking earlier."

Amanda wanted to offer reassurance, but Sheila should have known better. She balanced this new information with Zoe's declaration that Maria was no longer her friend. "I'm guessing your daughter knew about the mishap?"

"It's kind of hard to hide these things."

Her unapologetic tone set Amanda on edge. "Did Maria tease her about it?"

"You know how kids can be."

Amanda's heart sped up as anger pulsed through her. As the adult, Sheila should have stepped in. She was about to respond when the woman resumed talking.

"I corrected Maria, told her to be nice to Zoe. I explained that these things happen sometimes, and it could have just as easily been her."

Amanda appreciated that Sheila had probably done her best to smooth the situation. But Maria was just a kid. She could have been kind in front of her mother only to pick up ridiculing Zoe in her absence. *Poor Zoe.* This wasn't the first time Zoe had peed the bed either, though that was some time ago. She was probably feeling ashamed and that had her being distant with Amanda. "Thanks for getting back to me."

"Sorry it wasn't sooner."

Amanda ended the call as Malone pulled up in his SUV. He came for her, and Trent stepped over too.

"Bring me up to speed." Malone was a little out of breath.

"You all right?" She worried about his health more since his brain tumor.

Malone waved a hand of dismissal. "Just aggravated... Feels like I'm running behind."

Amanda nodded, appreciating that. Malone liked being on top of things and playing catch up would bother him.

"So, get talking," he prompted.

Amanda ran through the scene while Malone listened intently. He perched his hands on his hips. "What do you think is going on? First the girl, then Susie Valentine? What's the connection... well, besides the golf course?"

"I can't imagine there was one between Valentine and her killer," Amanda said. "Trent and I think that Valentine was killed to get her key to the club."

"Okay, but still, how did the killer know she had one?" Malone pressed his brows, and it had Amanda turning to Trent.

"Don't have an answer." Amanda was ashamed she hadn't thought of that before now either. She gave herself a pass that she would have eventually gotten there. In an investigation everything didn't hit at once. And a fresh perspective was always useful. The fact she was operating on a few hours' sleep in the last twenty-four probably didn't help her cognitive abilities. She went with what they had surmised. "We think the killer was privy to the club's practice of locking its doors to the public between five and six thirty."

"It was during that time we believe the killer brought in Reese's body and put her in the restroom," Trent said. "They signed off as Valentine on the cleaning log."

"All right. Back to Reese's body," Malone said. "What's to say the killer didn't have it on site beforehand and then slipped it into the restroom later? I read the autopsy report Rideout fired over, and Reese Thompson was dead on Friday."

"Yes, but Valentine was likely murdered Saturday morning. So the killer wouldn't have had a key until then."

"The ME tell you TOD?"

"Not for Valentine. Now a neighbor did see her Friday night but witnessed that man that I told you about."

"Right. Driving a white GMC van. We can't exactly issue a BOLO with so little."

She angled her head as if to say *obviously*.

"So we have one possible suspect. An unknown male."

The blunt summation had the images flooding her mind. Reese's young face, empty, shallow, hidden horrors. Then Susie's prone body, her eyes toward the ceiling, unseeing. "Pretty much. You might have read it in Rideout's report, but the chain used in Reese's murder was heavy duty, often used for general purpose. Our killer may be in construction or renovation, though I say *may* hesitantly."

"Or they bought the chain for a home project. *Or* just for the purpose of strangling the Thompson girl." Malone tossed out alternatives.

"It's best guess at this point," she admitted. "But there's a chain around Valentine's neck too."

"Same kind?"

Amanda shook her head. "Similar, but it has smaller links."

"If the killer's an outsider, how would they have moved about freely during the lockdown?" Malone set his hands on his hips.

"Who knows how many employees the club has," Trent

said. "But I wouldn't think it was a staff member though. They'd probably be able to get their hand on a key much easier than needing to kill someone."

"Well it seems the killer has or had some connection to Rolling Hills to know all they did—about the locked doors and the need for a key," Malone said. "You want to call the club's manager, Trent, and get a list of former employees?"

"Sure." Trent stepped away, pulling out his phone as he moved.

"This killer could have blended in," Amanda began. "As Trent hinted at, there are probably a lot of employees on the grounds at any given time. Might be worth noting club employees wear shirts with *STAFF* embroidered on the back."

Malone splayed his arms open. "See? It's even more possible we're looking at a former employee who held on to their shirt."

"Very well may be. But if this man in the coveralls is our killer, there's no way he would have fit into any of Valentine's clothes. At least basing that on the neighbor's description that the man was huge. Valentine's petite." Amanda's phone rang, and she flinched. Malone must have caught it as he smirked. She saw from the caller ID it was her mother. If she forwarded her to voicemail, she'd keep calling.

"Hi, Mom. It's not a good time right now," she answered.

"You could have given me a heads up you weren't coming for dinner tonight."

"I'm... sorry?" Not that she was, nor did she understand why her mother seemed upset by the fact. "Logan and Zoe should be there."

"Oh, they are, and they passed on your regards."

"You know the job, and I'm in the middle of an investigation." Two now, technically, but Amanda wasn't getting into the semantics with her mother.

"I know it all right. Your father would miss a lot of meals due to some case or other."

Before knowing about her father's brief and long-ago affair with CSI Emma Blair, Amanda would have taken her mother's words at face value. But now the possibility was real that on some of those occasions it wasn't his job as police chief that had him occupied. "Okay, Mom, I have to go."

"Fine, you do that, but it's bad enough Ava isn't here and now you. Just miss you both is all."

Amanda would rush to defend herself, stating she was there last Sunday for the family dinner, but her mind was stuck on something else. "Ava's not there?"

"Nope. Kristen said she's got a fever and isn't feeling well."

"So she's at home?"

"I'd think so. Yes."

Of that Amanda wasn't so confident. Little Sleuth Ava may have faked sickness to afford her leeway to sneak out and poke around. If Amanda was in Dumfries, she'd stop by the house to check on the girl. But she wasn't about to voice her suspicions to her mother. "Is Kristen there?"

"Yes, at least she showed up."

"Could you put her on the phone?"

"Uh-huh." The receiver was set down, and it clinked against a hard surface. Amanda heard her mother telling Kristen that Amanda was on the phone for her.

More scuffling, then, "Amanda, what is it?"

Apparently, her sister was still pissed off at her. "Ava's home sick?"

"What about it?"

"You really think she is?" As the accusation tumbled out, Amanda felt she was betraying her niece.

"Why would she lie? Oh my god, I'm an idiot."

"Listen, I'm not saying she's snuck out—"

"That's exactly what you're saying. But I saw the thermometer. She has a mild fever."

Amanda let her sister sit with that for a few seconds.

Kristen sighed. "That little shit."

"Again, Ava might be legitimately sick, but…"

"She likely held the dumb thing under her desk lamp. It gets hot as hell. Unbelievable. Erik!" Kristen yelled, possibly over a shoulder, but the volume wasn't dampened much. Back into the receiver, she said, "We're going home right now to check in."

"Let me know—"

Kristen hung up.

Huh. Amanda should probably get comfortable in the doghouse. Now, it wasn't just her niece and sister who were angry with her. Her mother would blame her for two more guests leaving.

"Everything all right?" Malone, who had stepped a few feet away, came back to Amanda.

"Let me guess, you heard the screaming from where you were?"

"Want to talk about it?"

So that's a yes… "Too much to get into." And she didn't want to. The last thing she wanted was to tell her sergeant—family friend or not—that her niece may be sleuthing around their investigation again.

THIRTY-THREE

Amanda stepped inside Susie Valentine's house. Rideout and Liam had been inside for some time, and they should have some information for her and Trent.

They were working on zipping the body into a black bag when Trent and Amanda graced the bedroom doorway.

"There you are," Rideout said. "Highlights, or lowlights if you wish, manner of death was obviously murder. Time of death I'd place preliminarily as Saturday morning between seven and ten."

She turned to Trent. "Think that man with the white van is even less of a coincidence now. He was seen in the victim's driveway around eight thirty." She'd added the latter part for Rideout and Liam.

Trent nodded.

Just how did they get from here to his identity? The neighbor didn't catch the plate on the van, but the vehicle type was often used in commercial fleets. Though sometimes Savanas were used in the construction industry. Either way, their witness said it was devoid of lettering.

"Cause of death?" Trent asked Rideout.

"I feel confident in saying asphyxiation caused by ligature strangulation. Petechiae was present and abundant."

Amanda nodded. "And was the chain the weapon?" Life experience taught her not to blindly trust what the eyes saw.

"It would seem so."

"He would have brought it with him," Trent said.

"Do you believe the victim was in bed, sleeping, at the time of the attack?" Amanda asked.

"I'd say it's most likely. There were no defensive wounds."

That would mean the killer found their own way into the house. The investigators would need to take a closer look at all access points. "All right. And when will you be conducting the autopsy?" She leveled the question at Liam.

"Tomorrow morning at ten."

She acknowledged with a dip of her head and led the way down the hall and back outside. "Let's touch base with the neighbor again," she said to Trent.

Beverly Robin stepped outside as Amanda and Trent started up her driveway. Amanda imagined the woman had been perched at her front window watching the activity across the street. Her hair was frizzy, and her eyes bulging.

"Something happened to her, didn't it?" The woman gathered the material of her shirt at her collar and flexed her hand.

"I'm afraid so," Amanda told her.

"She's dead?"

"Unfortunately," Amanda said.

"I wonder if it was that man who did it. The more I thought about him, his unlettered van… It didn't make sense."

"Why is that?" Trent asked.

"Don't these big companies make sure their name's slapped on their vehicles? But, I suppose the way he was dressed and carrying that bag must have given me the impression he was with the cable company anyway."

Amanda had forgotten about the duffel bag that Beverly

had mentioned on their first visit. It fit though. Running with the assumption this man was the killer, he'd need a means of concealing the chain. "Did you see him go into Ms. Valentine's house?"

Beverly slid her bottom lip through her teeth, squinted. "No, and I don't think he knocked on her front door either." Her forehead furrowed in concentration, and then she waggled a finger in the air. "Ah, yes, I remember now. He went around to the back of the house. That was another reason I thought he was with the cable company. I assumed he was checking on the wiring back there."

Typically, wired services were fed from the street to the front of the house. A quick look over her shoulder confirmed there were none. It must have connected from a back street in Valentine's case. "Thank you, Ms. Robin. You've been an incredible help."

"I hope you get the person who did this. Susie was always kind and patient with me."

"Thanks. And if you think of anything—"

Beverly's eyes widened. "Just remembered something. You asked me if I saw a license plate, and I told you no. I didn't, but the reason was because there wasn't one on the back. Maybe none on the front either. That I can't say."

Amanda thanked her again, and she and Trent left.

He turned to Amanda, and they stopped in the mouth of Beverly's driveway. "Both a front and rear plate are legally required. Getting more suspicious about this mystery man every minute."

"Please don't tell me you just said, 'mystery man.'"

"Isn't there usually at least one per case? That's what you've said before. We're just on par for a murder investigation."

"A golfing pun? Really?"

She smiled at the lightheartedness of their banter. "I know... *Groan*. But on a serious note, our killer might show the ability to plan out his next moves, but he's not entirely organized."

"And he takes risks. Walking into Valentine's backyard in plain sight of the neighbors, driving around in a van with at least one missing plate... Those are two things I can think of off the top."

"Slip-ups like these suggest strong emotions are involved. I'd say his reason for killing is very personal to him, possibly deeply entrenched. And I'm not suggesting he's a serial killer." She held up a hand to discourage her partner before he got carried away. "But when considering these crime scenes, there's such a high level of hatred evident, especially in Reese Thompson's case. But even to strangle—not one, but two people—watching the light go out of their eyes... That takes a certain type of killer."

"Yep. And there has to be a message in the fact the killer took the time to pose her just so. But a man taking an interest in the prom...?"

Amanda's mind recalled what Adrian had said about how girls made such a fuss over the event, even going overboard. "Huh. Did a prom queen hurt him in the past? Of course, I'm just spitballing."

"Could be. But Ms. Robin described the man as being in his mid-forties. His prom days are far behind him. Why now? What was it about Reese Thompson?"

She considered Trent's questions. "There had to be some personal tie or connection. I think Reese very well may have known her killer. She may even have gone with them willingly to start."

"That's a sad thought."

"Yep. And not an entirely new one." She pulled her phone and checked the time, more for a distraction than anything. It was going on 6:10 PM. "By chance, has Vince Galloway sent over the former employee list?"

"He said he'd get it over by noon tomorrow, latest."

"Why not before then?"

"He can only look it up by going through the physical files. Guess they have a cabinet that houses the files for former employees, but it's in alphabetical order, not based on last date of employment. And I asked for the last few months," he tagged on.

"And they don't have any digital record of this?" She found it hard to believe they wouldn't.

"They do, and that's why we need to wait until tomorrow. He's going to get the head of HR to get the information together."

"Can't do much about that then. We'll have to wait." *Just like with everything else*, she thought. They were already waiting on a warrant to watch the surveillance video and for Reese Thompson's phone records to come through from the provider. It felt like they'd been waiting forever for these things, but it was less than twelve hours. On the upside, Briggs in Digital Forensics would start looking at Laurel Wilkinson's phone and that text message within a few hours. Maybe he'd also come through with an update on Reese's phone.

Amanda's phone rang, and she immediately answered upon seeing caller ID. "Kristen?"

"She's not here," her sister rushed out.

Chills spread through her, fear for her niece's welfare foremost in mind. "Did you try calling her cell phone?"

"Of course I did—and she must have it as it's not where I put it—but she's not answering."

"But it's ringing?" There might be hope in that. Those criminally bent turned their victim's phone off to disable tracking.

"Yes," her sister hissed. "You need to find her, Amanda. If anything happens, I'm holding you responsible."

The phone suddenly felt hot in her hands. *I'm holding you responsible...* It had to be her sister's fear that was eager to lay blame should something bad happen to Ava. Maybe if Amanda thought like her niece, it might help pinpoint a place to start looking for her. Ava's drive thus far seemed to be wanting answers for her friend. It was reasonable to assume she might think returning to the crime scene was her best shot at getting them. "I'll find her," she pushed out.

"What? How? Where are you go—"

Amanda hung up and ran across the street, beelining for Malone. "I need to leave, Sarge."

Trent had hustled to keep up with her. Now he and Malone were looking at her with curiosity.

"There's a family situation." She glossed over the truth—that her niece was likely snooping around the investigation. Anything beyond that Amanda didn't even want to entertain.

Malone paled. "What's going on?"

She waved a hand. "Not a huge deal, but I need to check on it."

"Huh. Rather vague."

She remained silent, hoping that it would do the talking for her.

"Sure, go ahead. Suppose there's not much more you can do here right now anyhow."

"Thanks." She turned one step toward the department car, spun to Trent, and held out her hand. "I'll need the keys."

"I can drive," he told her but retracted under her gaze. "Then again, I could probably get a ride back to Woodbridge with the sarge."

"Why not?" Malone said.

"Great." Amanda wriggled her fingers.

Trent dropped the keys into her palm, and she wasted no time getting into the department car and gunning it down the road. Her mind was going mad thinking about her niece and the danger she might have gotten herself into.

THIRTY-FOUR

Rolling Hills Country Club was still open when Amanda pulled into the lot about six fifty. The days were getting longer, but there was probably only an hour until sunset. Amanda huffed it up the stairs to Vince Galloway's office and was grateful he was there.

"Detective Steele? I told your partner I'd get the list over in the morning."

"I'm not here about that. But now you brought that up, the sooner the better."

Vince's eyes narrowed marginally.

"Have you noticed a teenage girl, about five seven, long brown hair, straight— Oh, here's her picture." Amanda brought her photo up on her phone. "Was she on the premises this evening? She would have just been walking around, not playing golf with anyone. She might have been with another teenage girl." Amanda added that part in case her niece pulled Nadine into the fray too.

"She looks a touch familiar, but was she here last night?"

"She was." Amanda hugged her phone in her palm, wishing it were possible to reach out and hold her niece.

"That's probably why then. Since I came in to meet with you and your partner, I've been up here on the phone, talking with the club's lawyers. We're preparing ourselves for any possible repercussions from yesterday."

Vince had the business hat on and was taking necessary action, but somehow it felt shallow and cold in light of a young woman's murder. "I'm going to need to question your staff."

"Can I ask what this is about? Is this girl in danger or suspected to be hurt on the club's grounds?"

Amanda's stomach clenched. *Shove those thoughts aside!* "I don't believe so."

"I need to ask why you are looking for a teenage girl here." Vince leaned forward, clasping his hands on his desk.

She didn't want to get into the fact the girl under discussion was her niece. "After yesterday, students can become fascinated with death and poking their noses in where they don't belong."

"Ah." Vince smiled. "Someone's interfering with your investigation?"

As much as it pained her to admit such out loud, she said, "It's possible."

"Then, sure, I don't see what harm can come from you questioning my staff. But please keep your inquiries limited to this teen, nothing to do with the murdered girl from yesterday. If you have those types of questions, I'd kindly request you allow me to have the club attorney present."

"I understand." Amanda bounded from Vince's office and approached the first club employee she came across. She showed him Ava's photograph, and he hadn't seen her. She tried with a few more and still no luck.

"Excuse me, but who are you and what is your business here?" A lean man approached her, eyes full of suspicion. He presented himself as if he were the golf club's bouncer, but he wasn't built to toss anyone out.

She pulled her badge. "Detective Steele. Have you seen this

girl?" She held her phone's screen with Ava's picture toward him.

His eyes flicked to the photo. "I might have."

Anger and frustration waved through her. "Might have or did?"

"Did."

"Is she still here?"

He shook his head. "She left about an hour ago."

She glanced at the time stamp on her screen. It was currently 7 PM, so about six, depending on how accurate this man was at assessing time. Accounting for travel time, possible poking around, Ava must have left the house minutes after Kristen and Erik headed out for Mom and Dad's.

That little turd.

But the stark reality was Ava should have been home by now, so where was she? Her heart started to race. Where else might she have gone?

"She was a real treat too," the man added. "Wouldn't tell me what she was doing here. She said she was the daughter of someone on staff, but that was clearly a lie. I followed her through the back door and lost sight of her."

With every word from this man's mouth, the ugly scenarios painted themselves. "But you said she left an hour ago?" She'd cling to that tidbit.

"Uh-huh. I finally caught up with her. Well kind of, and then she was gone."

"What do you mean *caught up with her*?"

"I chased her to the lot."

Poor Ava. She must have been terrified. Though she never should have been here in the first place. Then a strange man runs after her. "And after that?" She rolled her hand impatiently. "You chased her, and she left. To where?"

Her phone chimed, but she'd look later. "Speak," she prompted the guy.

"She got into a vehicle."

Amanda's chest froze. "What kind of vehicle?" *Please don't say a white GMC van...*

"A Ford Focus."

"Did you catch the license plate or see the driver?"

"The driver was a white guy with brown hair, and I think it was a driving service. There was a Lyft sign on the dash."

She could call their customer support line and ask when the ride was completed, but would they answer that question? Likely not, but she had to try. She searched online and found the eight hundred number and called.

The man stood beside her as she inquired about the pick up from the club in Manassas about an hour ago. She provided the vehicle make and model and waited. There was a long pause. She was quite certain this was when she was going to hear they were not able to provide her information without violating customer privacy.

Instead, the woman said, "I probably shouldn't tell you this, but I'm a mom myself."

Amanda might have told a lie to get this far. She had no doubt if she approached from the law enforcement angle, the company representative would instantly get her back up and require a warrant to part with any information. "Oh, you have no idea what this means to me." Possibly a touch premature, but she was choosing to think positively.

"I'm seeing that the ride was taken to Dumfries and the fare dropped off at six thirty-two."

Roughly thirty minutes ago... "Six. Three. Two. You're sure?"

"Going by what the system's telling me."

She felt ill and lightheaded. "Where was the drop off?"

She listed an address which was a few blocks down from Kristen and Erik's house. What if Ava had gotten too close to the killer? He reacted and she was—

"Ma'am, are you still there?"

"Ah, yeah. Thanks." She ended the call and leveled her gaze at the club employee.

"Anything else I can do for you or...?" The man pressed his lips, as if impatient to be released.

Was there? Her niece may be in the hands of the monster who had strangled a teenage girl, stabbed her eyes out, glued her lips shut. She checked the message that had come through thinking it might be important to the case. It turned out to be Logan sharing a picture of him and Zoe at Amanda's parents' place. Zoe had gravy on her chin and was grinning. She must have been feeling better, but that happy place seemed a zillion miles away. Amanda cleared her throat and stuffed her phone into a pocket.

"You didn't by chance see a white GMC Savana in your lot, did you?" she asked the man.

"I kind of remember one driving behind them after they pulled out."

His answer had the blood in her veins turning to ice.

THIRTY-FIVE

Ava couldn't put off going home forever—even if she'd love to. When the Lyft driver had pulled around the corner about forty minutes ago, they'd passed her house. Mom's vehicle was in the driveway which meant both her and Dad had come home early from Grandma and Grandpa's. And her mom had been calling almost nonstop for the last half hour. She was so busted!

Ava directed the driver to drop her off a few blocks from home, and she'd been pacing the street, procrastinating. Her mother was going to kill her, and she wasn't going to count on her father for protection from her wrath. There were times she wondered if he feared her. And if all this wasn't killing her conscience, the T-shirt in her backpack felt like a heavy weight. What if it was a vital clue and she'd soiled it? She never should have snuck out and gone up to Manassas.

In the last few days—even before she and Nadine found Reese's phone—Ava had turned into someone she didn't recognize. She didn't like the reflection either. Lying to the people she loved and sneaking around wasn't who she wanted to be.

But she could justify it some. It was her best friend's sister's life. That weighed as responsibility on Ava even if she didn't fully understand why. She trusted her aunt Amanda, but she also knew police only had so many hours in the day to follow leads. What if some were missed?

She nudged out her chin. Yes, that's how she'd quiet the self-judgment.

Also what did her family expect of her? Law enforcement was in her blood. How many times had she listened to Grandpa Steele at the weekly family dinner talking about a closed case? Even Aunt Amanda. They were always so happy and light when they brought closure. That's the feeling Ava wanted.

Even though she knew it wasn't her job.

Even though she knew Amanda would find justice.

Even though she knew it was still early in the investigation.

Ava dropped down, sitting on the edge of a curb, her knees to her chin before she decided to stretch them out. The sun was growing weaker as the evening wore on, but the air was still warm.

She should probably turn in the shirt she'd found to her aunt. That seemed a no-brainer, but then what? No doubt she'd be on the receiving end of yet another lecture about how she shouldn't have gotten involved. How she'd messed up everything. She didn't need to hear it when she already knew it to be true.

Regardless of the trouble she'd be in, she had to let Aunt Amanda know about the shirt. To withhold it would be a grave mistake. Surely it had to mean something unless Ava had completely lost her mind. The fake appliqué alone told her something was off about it. But if it had been what the killer used to blend in at Rolling Hills, why dispose of it there and risk leaving trace? She'd seen enough TV crime dramas to know how just a tiny hair could lead to putting someone behind bars.

Ah, but they usually had a record, their DNA already in the system. That meant whoever had worn this shirt, presumably the killer, wasn't worried about that. He didn't have a record!

He'd used this shirt to blend in. It would have given him access to numerous areas of the building. He also must have had a way into the laundry area as that's the door she'd seen him come out last night. Besides, most wouldn't notice the makeshift job with the *STAFF* appliqué. People had short attention spans. Add to that, employees of the club were busy and people were arriving for the prom. He'd have been able to move about the premises freely and without attracting suspicion.

It seemed clear to her that whoever had worn this shirt had to be up to no good. Most likely the killer. She broke out in goosebumps and rubbed her arms. And what if he had found out she'd collected his shirt? Would it bother him? Had he been following in the white van?

A person knocked on someone's front door, the sound traveling in the evening air. Ava jumped a few good inches.

Jeez, Ava, get a grip!

She had best get a handle on her imagination, and hand over the shirt to Aunt Amanda as soon as possible. She stood up, prepping herself to face her mother.

Behind her, tires crunched along on the asphalt. She turned to see a white van slowing down.

A white van...? A wave of nausea rolled over her. Was it the same one she'd seen behind her on the way here?

She started walking faster.

The van inched forward, and the front passenger window lowered.

Ava refused to turn and kept her gaze ahead. *Just focus on getting home!* But her mind was still working...

She discreetly withdrew her phone and held it at her side and snapped a pic. Hopefully she got the plate, possibly the driver's face. She'd text it to Aunt Amanda later, but for now she just held her phone.

The van kept creeping along beside her.

Just go away!

She started to jog and found her father walking down the pathway from the neighbor's house toward the sidewalk.

"Ava? Oh my god, I'm so happy to see you."

Not as happy as I am! Ava snapped another pic. Her dad didn't seem to notice. Hopefully the person in the van hadn't either.

"Where have you been, young lady?" Softness in his voice and arch of his brow. Seeing his visible relief only had her feeling worse than before. She had been the source of his anxiety and fears.

"It's a long story, but I need to talk to Aunt Amanda right away."

The van's window went up, and it slowly pulled away.

"Long story or not, you're telling me and your mother first." Her father's tone had sharpened.

"Okay, I will," she consented.

The white van slowed at the stop sign down the street. There was no plate on the back. Weren't they required by law?

What would have happened to her if her dad hadn't shown up when he had?

Shivers tore through her.

THIRTY-SIX

The good news was Ava was home safe. The bad news was Amanda was at her sister's front door. Kristen had told her in no uncertain terms she didn't want to see her for a good, long while. If it wasn't for Ava's refusal to talk without Amanda present, who knows when that would be.

All Amanda had to do was twist the handle, knowing it would be unlocked. She hesitated.

The door swung open, and Kristen was standing there, hands on hips, a glower in place. "I'm not happy with you."

"That much is clear. Can I come in?"

Kristen flailed her hand and backed up to make room for Amanda to enter.

They joined Erik and Ava who were seated at the kitchen table. Her niece shied away from eye contact, but Amanda's brother-in-law lifted a hand in greeting. Her sister's tense energy permeated the entire house. For an ordinarily cheery person, when she was angry it pulsed off her in tangible waves.

"Would you like a coffee?" Erik offered and made a move to get up before Amanda even responded.

"That would be nice." She sat next to Ava and kept looking

at the girl, hoping to draw her gaze. Ava was preoccupied with picking at the end of her short shirtsleeve.

Kristen dropped into the chair beside Amanda. She was all about meeting Amanda's eye, but what defense could she offer for her niece? She had told Ava to leave the investigation to the police. Short of cuffing the girl to her bed frame, there wasn't anything Amanda could do. *And since that wasn't an option...*

"Ava, your mom said that you wanted to talk to me," Amanda said, wading in.

She nodded and now looked at Amanda. "But alone."

"Not happening, kiddo. Whatever you have to say we're hearing it too." This from Erik, who returned with a steaming cup of black coffee for Amanda.

She inhaled appreciatively and took a long draw. What was about to come was most likely going to be an uncomfortable discussion and given her niece's grim expression tack hours onto her night. "What is it, Ava?" Amanda encouraged kindly. "Whatever it is no one is going to get mad." She made certain she had Kristen's attention when promising that. Her sister gave a soft huff and crossed her arms.

Ava didn't seem to miss that either and took a deep breath. "I went up to Manassas, to the golf club." She paused there as if ascertaining whether this was new information for Amanda.

"I know that much, and I've told you that you need to leave the matter of Reese's murder to the police. To me."

"I want to. I trust you, but..."

"Right. It's the *but* part. What's going on?" The kid was rather deep, with many layers, and Amanda suspected something complex was motivating Ava to keep poking around.

"I just want to make things right for Nadine. She's my best friend, and it was her sister." A tear fell which Ava swiped away. "I liked Reese too. She saw me for who I am, not just some kid."

"I can understand why you'd want to do what you can to

help." Amanda felt the daggers that Kristen was shooting her way. She refused to buckle. "What happened at the country club, Ava?" She was tapping into her own cop intuition. Call it a feeling, but Ava had crossed the line somehow. "Did you find something, see something?"

Ava shrugged. "I was scared. I had this guy chasing me around, hounding me. I tried to get away from him."

"Amanda," Kristen blurted out. "She's going to get herself—"

Amanda held up a hand to silence her sister, and surprisingly it worked. "Your mom is right, Ava. You're putting yourself in unnecessary danger."

"I'm just doing what you would do," she snapped.

Amanda bristled. "Right, but I'm also a thirty-seven-year-old woman with a badge and a gun."

"I know," Ava mumbled. "That man wasn't the killer by the way. He just worked at the club. He wore one of those shirts. Ya know, with *STAFF* on the back."

Amanda tried to hide her pride. Her niece was certainly observant. But if she wasn't careful, it might get her into more trouble than she was in now. "How do you know someone on staff didn't kill Reese?"

"Um, I guess I don't.... But... Did you talk to that man who was whistling in the restroom?"

Kristen and Erik were watching Amanda with expectancy, as was Ava. Amanda recognized Ava's tactic of detouring the conversation so she could delay saying what she really had to share.

Amanda played along. "We did. His name is Clifford McIntosh. He's a substitute teacher at Potomac, Ava, for senior grades. And he can't whistle."

"What?" Her eyebrows pointed down. "Not Mr. McIntosh. I was talking about the other man standing by the food table."

The back of Amanda's neck tightened. *Another man?* She

searched her memory, and it wasn't coming through—not entirely. But there was a vague recollection of one—large build, wearing a short-sleeved collared shirt.

"He had big biceps. Come on, Amanda. Tell me you questioned him."

"I..." She hadn't, but an officer there would have. "What else do you remember about him?"

"He was probably about ten years older than you, brown hair."

The image was coming into better focus, and the description fit the man seen in Valentine's driveway. *Shit!* Had the killer been right there? Sticking around to witness the aftermath?

A span of silence fell over the room.

"Did you not talk to him?" Ava's face was a mask of panic.

"I didn't, but someone would have."

"Unless he slipped out before an officer had a chance. Aunt Amanda, this guy pretends to be who he isn't."

Amanda's breath froze in her chest. "How do you know that?"

"I found something. It's a shirt from the golf club, altered to say *STAFF* on the back." Ava turned to her mom. "It was an iron-on appliqué, like we've done together in the past." Ava reached down to the floor beside her.

"Wait." Amanda stood and put on gloves she had in her back pocket. "Let me get whatever it is."

Ava directed her to the main compartment of the backpack.

Amanda unzipped it and drew back. Mothballs. The same smell that was on the prom dress Reese wore. "Actually, Ava, I'll need to take your backpack with it inside. Less chance of further contamination."

Ava nodded. "But I don't think you're going to get anything useful from it."

Amanda snapped her gloves off. "What makes you say that?" She was curious to learn how her niece's mind worked.

"I say it belonged to Reese's killer. Who else would have a fake employee shirt? But if he was willing to toss it at the club, he's not worried about it tying back to him. He's not in the system, Aunt Amanda. Even if you find DNA, it will be useless."

Amanda sat back in her chair, impressed. Wow, her niece was incredible.

Ava added, "He might even have left it to mess with law enforcement. A sort of, look how smart I am."

Her impulse was to praise Ava for her amazing skill at investigating but wouldn't dare with her sister sitting right there. "Where did you find the shirt?"

"Behind the club in a garbage bin out near the maintenance shed."

"What took you back there?"

Amanda listened as Ava told her about a man who came out the staff door off the laundry room the night of the prom. When Ava finished talking, Amanda asked, "Could he be the same man near the food table?"

Ava's eyes snapped to Amanda's. "I think it might have been. Both were large build. Just the man inside wasn't wearing a staff shirt."

Simple enough. This guy posed as a club employee, ditched the shirt, and returned to the ballroom in a collared shirt. Brazen. But that fit with a killer who seemed to take risks. "About the shirt, what made you pull it out of the trash?"

"Just a hunch. It looked in great shape. There aren't any holes in it or anything, so why was it tossed?"

The more Ava said, the more Amanda wanted to get this shirt to the lab and analyzed. But she had a strong suspicion where the unaltered shirt had originated from. The Rolling Hills pro shop.

"Amanda, you need to do something about this..." Kristen flailed a hand toward Ava. "Please stress how dangerous it is for her to be playing detective."

"I know it is, Mom." Ava's voice carried a slight tremor, and the girl shrank into herself.

Amanda wondered what she wasn't telling them. "Is there anything else I should know?"

"Mom, Dad, can I please talk to Aunt Amanda alone?"

"Not on your life," Erik said, beating Kristen to likely saying the same thing.

Ava crossed her arms. "Then I won't talk."

Kristen and Erik looked at Amanda, then each other. "Five minutes, but remember, young lady, you're grounded for at least a month. Straight home after school, no phone."

"I get it. Completely cut off from life."

Kristen and Erik left, but Amanda was quite sure their steps stopped not far down the hall—within hearing distance.

Ava rolled her eyes and said, "I know you're still there."

Footsteps padded up the stairs, and all fell silent before Ava spoke.

"I, uh, am quite sure someone is following me. Mom and Dad would freak if they knew."

Amanda's heart fluttered, and her stomach tightened. But there was no point cautioning her again how risky it was for her to get involved. "Tell me why you think that." She was impressed by how calmly she put that out there.

Ava pulled her phone from a pant pocket. She fiddled on the screen. "Shoot, neither turned out."

"What is it?" Amanda's patience was tugged to the end of its tether.

Ava held her phone for Amanda to see. "I was hoping for the license plate or pic of the driver."

The photo on the screen was blurry, and the plate impossible to make out without guessing. Amanda didn't think Briggs would even stand a chance. Of more concern was the vehicle had a large grill, and the body was white. "Was this a van?"

Ava swallowed roughly and paled. "Uh-huh."

"A GMC Savana... big, boxy?"

"I think so..."

Amanda swiped to the next picture. It was blurred too; this one a shot of the cab. It was impossible to make out any distinguishing features on the driver aside from their bulk.

She shot to her feet and paced.

"Aunt Amanda? You're scaring me."

Amanda stopped walking, faced her niece. "You should be scared, Ava. Tell me everything. Where and when did you see this van?"

THIRTY-SEVEN

Amanda called Malone to update him on the situation that a white van had been following her niece. She requested an officer be posted on her sister's house and that one accompany Ava when she went to school the next day. She added, "The killer must know that Ava's related to me, and I'm working the case." Amanda was determined to leave out all mention of her niece's trip to the golf club. She'd figure out how to explain the uniform shirt when—and *if*—it became necessary.

"You think he's calling you out?"

"Could be a manipulation tactic. If I feel my family is in danger, he's counting on me to back off." She hoped it was nothing more than a mind game. But she also knew better than to underestimate the man. He was a cold-blooded killer.

"He should know it doesn't work like that. It's your job to put him away."

"Who knows what delusions run through the mind of someone like that?"

The call ended shortly after, and Amanda had gone home and crawled into bed. But her sleep was broken, and she felt like a zombie walking to her desk the next morning.

The events of yesterday were also weighing heavily on her mind. She was scared and pissed off—and she didn't like the combo. This killer, whoever he was, chose the wrong detective's family to mess with.

She entered her cubicle and found a takeout coffee from Hannah's on her desk. *Trent.* But he was nowhere in sight.

"There you are." He came up from behind her, possibly returning from the restroom. "How are you holding up? And Ava?"

She'd called him last night after Malone. "I don't even want to talk about it." She raked a hand through her hair and dropped into her chair. "Thanks for the coffee, by the way."

"Don't mention it. She'll be fine, Amanda."

"I sure hope so." And just like that, flashes from the Thompson crime scene entered her mind. The person they were dealing with was extremely dangerous—angry, volatile, unpredictable.

"So I made some calls about Clifford McIntosh. The principal at Potomac High confirmed his employment and his volunteering as a chaperone at prom. The care facility where his mother is backed up his alibi. He was there all day Friday, until after nine PM."

"So he didn't kill Reese."

"Nope."

"At least that's one off the suspect list. What did you gather from the Valentine scene after I left?"

"Nothing much aside from what you already knew before leaving. Upon second examination, there was evidence that one of the lower windows in the rear of the house was tampered with."

"The point of entry."

"Seems so."

"Then the killer let himself in and killed Susie Valentine while she was sleeping as Rideout thought."

"Again, seems so. You know the autopsy is being conducted this morning on her?"

Amanda nodded. "I remember. Rideout will provide us with the highlights. We need to be boots on the ground following leads." She filled him in on Ava's discovery of the shirt—they'd drop it at the crime lab in person that morning. While they were there, they'd ask the CSIs for any updates on evidence collected at either murder scene. She also showed him the pictures that Ava took. "I ended up forwarding this along to Jacob in Digital Crimes last night. Not holding out much hope, but he might be able to clean them up."

"If anyone can do that, it's him. Did he say any more about Laurel's phone or Reese's?"

"Just that he would get to it ASAP. Guess something else landed in his lap."

"What did Malone have to say about Ava's sleuthing?"

"About that, he has no idea, and I'd like it to remain that way."

Trent nodded. "Your secret is safe with me. It's interesting the shirt smelled of mothballs."

"Possibly transferred from the prom gown."

"You said you thought he'd purchased a new one from the pro shop to alter. We could check with the shop, see if they recall a man of large build buying a shirt lately."

"A complete shot in the dark, much like another path I'd like to explore." She told him that she had been mistaken to assume Ava had pointed out Clifford McIntosh. "We need to find out if any officer spoke to this guy, but I'm not sure where to begin. And he may have slipped out and not been interviewed." She had to dive into the investigation, or she'd go insane with worry about Ava. "Where are we with the warrant on the security video?"

"You requested that."

"I know that, but Malone was to follow up. Hear anything?"

"No email from the judge when I checked five minutes ago."

"Same for Reese's phone records."

"I can pressure them if you want."

"Let's. I'll follow up on the phone records."

He left her to go into his office space and while he was there, she fired off an email about Reese's phone records.

"Malone assures me he's all over the warrant." Trent joined her a few minutes later in her cubicle.

"If he was all over it, we'd have it already. Let's get moving. We'll hit the lab first, drop off the shirt, and get any updates they might have for us."

"Sounds like a plan."

"Now Ava saw the suspect come out of the laundry room of the country club. We might want to take a look around in there."

"Could be worth a trip."

"Could be," she agreed. But if the laundry room somehow factored into the journey of the killer getting Reese into the restroom, that evidence was now compromised. It had been two days ago when this investigation had started, and already it was hard to keep it all straight. And the lack of solid sleep was starting to take a toll. She just hoped she and Trent could keep it together to do the case justice.

THIRTY-EIGHT

CSI Emma Blair looked up when Amanda and Trent walked into the lab. Evidence collected from the Thompson scene was spread out on the table in front of her. Each piece was tagged and bagged waiting its turn.

"Just started digging in," Blair said, her tone slightly guarded, along with her rigid body language.

"We brought another gift." Amanda handed over Ava's backpack, and it garnered a strange look from Blair. "It's what's inside," she clarified.

"And that would be?"

Isabelle Donnelly came into the room and offered a chipper "good morning."

"It's a shirt that was collected from a garbage bin at the golf club," Amanda said.

Blair angled her head. "And you just happened to pluck it out?"

The investigator had this look of a mother in her eyes—piercing, unrelenting, and expectant of a straight answer. But for her sake and Ava's, she wasn't giving the CSI the entire truth. "Sure. Why not?"

"And the backpack...?"

Amanda should have known better than to think she could have pulled off the deceit. "Fine. But what I say remains between us. It's not ever to get back to Malone. Understood?"

"Oooh, this is going to be an interesting story." Donnelly rubbed her hands together.

At least she was having fun... "My niece Ava found it. She knows she's not supposed to be poking around, and she won't be anymore."

"All right, but even if I find anything, it's not going to hold up in court," Blair said. "Any DNA? It's out, even mention of the shirt itself."

"I realize that. But it might help Trent and I know where to concentrate our efforts." Amanda was talking confident, but like Ava had said, the killer probably wasn't worried about leaving trace because he wasn't in the system to find. It might suggest Reese Thompson was his first victim. But he'd killed Susie Valentine after that. Trace from the shirt could tie back to forensic discoveries at both crime scenes. Why take such a risk? After all, he couldn't have known it would become tainted evidence.

"And what makes you think this shirt is vital to the investigation?" Blair quirked her eyebrows.

"It was altered to look like a uniform shirt club employees wear, and it smells like mothballs," Amanda said.

"Huh, like the gown. Okay, leave it on the table, and I'll get to it." Blair gestured to an opening.

Amanda put the backpack down where Blair indicated.

"We'll get to it as soon as we can."

"There is something else we need you to look at," Amanda began. "The cleaning log from the restroom. It had the signature of Susie Valentine, but she was dead by that time. Can you see if you can lift any prints from the frame or sheet?" The need to compare signatures became moot with the timing of Susie Valentine's murder.

"All right."

Amanda pressed on a smile for Blair. "Anything you can tell us?"

"We haven't gotten far, but I will share our initial observations," Blair said. "In the Thompson case... The dress is a nineties design and smells of mothballs."

"Likely stored then opposed to being purchased in a vintage or secondhand store," Trent inserted.

"Why jump one way or the other?" Amanda didn't like shooting down her partner's theory, but she wasn't swayed yet. "Rideout mentioned that the tiara had some patina. Does that gel with the gown being stored safely while it was left to age?"

Trent leveled his gaze at her. "Or we're looking at two things? The gown came from the killer's own closet."

"Who we suspect is a man..." Amanda raised her eyebrows.

"I'm sure he had a girl around at some point in his life."

She nodded and waited for him to continue.

"The tiara might have been picked up somewhere. Either way, we should stop in at vintage stores in Prince William County and area," he suggested.

She realized he'd tagged on the latter because technically Manassas wasn't part of the county anymore. "Yes, we'll add it to our list. I'd start in Dumfries though."

"Why?"

"As we seem settled on, Reese Thompson wasn't a random murder. Not with how and where she was posed. The killer knew about the title and the prom."

"Right. Okay."

Blair cleared her throat and inserted, "You should also know that the dress wasn't a fit for her. I'd say at least two to three sizes too big."

"Like the foundation was too dark," Amanda said. "Know any more about it?"

"I'd say it is quite old, possibly a cheaper brand as well," Blair said.

"Why is that?" Trent asked.

"When I tested it, there was a high amount of toxic chemicals present. I'd say the foundation could be decades old even. Newer regulations are far more strict." Blair made eye contact with Amanda as she continued. "When you really look at makeup, you need to be so careful. Many foundations include chemicals that disrupt the endocrine system of the body. That being what regulates the biological processes in our bodies. At least one of these chemicals, methylparaben, has been proven in studies to cause cancer."

Amanda wore the stuff but might rethink doing so after this enlightenment. As if she needed one more thing to worry about. But these days it felt like everything caused cancer. "All right, well, with no idea where or when it was purchased, it's not like we can follow that angle." A solid lead was feeling like too much to ask for. She might need to be satisfied with what they had already. She paced a few steps. "So we have an older dress, from the nineties, and foundation that's presumably been sitting around. It's possible the killer held on to these items all this time. But we suspect a man..." She was trying to make sense of all that.

"As I said a moment ago, he probably had a woman in his life at some point," Trent said. "He could have had these things on hand from a sister. Maybe one he lost, for all we know. We'd need the killer in custody to find out."

"You're supposed to be the positive one," she mumbled.

"Hey." Trent held up his hands. "I'm not going to blow sunshine up your ass unless I have some."

"At least we're not without avenues to explore. We have those places she frequented in Manassas with her friends.

Someone could have latched on to her there." She tossed out the hypothetical, trying it on though unsure how it fit just yet.

"For sure," Trent replied.

"Sounds like you two have work to do. So if you'd just..." Blair jabbed her gaze from Amanda to Trent, back again.

Amanda laughed. "Fine, we'll leave if that's all you have. Any insights on the glue that was used on her lips?"

Blair and Donnelly shook their heads.

"On the list," Blair said.

"All right, we'll leave you to it. I'm assuming you haven't started on the Valentine case?" Amanda plastered on a cheesy grin to ease the pressure.

"You assume correctly. Now go. Let us get to work." Blair pointed toward the door. Her expression was serious at first, but it softened before Amanda and Trent turned to leave.

Amanda and Trent loaded into the department car, and she turned to Trent as she did up her seat belt. "Well, it seems obvious the killer held on to the foundation. It's not like you can go out and buy decades-old makeup."

"Yep." Trent had turned sullen.

"What is it?"

"Just something I thought back there, the bit I said about the killer possibly losing someone. That might explain holding on to it all these years. He wasn't able to let it go."

This revealed the reason for the shift in his mood. The hypothetical smacked close to the recent investigation that had the killer using Trent's gun to shoot himself. "But if that was the case, what made the killer bring it out now to use on his victim?"

"Something likely triggered him about Reese Thompson. But what? And why did it ignite such a level of hostility?"

"Someone with a lot of hatred in their heart and a message to get across." That part seemed simple. Getting from there to slapping cuffs on the killer not so much.

THIRTY-NINE

Motive wasn't always uncovered, but theorizing the possibilities did affect the direction of an investigation. Amanda's mind struggled with finding what might move a middle-aged person to murder a teenage girl. Even if the man had a sister at some point, how did that lead him to murder? And given the age of the makeup alone—decades' old—surely whatever prom dreams existed had been long shattered, so why kill now? Regardless of the answer, it was clear that whatever happened had profoundly shaped their killer's life. It had stayed with him over the years, rooted deep within. Jealousy? She looked over at Trent in the driver's seat. "What if something about seeing Reese's good looks and popularity were the trigger? Our killer didn't have the prom he'd wanted, and it affected the shape of his life."

"It's not like he could have been voted prom queen."

"Nope, but prom king. Oh, and he might have had a date with the prom queen, but something happened to the relationship. He might have bought the gown and tiara, but that doesn't explain the old foundation."

Trent pressed his lips and shook his head.

She went on. "And if the killer was that man Ava had tried to point out to me..." She stopped, roiling with guilt at not specifying which man that night. It's just usually she and her niece were in sync. Amanda was certain she'd been indicating who they came to learn was Clifford McIntosh. "He didn't look like an outcast type either."

"Huh. Well, it's hard to say. We're talking several decades ago now. Looks can change drastically."

"You're right. Now, he was a big guy... It wouldn't be the first time a person turned to weightlifting to compensate for being unpopular." She felt like she was spinning now, trying to find something to grab hold of.

"Who knows, Amanda? Without finding out who he is and talking to him anyhow."

"Well, if he was an outcast, and bullied possibly, those type of scars last a long time. For some they never go away."

"Okay, well, let's say we're onto something with this angle. Who in Reese's world comes close to that description? If that man who was at the food table is the killer, did he know the Thompson family?"

"Ava didn't know him. Seems like she was very close to the family."

"Doesn't mean she knows everyone they do. Heck, it could be a neighbor... anyone really."

"Jeez, that's helpful. Why don't you take us to Thrifty's first. It's a vintage store, and it's on the way to the Rollerblade rink."

"Thought you wanted to start with the ones in Dumfries."

"Please."

"You got it."

"In the meantime, I'm going to call Clarissa Thompson and see if she knows of any well-muscled men."

"That ought to be an interesting conversation."

"No doubt." She pulled her phone and made the call.

When Clarissa Thompson answered, Amanda said, "It's Detective Steele."

There was a brief silence, then a sniffle followed by, "Do you know who killed my baby?"

Amanda pinched her eyes shut. She should have expected that would be the woman's first question. "We're still following leads, but I have a question for you. Are you aware of anyone close to the family who would know about Reese's accomplishments, and possibly showed any signs of jealousy? Possibly someone who is quite strong, muscled?" As Amanda asked, she realized there was another thing to add to Reese's attributes—her gift as a fashion designer. Her sketches were incredible and showed real talent, at least to Amanda's untrained eye. Was it somehow a sore point for the killer too?

"Not that I can think of."

"Did you share with anyone about her being prom queen?"

"Anyone who would listen."

"All of these people were close to you?"

"Not all, but I don't remember anyone heavily muscled."

"Would you be able to get together a list of the people you told?" Even that was a long shot. The killer may be someone who had heard secondhand.

"I'll do my best."

"All I can ask." Clarissa had her email address from when Amanda had sent the list of club and catering staff. The woman promised to send something over.

Amanda repeated the inquiry with Melvin Thompson, and he told her the same thing. That he couldn't think of anyone that fit Amanda's specifications.

"I did tell people at work though."

"Please send me a list of their names." Like Clarissa's, Melvin's list might include someone simply adjacent to the killer they were after. In that case, she and Trent would be none the wiser.

By the time she'd finished with Melvin, Trent had parked in the lot outside Thrifty's.

"So?" he prompted.

She filled him in.

"Sorry to be negative again, but it sounds like a dead end to me. At least short of prying into the lives of everyone they send over to see if we can find a large man."

They got out of the car and entered the store. Amanda was struck by a cacophony of odors, but she didn't detect mothballs in the mix. No one who worked there was within sight, and she and Trent moved through the store to a section dedicated to formal attire.

Trent moved dresses and suits along the racks. "Nothing appears to be that out of date here. Certainly not decades' old."

"Agreed."

"Can I help you?" A tall, slender woman with ink-black hair walked up to them.

They both pointed to their badges that were clipped to their waistbands, and Amanda pulled her phone. She brought up a photograph of the gown Reese had been wearing and held the screen toward the woman. "Does this look familiar to you?"

The woman leaned in and, shortly after, drew back shaking her head. "Heavens no, with a style like that it's got to be at least thirty years old. We sell gently used items and ones from within the last decade." A prim smile, hinting at conceit, as if she were working in a fancy clothing boutique instead of a secondhand store.

"All right. What about this?" Amanda showed her a picture of the tiara.

"Doesn't look familiar either. Again, it looks quite old." She swirled a fingertip, pointing out the patina.

"Do you know of vintage stores in the area that might carry older items?" Trent asked.

"I'd say most vintage stores don't have the standards we do here at Thrifty's. But, still, these items are quite old."

All right then... "Thank you for your time," Amanda said, and she and Trent left the store.

"I don't think either of us expected to walk in and get the answers we wanted right off the bat."

She looked over at him as she rounded the rear of the department car to the passenger side. "I really think my negativity might be rubbing off on you."

"Why? Just because I'm not Mr. Sunshine all the time?" He smiled and got behind the wheel. He started the car, got the air conditioning started up, and pulled his phone. "Heard a chime when we were on our way out..."

She took out her phone too, hoping there would be a good lead in her inbox.

"I received that list of former employees at the golf club," he said. "And we have Reese's phone records."

"I have the signed warrant for the video footage we needed for Protect It." She updated him as she forwarded it to the security company with the request for all available footage from Friday night until Saturday midnight. She provided a link to the department's secure server. "There. Protect It now has it. Hopefully they'll get us what we need quickly."

"I take it you emailed them?"

"Yes."

"Let me call to apply some pressure." He got on the phone with Protect It, and she heard him taking care of that.

In that time, she received a text from Malone. *Search of Prince William Forest Park concluded. No obvious leads.*

As she was reading it, another message popped up. *When it rains it pours*, she thought.

This text was from Donnelly, and it had Amanda's stomach turning to lead.

By the time Trent got off the phone, the air conditioning

was blowing out ice-cold air. Amanda adjusted the fan speed and directed the flow away from her.

"We should have the footage within the hour," he said.

"Awesome job. I have some updates too. Malone said the search of the park is concluded, and there was nothing there connecting to Reese. But Donnelly also messaged."

"I sense it wasn't good...?"

"Yes, and no. They had collected the cleaning log from Rolling Hills and lifted several prints—all of which are being run through the system. Here's what is occurring to me now. Why even record in the cleaning log?"

"Huh. Now you mention it..."

Her phone rang, and she answered without consulting caller ID. "Steele."

"Detective." The voice was young and small. "This is Nadine, Reese's sister."

Amanda's heart broke with how the girl identified herself. "Hi, Nadine, what can I help you with?" She resisted the impulse to ask if everything was all right. That question was a potential landmine.

"Mom said that you called here wanting to know if anyone was strange with Reese?"

That wasn't exactly how it was put, but roll with it... "That's right." Amanda turned to Trent, widened her eyes and pointed at the phone. She'd put Nadine on speaker, but didn't want to risk discouraging her from talking.

"I didn't remember this until now, but she complained about some man at the roller rink. She said he was creepy the way he watched her."

"When did she tell you this?"

"Two Fridays ago. I called her when she was there with her friends. She griped and said she was moving outside to get away from him."

Tingles ran through Amanda. Could this be the solid lead they were waiting for? "Did she ever mention him before?"

"I don't think so. Probably just the once and that's why I had forgotten."

Who knew how long he'd been harassing Reese? She might not have had a reason to mention him to Nadine before. "Did she say anything about what he looked like?"

"No."

"Okay, Nadine, this is good. If you think of anyone else, let me know."

"All right." The girl hung up, and Amanda held on to her phone.

"We just got an interesting lead." Amanda filled Trent in on the phone call.

"Next stop Rock n Rollerblade?"

"You got it." It was only creeping up on eleven in the morning, and Reese and her friends would go to the place Friday nights. She didn't imagine the place being too busy this time of day or drawing the same clientele. People Reese's age would still be in school. But they had to follow the lead.

"So Nadine knew about this guy, but why haven't any of Reese's friends mentioned him?"

"That I don't know. Maybe they didn't make as much of it as Nadine did. I also know the sisters were close. Could it be that Reese downplayed her dislike for this guy to her friends for the appearance of bravado?" Amanda wasn't even sure she bought her suggestion but hated getting weighed down in all the questions and doubts. Hopefully the trip to the roller rink would give them some clearcut answers.

FORTY

The parking lot for the roller rink was a ghost town. There was a grand total of five vehicles, including the department car Amanda and Trent were in. Inside, Taylor Swift was belting out her latest over the sound system. Amanda didn't listen to music often, but she recognized this one from a streaming app she turned on when cleaning the house.

The lighting was low, and colored strobes crisscrossed across the rink. Two people were skating. It was curious why the place bothered being open this time of day.

Amanda and Trent walked to the counter, and a man in his fifties limped over. "Two?"

She lifted her badge. "Prince William County PD. We're here with some questions."

The man drew back at the sight of the gold shield. "What about?"

Amanda showed the man a photo of Reese. "Do you know this girl?"

"Of course. Girl's a regular. In here every Friday night."

"You work that shift?" Trent asked.

"Sure do. Pretty much every shift. I'm the owner. Pete Matheson. Never been good about delegation."

"Did you ever notice anyone leering at the girl or her friends?" Amanda realized how vague the question might come across.

"Friday nights it's quite packed in here. Lots of teens and lots of guys who gawk at the girls. No law against that."

Amanda stiffened. "Grown men checking out children, there should be."

Pete held up his hands. "I don't like to judge people. Besides I've never seen any of them touch the girls. I'd step in then."

"*Any of them?* Do you have specific people in mind?" Trent must have latched on to the same phrasing Amanda had, beating her to the question.

"There are a few guys who come in on Friday nights, but they've been comin' in here for ages."

"They make moves on teen girls?" Trent's tone didn't muffle his obvious disgust.

"Again, not that I've seen, but they always do *watch*."

"Do they skate or just gawk?"

"They skate some, yes, and drink beer. Lots of that. Sometimes they talk to the girls."

Apparently, cash in Pete's pocket made him look the other way. "You know the names of these guys?"

"There are three of 'em. As I said, they've been comin' in here for ages. They're all in their late forties and married."

"Doesn't mean anything to some," she countered, not even pointing out they obviously had no qualms about *watching*—young women at that.

"Can you tell me what this is about?"

"That girl I showed you," Amanda said, "was murdered."

"Oh dear God." Pete signed the cross and backed up, leaning against a back counter.

Amanda squared her shoulders. "Now I'm sure you can

appreciate why we're so interested in getting our questions answered."

Pete nodded, but the action was minimal and barely perceptible. "Those men I mentioned, they all hold respectable jobs. Never caused problems here. I can't imagine any of them doing anything to anyone."

"We'll determine that. I'll ask again, names?" Trent said, pen poised over his notepad.

"I know first names. Colin, Dale, and Hammer. Though I'd wager that last one is his nickname."

Safe bet there... "Any of them a rather big build?"

"Hammer is."

"Why the nickname?" Trent asked.

"No clue. It's not like I chat with them and know everything about their lives. What I know, I've picked up and pieced together over the years."

That was one downfall of the world today—indifference. "You mentioned they had respectable jobs, what were they?"

Pete told them that Colin and Dale had office jobs, banking he'd gathered, but he wasn't sure about Hammer.

The nickname could have been earned for an endless number of reasons. Amanda's mind served up one that had a potential connection to the case. It stemmed back to the intended purpose of the chain that was used to strangle Reese. "Could it be he worked in renovation or construction?"

"Hey, you know what? I think so. As I said big guy, muscular, and he must work with his hands because they are often calloused."

"Can you remember any more about this man?" Amanda asked. "Does he drive a white van?"

Pete pressed his lips. "Again, no idea what he drives."

"You said he's a regular. Just on Friday nights?" She had her fingers crossed he was in more often than that. Then she and Trent would return later tonight to question him in person, get his real name, feel him out and see whether he should remain suspect or not.

"He's in here most nights. He'll likely be in tonight."

"Time?" This from Trent who sounded as eager to move on this as she was.

"Probably around seven."

"We'll be back. Don't say one word about our visit here or that we'll be coming to speak with him. Understood?" Amanda said firmly.

Pete nodded. "You have my word. Gotta say, you got me reeling here. That poor girl."

She scanned his eyes and sensed he was being genuine. "Okay. Thank you for your cooperation." She considered advising Pete that if he warned Hammer, he'd be seen as interfering with an open police investigation but didn't feel it was necessary.

Amanda gave him her business card, and she and Trent left the place.

FORTY-ONE

He had to make this fast and get back to work before his boss questioned what had taken him so long. But if he pushed too much, he'd just kill him too. The fantasy alone brought pleasure, but he'd need to suppress his urges or he'd wind up behind bars.

He was parked down the street from Potomac High knowing that they'd be dismissing for lunch any minute. He'd keep his eye out for the brown-haired girl, and if luck was on his side, it wouldn't take long to spot her. Then he also had to rely on the girl ditching the cops who were there to watch over her. That part of the equation felt reliable.

She certainly seemed to have an independent streak, if her snooping around was any indication. What he failed to understand was why she cared so much about Reese Thompson's fate. She was obviously the sister's friend but what beyond that? It was like she had a need to play cop.

With that thought, he remembered her at the prom. She was relaxed and poised when she'd spoken to that cop with the red hair. Shouldn't a teenager be uncomfortable around officers of the law? Whereas this one's body language communicated she was at ease, and he was quite sure they had the same shape chin. Could it be the detective and the girl were blood relatives? *Bonus.*

That thought made him smile.

How would that detective feel when she failed to save her own blood? And right under the noses of the PWCPD, at that.

A uniform was posted outside the girl's house and school. They must have been alerted to him and his threat against her. But he had messed up when he'd tried to lure her to his van last night. She was obviously spooked, the way she'd ignored him and hustled down the sidewalk. And he was quite sure she'd snapped a picture or two with her phone. If it hadn't been for the man—her dad?—she might already be dead.

The police would be on the lookout for a white van, but it was the best he had at his disposal. The only thing soothing his anxiety was there were a lot of white vans out there. He should blend in. He also had both plates affixed to the bumpers again.

Unless the girl did capture his face in one of her pictures. And that made it even more imperative to silence her—and the sooner the better.

It's not like he had any qualms about killing again. In fact, he looked forward to it. And beating the police would serve to elevate his confidence further. He'd already gotten away with murder twice.

It had made looking at himself in the mirror easier. His demons were finally banished, and the voices that screamed he was a loser had finally been silenced. If he'd known killing was all it would take to feel like this, he'd have started years ago.

But not just any victim would have given him this level of liberation. Reese had been perfect, representing so much of what had wounded him—and his injuries had left deep scars.

Just seeing and hearing Reese speak, being witness to her accomplishments, had his past hurts bubbling up for healing. And he had refused to listen to the voices anymore. They needed restitution. Now these wounds had been treated, he had zero regrets. He'd do it all over again. In fact, he planned to. Maybe he'd even use this girl as leverage to draw out that detective.

But he had to be careful or he'd be locked away. The public would view him as some monster, this time likely ascribing him with a mental illness. What people didn't understand, they tried to explain away. Regardless, he wasn't ready to be a chew toy for the media.

He gripped the steering wheel, grinding his palms against the hard leather. He had to get her into his van before the cops clued in, but he'd need some cover story to get her close. He had a feeling she was smart, and she was already suspicious of him.

The school bell rang in the distance and with his window down, he heard students' voices as they streamed out the front doors.

He sat up straighter, leaning his torso against the wheel, but was careful of not hitting the horn.

Then he spotted her. She was alone, looking left and right. He didn't see any cops around her; she must have ditched them! And she was coming right down the street toward him.

What a rush!

He'd picked the right side street! It wasn't until she got rather close that she seemed to notice the van. She stopped and stared. He'd need to play this next part smoothly and to script. He turned off the vehicle and got out, slowly and methodically so as not to alert the "rabbit" and have her hopping off in a panic.

"Excuse me." He spoke in the most pleasant, nonthreatening voice he could muster. "You're a friend of Nadine Thompson's, aren't you?"

He worked at closing the distance and was within a few feet when she backed up.

"No need to be afraid of me."

Her eyes narrowed, cautious, assessing. "Who are you?"

"I'm a friend of the Thompson family. I've noticed that you're helping Nadine through this time."

"She's my best friend." Spoken defensively with squared shoulders.

"It's great to have a best friend." Hatred swirled through his insides, twisting, tightening. He'd had a *best friend* once. "Do the police know who did that to her sister?" It took all his acting skills to play the innocent. The sights and sounds of Reese's demise were still potent.

The girl barely shook her head.

"Hopefully they find out soon." He turned to leave. This was to be the bait and hook. He'd almost made it back to the van when he heard her voice close behind.

"What's your name?"

He stopped walking and pivoted around to face her. "You can call me MP." *Moon Pie.* An inside joke, but he had no urge to smile.

"What does that stand for?"

"Myron Powers." The name came out like he'd given it advanced thought. *I am awesome!* "What's yours?"

"Ava."

No surname, but the girl was already breaking a rule she'd have been given as a child: don't talk to strangers. "You might have noticed me. I tried to talk to you last night. I'm Reese's estranged uncle, on her father's side. But it doesn't mean I don't watch the family, keep tabs on them. When I found out about Reese, I wanted to find who did this to her. I see you're trying to get answers, so am I." He tagged on a solemn smile.

Her eyes narrowed, disbelieving.

"But I need to head out of town now, and I was wondering if you would give something to the Thompson family for me." Again, he smiled, this time letting it reach his eyes.

"Why can't you give it to them?"

"As I said, estranged. They wouldn't be happy to see me. Just thought if I found you, then I could have you pass it along."

"Okay. What is it?"

"It's just in the back." He turned to walk to the rear doors and heard her following.

Like taking candy from a baby...

FORTY-TWO

Amanda and Trent picked up some food from a drive-thru on the way back to Central. They had a lot ahead of them—the video footage from Protect It covering the golf course, the former employee list, and Reese Thompson's phone records. They decided to start on the latter first.

Reese's phone last pinged in the area of Prince William Forest Park on Thursday afternoon at 12:12 PM—the time that Laurel received the text message. Any question about whether it was sent using Reese's actual phone was answered; it had been. Amanda keyed a quick text to Briggs to let him know not to worry about looking at Laurel's phone trying to source the origin anymore.

"Is it possible Reese's abductor didn't take her until Thursday?"

"If so, where did she spend Wednesday night?"

"The alternative is we assume the abductor returned to the park to fire off that text? And if so, why?"

"A taunt? The killer trying to communicate he is smarter than everyone else. Untouchable, as it were. He had to know Reese's disappearance would be investigated."

"Honestly, I don't put anything past these sickos anymore. But you're probably right. If it was just a matter of trying to make Reese appear fine, he would have carried out the ruse from the start. He would have at least responded to Nadine by text."

"Good point."

"Yep, and I'd say we have ground zero. We have what we need to get that warrant for surveillance cameras in the park now. They might have one on the parking lot and/or the exit. We can see where we get with that."

Trent scribbled madly in a notebook in front of him.

"Hopefully we get somewhere with that. We also know if the killer returned to the park to dispose of the phone on Thursday afternoon, they had someplace to hold Reese without fear she'd be found or get free, all the way from Wednesday until they dumped her body at the golf club." At face value it might seem cold to talk about the crime in such a blunt manner, but it helped enforce objectivity.

"We're always thinking someplace rural."

"Yes, but you raised a good point earlier in this investigation about the privacy of garages too."

"A garage would allow the killer more freedom to get Reese inside. He could have kept her incapacitated, unable to call for help."

"Exactly. And as we've batted around a lot, I think Reese knew this person... possibly familiar enough to go with him willingly."

"Right, so even if we get our hands on video footage from the area of the park or even its lot, it might not look like a kidnapping."

"It probably won't. It will likely just be Reese walking along calmly with the killer. But the video might give us this person's face, possibly the license plate on the vehicle they drove. The killer may have more than a white van at his disposal."

"Yep, and there's also the possibility the killer lives within walking distance of the park..." He pressed his lips, raised his brows.

"The possibilities are endless."

"I'll make a quick call to the county offices." Trent got on the phone.

While he was busy with that Amanda continued to look at the tracking history on Reese's phone. She did go to the park a lot, and there were pings in Manassas on Fridays and Saturdays, from her outings to the Rollerblade rink and the rock-climbing place no doubt, and wherever else the teen and her friends would go. The history confirmed Reese also visited the homes of the "sisterhood"—Laurel Wilkinson, Hailey Garner, and Ella Maxwell. But there was one area where her phone had been a week ago Monday that needed an explanation. The address felt familiar.

Amanda keyed it into her phone. "I'll be," she muttered to herself.

Trent ended his call and pushed his cell phone into a rear pants pocket. "All right, so the park has a camera on the parking lot. And they're going to send it right over."

"No warrants needed? That's great. Look at this." She held her phone's screen for him to see over the partition.

"What is it?"

"The Mann family."

"Now you've lost me." Trent came around and entered her office space.

"There was an address in the tracking history from last Monday, and it ties back here."

"The Mann residence?"

"Yep."

"Aren't Reese and Makayla mortal enemies?"

"That's how we heard it the first time. But the phone records don't lie. Reese was at the Mann house."

"Huh. So why didn't Makayla or her mother mention this to us?"

"Let's go find out." Amanda was already to her feet and headed toward the department lot.

"We should have said something when you were here last." Gloria Mann was sitting, back straight, on the couch with her hands on her knees. Makayla was seated next to her mother, tucked tight against the arm.

An admission didn't explain their reason for withholding this information. "Why didn't you?"

"Is that important?" Gloria primly crossed her arms. "You know now."

"Why was Reese here?" Amanda tamped down her irritation at the mother's stonewalling.

"Reese wanted to make sure I was okay." This from Makayla, who wouldn't look her or Trent in the eye.

"Why would she do that?" Trent asked. "You made it clear the last time we were here that you and Reese hated each other."

"She was delusional—and two-faced. She acted one way toward me when her friends were around, another behind their backs. But that doesn't make the way she treated me okay! I hated her all the time."

"Makayla," Gloria gasped at the phrase.

The teen shook her head. "It's the truth."

Amanda inched forward on her chair. "You said she wanted to make sure you were okay... about not being prom queen?"

"Oh, believe me, that came up. But her primary *concern* was about what she and her friends did at school that day."

"That was the day with the juice box incident," Trent said.

"Yeah. But whatever. I'm over it now."

"And you said she checked in on how you were about losing prom queen?" Amanda asked.

"Just to rub her winning in my face more. *Runner-up.* Trust me she stressed that during the conversation, while apparently checking on my welfare. Give me a break."

"You were terribly upset about both things, Makayla," Gloria pointed out.

Makayla didn't say anything but looked at the carpet.

"So how did you react when she turned up at your door?" Amanda was prodding, running on a feeling.

"I was pissed. She just needed to leave me alone."

The evidence was leading to a man, but Amanda saw how much hatred this girl harbored toward Reese. "Did you tell her that?"

"Repeatedly. She didn't care. Trying to clear her conscience or whatever." She crossed her arms, shook her head.

"When did you see Reese last?" Another question from their initial visit but another truth might slip out this time.

Makayla worried her bottom lip.

"If you know something, you need to tell us," Amanda said gently.

The girl drew a deep breath and squared her shoulders. "I saw her at the park on Wednesday night."

Amanda stiffened. The girl may have been the last person to see her alive. She could have seen the person who may have abducted Reese. "What time?"

Makayla shrugged. "About six."

"My daughter goes there to be alone, Detective. There's no crime in that."

"Why didn't you tell us about seeing Reese Wednesday night when we spoke?" Amanda was peeved. How much further along might the investigation be if Makayla had come forward sooner?

"Why would I?" Makayla snapped, rage flashing in her

eyes. "I hated her. She can't just turn nice whenever she wants and treat me how she does in front of other people."

"Did you do something to her, Makayla?" Amanda didn't peg the girl as Reese's killer, but wondered now if she were somehow involved. "Please tell us."

"I..." Makayla wiped her eyes and clenched her jaw, her guilt tangible. "I didn't do anything she didn't deserve."

"What did you do?" Trent interjected.

"Gah." Tears hit her cheeks. "She was doodling in that stupid sketchbook like she always did. As if she was going to make something of herself. Pu-leeassse."

"Makayla Flora Mann. What. Did. You. Do?" Her mother's question laid out each word as its own sentence.

"Fine. Here goes. I went over to make nice, like she tried to do here on Monday. But she was really upset. Her eyes were all bloodshot like she'd been crying a lot. I sat next to her and..." Her eyes darted back and forth between Amanda and Trent. "You promise not to get me in trouble?"

"We can't promise that, Makayla," Amanda said, "but things will go better for you if you talk to us."

"I gave her a pill."

Gloria gasped as she shot to her feet. "You what? Have you lost your mind?"

"Mrs. Mann," Amanda said. "Please sit. Let's hear your daughter out."

Gloria did but with a huff.

"What kind of pill?" Trent asked.

"I probably shouldn't say anymore." Makayla crossed her arms.

"Like hell," Gloria snapped. "You get talking, missy."

Makayla pressed her cheek into a shoulder. "I take them sometimes to take the edge off."

"What are these pills, Makayla?" Amanda asked.

"Just some oxy, okay?"

"No it's not okay." Gloria shot to her feet again and started wagging a pointed finger at the girl. "Did you take them from my medicine cabinet?"

"Ms. Mann, I appreciate this is coming as a shock to you, but it would be best for everyone if you were to be calm," Amanda said, her voice level.

"Fine." Gloria sat down again. To Makayla, she said, "You're grounded for a year." She slumped and shook her head. "I was prescribed oxy earlier this year for a back injury I got from a car accident."

Amanda could have pointed out Gloria should have safely disposed of any unused pills. At the same time, she certainly wasn't to blame for her daughter's actions. "Why did you give one to Reese? To hurt her?"

"No. I was... being nice." Makayla hitched her shoulders. "They just relax me, and I thought it would help Reese."

"You drugged the girl," Gloria muttered under her breath.

"I didn't force it down her throat!" Makayla yelled.

Amanda hated to think the oxy might have played a role in Reese's abduction, then subsequent murder. The drug was known to relax a person and affect social behaviors, including making one more trusting. Reese presumably would have been more vulnerable to her killer's advances.

"That pill didn't kill her." Makayla's voice was barely above a whisper, and tears were falling down her cheeks.

How to break it to the teen that her actions may have led to Reese's abduction and murder? Gently was the only answer. "It wasn't her cause of death, but the drug might have made her more relaxed and malleable... trusting." Amanda set her lips in a straight line, and her heart broke as the girl gasped a sob and rocked back and forth, piecing together the implication.

"Oh my god." Gloria put a hand to her forehead. "Should we get her a lawyer?"

"It might be a good idea." Depending on how this shook out,

Makayla may be facing a civil suit from the Thompson family. "Makayla, you were probably one of the last people to see Reese alive. It's very important that you remember back to Wednesday night at the park. You said that Reese was drawing in her sketchbook."

"Yeah, and after she took the pill, I... I snatched her book and ran off with it."

And it gets worse... Amanda had lost touch with just how spiteful teenagers could be.

"Why would you do that?" Gloria looked at her daughter as if she were a stranger.

"I hated her. Don't you get that yet?"

Makayla's motive in giving Reese the oxy wasn't birthed from kindness, rather urged on by an underlying resentment that wanted to see if the drug would hurt her. "Did Reese try to get her book back from you?"

Makayla palmed her cheeks. "She tried, but she couldn't keep up."

Probably due to the oxy... "Did you see anyone else with Reese at the park, someone who might have been paying her attention?"

"I'm not sure..." Makayla hiccupped a sob.

"Anyone around at all?"

"There were families there."

"You're sure no one was paying her any particular attention? What about anyone, say tall and of muscular build?"

Makayla's forehead wrinkled in concentration. "Don't think so."

"Did you happen to cross through the parking lot?" Amanda was teeing up for a question that might be a stretch.

"Yeah. What about it?"

"Did you happen to notice any white vans?"

The girl shook her head.

"And what time did you leave the park?" Amanda asked.

"Six thirty."

Amanda recalled Nadine said she had gone to the park about seven and hadn't seen Reese. Her killer must have taken her between six thirty and seven on Wednesday. "Okay, you remember a van or think of seeing someone after we leave, you call me immediately." Amanda handed the girl her card, and she and Trent left but only after Makayla got Reese's sketchbook.

"If it wasn't for that pill, we might not be in this situation," Trent griped on the way to the car.

"It might not have helped the situation."

"What bothers me is Gloria."

"The mother?"

"Yeah, she must have suspected her daughter of something or why withhold information on our first visit? She just let us go along believing the two girls detested each other."

"One thing with mothers, Trent. Most will protect their young until the end, consequences be damned."

"Still don't like it. What do you suggest we do about Makayla Mann?"

"Legally, there is nothing unless we prove the oxy contributed to Reese's death. And considering Makayla gave it to Reese Wednesday and time of death is Friday..."

"That's not going anywhere."

"Not by us. A civil suit is a different matter."

"I hope she learned a lesson from all this though."

"I'm sure she did."

"By the way, I received a message while we were in there," Trent said. "The video from the park is available for us to watch."

"Let's get on it."

They got into the vehicle and headed back to Central. Amanda hadn't known what she'd expected when she discovered Reese had been at the Manns' house, but she hadn't anticipated what they were walking away with. An eyewitness placed Reese at that park about an hour after she ran away from home and admitted to, essentially, drugging her.

Amanda ran her hand over the sketchbook in her lap. At least she had this to return to Reese's mother. Even if it wasn't the justice Clarissa was after. Unfortunately, that would still need to wait.

FORTY-THREE

Amanda grabbed a coffee for herself from the bullpen, and would have gotten one for Trent too, but he'd declined the offer. Her phone notified her of a text message, and she found it was from CSI Blair. Trent would want to know what she had to say.

She found him in his cubicle with the video from the county queued up and ready to play. "Just heard from Blair," she said. "Not good news, but they're updates, nonetheless. The glue used on Reese's lips was likely commercial grade—but that's all they can give us. No unusual prints or trace at Valentine's. There was some epithelium on the golf shirt, but no DNA or forensic trace at Valentine's place or in the restroom stall that is deemed relevant for comparison."

"What about the prints on the cleaning log?"

"Nothing came back in the system."

"He must have paid particular attention to his movements most of the time, but didn't think twice about tossing the shirt at the country club. The same place he'd disposed of Reese's body no less. Not sure I can figure this guy out."

"Who knows? But a guess. He ditched it and then returned to the prom to witness the aftermath of his actions."

"Sick prick."

"Yep. He's conflicting too. Someone who may be opportunistic, but only to a point. Then it seems he goes to great lengths to orchestrate everything just so."

"I agree. It's not like he could have known that Reese would be at the park that night."

"Unless he'd picked up on her routine. Suppose until we know exactly who we're looking at, we can't leap to any conclusions." Sometimes it felt like investigations spun them in a circle. "This thing ready to go?" She turned her attention to Trent's monitor and the paused feed. The timestamp in the bottom corner was five fifty, last Wednesday evening.

"That it is." Trent hit play on the video.

It didn't take long to see that there was no white van in sight. "This covers the entire parking lot at the park?"

"Yep." Trent pointed out the edges as the feed continued.

As the minutes trudged on, closer to six when Makayla said she ran into Reese, there still was no white van or anyone who resembled the build of their suspect. And Makayla must have entered the park out of view of the camera.

Trent forwarded in slow motion. Vehicles came and left—no white vans. Once the video hit 6:35 PM, Makayla crossed the lot alone. Amanda sat straighter and pointed into the distance, behind the parking lot. "Is that Reese?"

"If it is, she's not alone."

"Can you zoom in?"

Trent did his best, but the feed got grainier as it was enlarged. The person was wearing a hoodie, and their face was obscured with black shadows.

"Just show your face, you bastard," Amanda seethed.

But as they continued to watch, there was no clear shot. It was like he had purposely avoided looking directly at the camera. "He knows about the cameras."

"Or got lucky. But who gets *that* lucky?"

"Wait. Stop it right there. Back up a second..."

Trent hit pause just as the mystery man's stride put him slightly in front of Reese's. No face, but it was possible to make out his size and structure.

"Size wise, he could be a fit based on what we've been hearing." Amanda drew back, staring at the screen, now studying Reese's body language. It was relaxed, and she was gesturing as she spoke. The pause had her arms in midair. "She's comfortable with him." She pointed out what she was seeing.

"You're right. Nothing to indicate she was fearful of him. The oxy wouldn't have hurt there, but I still think Reese knew and trusted him."

Which made matters worse. To consider that level of brutality and mutilation had been at the hands of someone Reese had trusted burrowed an ache in Amanda's chest.

Trent resumed playing the video. "They're not headed toward a vehicle."

"Not one in the lot anyway. He could have parked on a surrounding street."

"Or his house is within walking distance of the park, as I've theorized before?"

"Or that."

Trent stopped the video as Reese and the mystery man left the feed.

"We need to salvage what we can and take the best image over to Clarissa and Nadine Thompson, see if they recognize this person. If they don't, we'll ask Reese's father. And we'll take that list of former Rolling Hills employees with us and see if one of the names rings any bells."

Trent rushed into action, taking shots from the video and saving them as JPEGs and forwarding copies to himself and Amanda.

As Amanda watched him work, she prepared her mind to face Reese's mother yet again without news of an arrest. At least they wouldn't be showing up empty-handed. They had Reese's sketchbook.

FORTY-FOUR

Ava couldn't move and not just because fear had her paralyzed. She must need her head examined for taking this risk—and what had she been thinking to dodge her police escort? How egotistical to think she could lure out the killer and remain unscathed. To compound the matter, she'd gone along with the cover story he'd fed that had been utter crap, still figuring she was in control. *Stupid, stupid, stupid.* But she'd told herself that her aunt Amanda wouldn't be afraid, so Ava had summoned her courage. She'd reasoned even if he abducted her, she'd somehow be able to manipulate things, and get free. Then she'd tell her aunt right where to find him. But the stark reality was she wasn't going anywhere.

Ava had felt his strength firsthand when he'd gripped her arm and tossed her into the van like she weighed nothing. And he'd suppressed her screams before they birthed by slapping silver duct tape over her mouth. No matter how hard she'd pounded on him with her fists and kicked her legs, her efforts had zero effect. Her hands were also bound together with the tape, and he'd taken her phone.

They traveled for what Ava would guess was fifteen minutes. Then the van stopped.

Ava braced herself. The instant the back doors of the van cracked open, she kicked out both legs at him. Her feet glanced off him. Next thing she knew she was lying on a concrete floor, the wind knocked out of her.

He hauled her to her feet, and Ava found herself in the bay of a garage. The metal door was closed.

He yanked the tape from her mouth, and she cried out from the pain.

As it eased, she said, "Where are we?"

"Don't you worry about that." He grabbed her arm again and directed her around like a limp doll.

He stopped at a doorway and pushed her in ahead of him. It was a small room with no windows.

Ava spun and charged at him, ran right into his chest and looked up. She drew back. *What the...*

He yelled for her to sit with her back to a plumbing pipe that was sticking out of the floor.

"No."

"Do it, or I'll make you."

Her mind was still spinning on what she *didn't* see when she had looked up at him. It had certainly taken her by surprise.

"Very well." He forced her to that spot and wound more tape around her wrists and included the pipe. She wouldn't be going anywhere. "You look all nice and cozy." Another sinister smirk, and he slapped tape over her mouth again.

A tear ran down Ava's cheek, and she cursed at showing him any fear.

He turned and left the room, closing a door behind him, and abandoning her to the darkness. She heard his whistles from the hall. It was the same tune she'd overheard at the prom.

She had been right about him, from the start. But she didn't get everything right. In addition to underestimating him, there was another thing she got wrong. She'd noticed it when she looked at him closer up. The observation, though surprising, didn't change the fact she was still in grave danger.

FORTY-FIVE

Amanda and Trent had spent a couple hours visiting Clarissa and Nadine and then moving on to Melvin Thompson. Clarissa and Nadine had sobbed when Amanda handed over Reese's latest sketchbook and told them about Makayla and the oxy. To hold that back didn't feel right.

The three didn't recognize the man with Reese in the park from his size and shape, or any names on the list of former golf club employees.

Amanda's phone rang as she was walking from Melvin's house to the department car. It was Kristen showing on the ID, and it had Amanda's blood running cold. She stopped next to the passenger door. "Kristen, everything okay?"

"No, I don't think so. It's... it's Ava." Kristen's words were hacked by sobs.

"Talk to me, Kristen," Amanda said firmly.

"Ava's missing."

Amanda leaned against the vehicle, relying on it to hold her up. "Are you sure?"

"She's missing," Kristen snapped. "The psycho who killed that girl probably has her!"

"All right, let's just take a deep breath."

"Amanda, no. She's in trouble."

Amanda's hands were shaking as worst-case scenarios fired through her head, but it was her job to keep her sister calm, to approach this with objectivity and logic. "What makes you think she's missing?" This wasn't making any sense. They had officers watching her.

"She should be home from school by now, and she's not answering her phone."

Amanda looked at Trent who was watching her with concern. He touched her shoulder, and she let it stay there. "Is it ringing straight to voicemail?" If so, that meant it was offline.

"Yes. Please do something, Amanda." Her sister broke down.

"I will. I promise. Is Erik there with you?"

"No, but he's on his way home from work."

"Okay, both of you stay put at the house."

"In case the monster who has her calls? We don't have a lot of money, Mandy, if they want a ransom."

"Just so you're home if Ava returns. Okay?" Pointing out this killer was more interested in torture and murder, opposed to looking for a payday, wasn't a good idea.

"Okay."

"I'll get her, Kristen." With that, Amanda ended the call and turned to Trent. "I think our killer has Ava." The words spilled out, and with them, her legs buckled. Trent rushed to keep her upright. She withdrew from his arms. "We've got to save her, Trent. No other option."

"We'll get her."

"But how?" She swiped at a rogue tear that threatened to give away her volatile state. She was a cop, daughter of a cop, and she was to be built of tougher stuff.

Trent took her hand and peered into her eyes. "You have

the right to cry about this, Amanda. But it won't do any good. It won't get Ava back. She needs you, now more than ever."

She sniffled and nodded.

"I'll get Ava's phone tracked," Trent offered.

"It's off, but it should give us her last location."

Trent nodded, pulling out his phone. "Just remember, there are still avenues we haven't broached. It's too early to go back to the roller rink in hopes of meeting up with Hammer, but we have the videos from the golf course. We'll see if we can spot that man who had been standing near the food table. The one who was suspicious to Ava."

"Why would she do this to herself?" Anger and frustration battled within her for dominance. She hated that it directed blame to her niece. "If she hadn't poked and prodded... He must have caught on to her, Trent."

"We'll get her back safely."

"I appreciate the confidence, but..." She couldn't bring herself to finish that sentence.

Trent placed his call, and she got in the car and apprised Malone of the situation. She even fessed up to Ava playing Nancy Drew and finding that golf shirt. "If this killer is trying to call me out, guess what? Success. I'm going to find the son of a bitch and—"

"Detective Steele." Malone's tone was cool and professional, just what she needed to hear, and how she needed to hear it. A reminder that she was qualified to save her niece and that objectivity was the key to that end.

"What happened to the officers that were supposed to be watching her?"

"You can be sure I'll be finding out."

"Best you do, and I don't," was what Amanda said before hanging up.

FORTY-SIX

Amanda's phone rang, and she flinched. Her caller's identity had more guilt spiking through her. "Libby, I'm so sorry. I..." She snapped her mouth shut. Libby was returning Amanda's message to call. Now she'd have to come out and put the nightmare into words. "Ava's missing."

Libby's end of the line was silent.

"She's... well, she never came home from school, and no one can reach her. We have officers out looking for her, of course, and I'm doing all I can to..." Amanda rubbed her neck and pinched her eyes shut.

While she spoke on the phone, Trent let the video from the Rolling Hills Country Club continue to play. They'd already watched the footage from the pro shop, hoping to spot their prime suspect, but they didn't have access to days' worth of video—just Friday and Saturday. The killer could have bought the shirt on the Thursday, or months ago.

"Amanda, I don't even know what to say, but I'm sorry you're going through this. I hope you find her and soon. In the meantime anything I can do, I'm here for you."

"Well, that's why I called. Can Zoe sleep over at your place tonight?"

"Goes without saying."

"And don't tell her about Ava," Amanda rushed out. The two had a strong bond, and there was no need to upset Zoe at this point.

"I won't. Good luck, and I'll be praying for you."

Amanda ended the call, her mind ripping apart Libby's last promise. Prayer didn't do an ounce of good—not in Amanda's experience. It hadn't kept Kevin and Lindsey alive, or Amanda's unborn child. God was either too busy to hear her pleas or wasn't interested. She put her faith in police work, following leads, and seeing them through.

She glanced at Trent's monitor and what was playing out on the screen. The angle of this camera was out the back door, overlooking a walkway that circled the club and covered some of the greens.

Malone shadowed the doorway of Trent's cubicle, and Trent paused the video.

Malone said, "Ava's phone last pinged just after noon, near the school."

"Where was the officer?" Each word came out in equal measure. Her temper and frustration were burning hot and not far from the surface.

"He was there, where he should have been, but he said a load of students exited the school at lunch. He looked for Ava but didn't see her, so he assumed she was eating in the cafeteria."

"Assumed." Amanda clenched a hand into a fist. She'd like to believe her niece was smarter than ditching the cops, especially after her scare last night. They needed to apply pressure to Jacob Briggs about the license plate more than ever. Even if they couldn't get a clear enough shot to run the driver's face through facial recognition databases, that was fine. The person would need a criminal record to be stored there anyhow.

"Detective Steele, can we talk a minute in private?" Malone asked.

"Ah, sure. Trent, see if you can reach Briggs and if there's anything he can do with those pictures Ava took. A license plate would be really helpful about now. Also, where are things with Reese's phone? We've never heard."

"Consider it done."

"Thanks. And go ahead with the video without me too."

He nodded, and she left with Malone, heading toward his office.

After they got there, he shut the door behind them. "I've got officers out scouring the area around Potomac High."

"Make sure they ask about white vans. Specifically GMC Savanas."

"Noted, and they are. But the main reason I asked you to come into my office was because we need to talk." He rounded his desk and sat down.

She took one of the chairs across from him.

"I'm going to do what I can to keep the details from hitting the ears of the police chief. If he finds out that Ava was interfering with an active police investigation, there might be trouble for her and you."

"Then just don't let that part get back to him. It's enough to know that she's best friends with the vic's sister, goes to Potomac High, and I'm her aunt."

"You think the killer is doing this because of who you are?"

"Of course that's why." A lump rose in her throat, and her chest tightened.

"Whatever is motivating this killer, this isn't on you."

"It just pains me to think Ava's with a killer right now."

"It is possible there's another explanation."

"I don't think so. Neither do you." It was evident in his eyes that he was trying to germinate alternatives in her to make her feel better—not that he offered any.

"We're doing all we can. *You're* doing all you can. Just remember no matter how this turns out, none of this is on you. Promise me that you won't take it upon your shoulders."

"I promise." But the vow was flatlined and meaningless. If something happened to Ava, Amanda would assume all the blame. Ava needed her aunt, and it would be a matter of Amanda letting her down. Even Malone was attempting to prepare her for the worst-possible outcome—which she couldn't stand to think about. "Can I go now?"

Malone nodded, and she returned to Trent and the video from the golf course. He paused to say, "Briggs has bad news and bad news. Whatever was on Reese's phone is lost. He also took a quick look at the photos, but he can't clear them up."

"Thanks for checking."

He resumed the video, without making any attempt at small talk. She appreciated that—she just wanted to keep moving forward.

"Stop," she called out. "There." She pointed at a man pushing a wheeled janitorial bin. "He sure looks like the guy we're after."

"That he does." Trent paused the feed and brought up the one of Reese walking with the mystery man and put them side by side. "I'd say that's a match."

"We need to know who this is. Can you check earlier times from another camera, maybe one that shows the lot?"

"You got it." Trent did just that, and they quickly had their horrifying truth.

The man had arrived in a white GMC Savana with no rear plate—that end facing the camera.

"Trent, can you go back more, see if you can find when he entered the lot?"

He rewound, and the van came in at five precisely.

"No front plate either. What the hell? All right, back to where we were, please," she said.

They watched as the man left the feed and returned with a janitorial bin and wheeled it to the vehicle's back doors. Next, he removed a large garbage bag from inside and put it in the bin. It took up most of the realty.

"Reese is probably in there." Her stomach turned. "I can't believe we have this."

"Makes two of us. Now we just have to find this son of a bitch, and his ass is nailed." Trent zoomed in on the man's face.

"He must not know about the camera locations. But how does that fit with him knowing about the protocols for evening events at the club?" Her eyes fixed on him—beyond his size he was rather ordinary looking.

"I don't know."

"Another thing, staff from Protect It doesn't blink an eye when they see this guy taking what looks like garbage out of his van?"

"Guess not. Same for club staff. It's like he was invisible."

"A sad reflection on the world today," she said. "People don't pay enough attention to other people. But I hope we start figuring some things out. Let's go talk with Vince Galloway immediately and see if he recognizes this person."

Amanda brought up the number for the golf club and was told that Galloway had left for the day. "It's an urgent matter, and I need to speak with him." The woman on the other end already knew who she was. "Cell phone number?" Amanda prompted.

The woman prattled it off, and Amanda hung up and tried the number. "Mr. Galloway?" she said when a man answered.

"It is. Who is this?"

"Detective Steele. There's an urgent situation that you may be able to help me with." She told him about securing the video from Protect It and the man with a wheeled bin.

"Sure, send his picture over and I'll look right now."

Amanda asked for his email and let him say it on speaker as Trent got to work compiling the email with the attachment.

"I'll hold the line while you take a look."

Every passing second felt like a stab to the heart, and her lungs expanded and contracted painfully as if full of slivers. Eventually, she broke the silence. "Mr. Galloway," she prompted. Nothing came back at first, and she deduced he was studying the photo.

"I do recognize him," he eventually said.

"A former employee?"

"Nope. We had some construction work done at the club's restaurant back in February and March—drywall, plumbing, that kind of thing. They also helped pull a few stumps from trees that didn't make it over the winter. I think this person was with them."

The chain that had been used to strangle Reese was intended for things like stump removal. "The business's name?"

"Gray's Building Projects. They're out of Woodbridge but came highly recommended."

"Do you know the man's name... the one in the picture?"

"My memory's good, but not that good."

Amanda thought back to Rock n Rollerblade and one string they were waiting to tug—the man who worked in construction and regularly leered at teenage girls including Reese. "Does the nickname Hammer sound familiar to you?"

"Hammer," he said as if trying it on. "Yes, I think that's it."

Amanda's hand was shaking, and she set her phone face up on the desk. "Another question quickly before I let you go. Have you changed the locations of your security cameras in the last few months?" She was curious if it was after Hammer had finished up his work there.

"Yeah, we did."

"I'm mostly interested in the one that is over the end of the parking lot."

"Oh that one? It's brand new."

Amanda looked at Trent, thanked Vince, and ended the call. "Hammer didn't know about the new camera. He thought he was going about his deeds undetected."

"And there's some luck for us."

"About freakin' time. And we now know he goes by Hammer. We just need to call Gray's and ask for the real name that goes with it."

"We thought the killer was someone in construction."

"Drywall... Vince said they did some drywall work." She swallowed roughly as a picture formed. "We were never able to determine what was used to stab Reese's eyes. We just know that it was sharp and serrated. When Kev and I bought our place, we did some reno work. He hated drywall most of all, but he did his best to save us a few bucks. To cut it he used a drywall saw. Handheld and—"

"Sharp and serrated," Trent interjected, capping off what she was going to say.

She picked up her phone and brought up the number for Gray's Building Projects. A man named Robert Gray answered immediately. Amanda told him who she was and what she wanted to know. Within a few seconds, she had Hammer's true identity. "His real name is Warren Chaney."

FORTY-SEVEN

Amanda and Trent set off for Manassas without an arrest or search warrant, but Sergeant Malone said they'd have it by the time they got to Warren Chaney's house. And while he let them go ahead of the paperwork and Special Weapons and Tactics, they were to take backup and wait on scene.

Amanda pulled a background on Chaney prior to leaving Central. He didn't have a criminal record—just as they'd figured their suspect wouldn't.

Trent was parking out front of Chaney's when the search and arrest warrants came through. No garage, and the sedan registered to him wasn't in the driveway.

There still wasn't any sign of SWAT, but a police car pulled up. The officer inside would qualify as backup.

She got out of the car and trudged toward the front door.

"Amanda, where are you going?" Trent asked.

"If you think I'm just sitting around waiting on SWAT, you have another thing coming." She rushed up the stairs and banged on the door. "Prince William County PD! Open up!"

Nothing.

She banged again, the screen door rattling loudly in its frame.

"As you told me before, you break it, you bought it," said Trent from the stairs behind her.

"Send me the bill." She let loose on it a third time.

"I don't think he's here."

But how was she supposed to leave when Ava might be inside? Technically, protocol in situations such as this necessitated that SWAT breach and clear. She flung the screen door open and shook the interior one by its handle. She stood back. "Bust it down."

"We need to wait on SWAT."

"Trent. Please."

He stepped back as if he were planning to build momentum before crashing into the door, but she stopped him.

The commander vehicle for SWAT had just arrived. She barked orders, and while they did as she was saying, she wasn't confident they were actually listening to her. Rather following their training. They got through the front door in seconds with a battering ram.

After about ten minutes, the SWAT officers came back outside. The team leader beelined to her and Trent.

"No sign of the perp inside, or the girl," he told them.

Amanda wasn't sure if this had her breathing easier or harder. A quick check hadn't shown any other properties registered to Warren Chaney, and he certainly wasn't a man of means. The house was nice but modest.

"Thanks," Trent told the chief, who dipped his head, and he and his men headed back to their vehicle.

Amanda turned to Trent. "We'll get officers searching inside for anything useful."

"Where are we going?"

"No way I'm just standing around to see if and when

Chaney returns." She left him to follow in her wake. "Take us to the Rollerblade rink."

"Yes, ma'am." Trent got into the department car after informing the backup officer where they were headed and to start the search.

She keyed a quick text to Malone to bring him up to speed, and Trent couldn't get them to the rink fast enough. Now if Warren Chaney wasn't there, they'd get a BOLO issued for his sedan, but that did little to appease Amanda's nerves.

"Just stay positive," Trent said, almost as if reading her mind or sensing that she was starting to feel hopelessness ebb in.

"Trying."

He pulled into the lot for the rink, and she looked around for Chaney's sedan. It was nowhere in sight.

She didn't wait until the car came to a complete stop but hopped out slightly before and rolled with the motion of it. She found solid footing and entered the building ahead of Trent. A text came through from her sister to say they still hadn't seen or heard from Ava. She was looking for an update from Amanda. She keyed back that they were following a lead. While it might provide more hope than it warranted, Amanda wanted to give her sister something to cling to.

Amanda looked around, desperate to spot Chaney, but it was hard to make out faces due to the dim lighting of the place. She walked to the counter and asked for Pete Matheson. He came out of a back office, and Amanda rushed out, "I need all the lights turned up and the music off."

"I can't just do that."

"You can, and you will. Just a few minutes should be long enough."

"Tell me what this is about."

"We're looking for Hammer." She provided the name the owner would be familiar with.

"I can tell you right now I haven't seen him tonight."

"You said he was in most nights around seven, drinking with his friends. It's seven ten. Are they here?"

Pete pointed at a table where two men were drinking beer and laughing it up with a couple of teenage girls. The teens appeared to be tolerating them. Amanda headed over, Trent with her.

"We're looking to speak with your friend Warren Chaney, or as you might know him, Hammer." She held up her badge for more incentive. "Any idea where we might find him?"

The two men's expressions sobered quickly.

The one said, "He should be here any minute."

The other pointed toward the door. "That's him now."

Amanda turned and saw that Warren Chaney had indeed just walked into the building. She wasted no time hustling over to him.

"Warren Chaney?" she said as her mind computed she was looking at a killer who had mutilated a young girl, strangled a woman, and kidnapped her niece. He looked a little different in person compared to his driver's license photo and what was captured on video, but that wasn't unusual.

"Yeah. And you are?"

"Your worst nightmare," Amanda said. "Where is she?"

"Where is who?" His brows furrowed down, like writhing bushy caterpillars.

"The girl you took."

"I didn't take anyone." His face grew red.

"Play it how you want, but I'll get it out of you. Now turn around." Amanda twirled a finger.

"Who are you people?"

Trent answered, "Prince William County PD, and you better do as she says."

FORTY-EIGHT

"I swear to you I have no idea who you're talking about." Warren was pale under the fluorescent lights of the interrogation room back at Central.

Amanda tapped the photograph of Ava she'd placed on the table at the start of the interview. "Look real close."

"I've never even seen her before. Should I get a lawyer?"

"You've been brought in for questioning pertaining to the murder of Reese Thompson and Susie Valentine and the abduction of Ava Rollins. Up to you." She put all this out drily, letting the man then run to his own conclusion. She certainly wasn't going to suggest an attorney. Things would move along a lot faster without one present.

"Murder?" Warren gulped, his Adam's apple bobbing and beads of sweat dotting his forehead.

"Reese Thompson, eighteen." Amanda withdrew her photograph from a folder she had with her.

Warren looked at it but shook his head.

"Don't tell us you haven't seen her," Trent inserted.

The man's eyes flicked to Trent. "I've seen her."

"And where was that, Mr. Chaney?" Amanda asked.

"At the Rollerblade rink."

"You like to watch teenage girls with your friends, laugh it up, hoot and holler," Amanda said, even though doing so made her sick.

"We, um, like to do that, but that's all. We never, ever, take things further."

"So you never make unwanted moves on them?" she pressed.

"No. I swear."

That two-word phrase was a favorite of Hammer's as it turned out. "Where were you last Wednesday evening between six and seven o'clock?"

"Out for dinner with my friends, then we went to the rink."

"When did you last see Reese Thompson?"

"There you said her name again. I didn't even know it before."

She resisted the urge to say you don't need to know a person's name to kill them. "Answer the question." Amanda's patience was gone. Her niece was being held somewhere, and the man across the table held the answer.

"I swear, I don't—"

The door to the interrogation room swung open, and Nathan Steele bowled through. He lifted Warren from the chair by the scruff of his shirt and pushed him against the back wall. "Where is Ava Rollins? I won't ask again."

Amanda's gaze was fixed on her father. She should get up and stop this from happening, but she was unable to move. Her father, the former police chief, was doing something she wouldn't dare do, blowing past a line she'd never cross if she wanted to climb the ranks. But desperate times and all that...

Warren's eyes were bugging out, and he was swatting at Nathan's arms.

Trent stood and cleared his throat. "Put him down."

Nathan thew a glare over a shoulder at Trent, and Amanda was happy it was her partner on the receiving end and not her.

"He's right. Stand down!" Malone barked as he swept into the room.

Nathan released his grip. Eventually. When he was good and ready, knowing her father.

Warren was heaving for breath, and the four of them left the room and entered the observation room next door.

"What do you think you were doing?" Malone's voice shook the room as he spoke to her father. "I said you could watch, not intervene."

"That man"—her father thrust a pointed finger toward the two-way mirror—"has my granddaughter, and you think I'm just going to stand back and do nothing?"

Malone let out a sigh of disgust and shook his head. "I should have known you'd barge in there all bullheaded."

"Would you two cut it out?" Amanda shouted to be heard.

Both men looked at her as if scolded by a parent. Though one was her father and the other like a second one. "We need to keep our heads. For Ava's sake."

An officer appeared in the doorway, cheeks flushed. No doubt he'd heard everything from down the hall. "Ah, excuse me?"

"What is it, Tucker?" Malone asked.

"The search has finished at Chaney's residence, and there wasn't anything that tied him to Reese Thompson or Ava Rollins."

Malone threw his hands in the air. "Just great, and now we're no closer to finding Ava and Chaney might sue the department."

The officer slinked back into the hall and out of sight.

"He could have still done this," Amanda said evenly. Somehow witnessing her father's act of impulsiveness had her thinking more rationally. "He certainly looks like the guy we have on video unloading a huge garbage bag from the rear of the van."

"Except, I'm starting to think we might be missing something here." This came from Trent, and they all turned to face him. He spoke to Amanda. "She was relaxed with that man in the park. We saw it with our own eyes."

"Yeah, due to the oxy in her system," Amanda kicked back, not sure where her partner was headed.

"But answer this. Even still, she'd see Chaney as some strange older man who hollers at her when she skates with her friends on Friday nights. She even told her sister she wanted to get away from him."

"But it's his face on the video," she said.

"Everyone supposedly has a doppelganger," Trent countered.

"Show him stills from the park video and ones taken from the golf club. See what he says to that," Malone said.

"We don't have time for all this," Nathan seethed. "My granddaughter is out there terrified for her life."

Malone set a firm hand on Nathan's shoulder. "We'll find her. I promise."

Nathan batted his friend's hand away, along with his assurance. "No promises in this line of work, Malone. You should know that by now." Her father left the room, passing by Amanda with a subtle dip of his head.

She'd see her father in a different light moving forward. Though she always saw him as an alpha male who would go to any lengths to protect his family, she never imagined he crossed the line in an interrogation room. But the way he'd moved in on Warren Chaney, she had reason to suspect it wasn't the first time he'd pressured a suspect with physical violence. He might have another toe hanging over the edge of the pedestal she had him on. Though there was another part of her that was proud he was her dad. But she'd sort through her feelings later.

She returned with Trent to the interrogation room. This time she was armed with the photographs Malone had directed them to show Warren. Surely, confronted with his own face, he would have no recourse but to own up to his crimes—and Ava's whereabouts.

The first one she put down was of the man with Reese in the park. She pushed it across the table facing Warren. "What were you doing with Reese in this picture?"

Warren leaned in, then seconds later scrunched up his face. "Ah, that's not me."

Amanda plucked one picture after the other from the folder. These were various angles obtained from the Rolling Hills security footage. "Bet you're going to say the same thing about these ones."

Warren shuffled through them. "You bet because that's *not* me."

"This is you, Mr. Chaney." Amanda pressed a finger to the photo on top that had a rather clear image of Warren's face.

"Nope. That's Leslie Hansen." Warren leaned back in his chair.

"And who is Leslie Hansen? Another alter ego?" Amanda was getting more pissed by the second.

"Ah no. She, or should I say *he* to be politically correct, works for Gray's too. Just to further prove this isn't me, I have an Adam's apple whereas Leslie doesn't. I'll bet if you enlarge these photos you'll see that." He casually leaned back and clasped his hands over his lap. "I'll wait."

Amanda looked at Trent. She normally didn't take orders from a suspect, but some pieces of the investigation would make more sense if the killer was born anatomically female. Like the dress, tiara, and makeup. She led the way from the room.

"You got this?" she said to Trent.

"Yep, I can figure it out." He sat down and brought up the section of video that had provided most of the still shots. He enlarged each one in turn. No shadows were cast to indicate an Adam's apple.

"Hate to say it, but Chaney's right," Trent said.

"You must admit this makes sense. The older prom dress, the tiara, the decades' old makeup that had to have been sitting around. It would also explain why he was coming out of the men's restroom when Ava heard him whistle. Leslie must have started identifying as male at some point. My guess is around the time of his prom. And I would bet that something drastic happened to him at that time that affected him deeply and stayed with him all these years. Was there something about Reese that triggered that hurt and those memories?"

"It very well could be, but no matter what Leslie Hansen had gone through, he's a killer now. Let's get the warrants we need and pick him up."

It couldn't happen fast enough...

FORTY-NINE

Amanda and Trent beat everyone again, and that was taking the time to pull some information on Leslie Hansen before leaving Central. His background was clear of criminal charges—as they'd suspected. It would limit Leslie's risk in leaving DNA trace that would tie back to him, though it wouldn't stop it from being used to implicate him after the fact. They also did a database search and found that Leslie Hansen held the mortgage on one property. It was a house located just a few blocks from Prince William Forest Park, close enough to be within walking distance, and it was also located along the route Reese took when she rollerbladed. If Leslie had a habit of going to the park like Reese, it was possible that the two had made unlikely acquaintances. Stranger things have happened.

They referenced notes from the canvassing officers who covered the street, including Leslie's neighbors. No one had seen anything, and Leslie's house had been marked not at home.

"I can't believe her killer has been right here from the beginning," Trent lamented as he gestured toward the compact bungalow with an attached garage.

"I've gotta go, Trent. Ava could be in there." She reached

for her door handle, prepared to go rogue, just when SWAT rolled up.

"Shouldn't be long now," he said.

Amanda got out of the car but stayed back and watched as SWAT did their thing. Trent stood next to her.

SWAT officers knocked and announced themselves, but no one came to the door. They rammed through it like they had at Warren Chaney's. Calls of "Cleared" carried from inside out into the night air. With every one, her heart sank further.

After a number of painful minutes, SWAT came out. The leader came to her. "No sign of Ava Rollins being here or having ever been here."

"That doesn't make any sense. Take a harder look."

"I'm sorry, Detective."

If he knew that Ava Rollins was her niece, he might be more genuine with his apology.

"Amanda, we'll find her, we will." It was Trent with the pep talk, and he was rubbing her back.

She wanted to believe him, but with every passing second a happy ending felt further out of reach. "Can I go inside?" She had directed the question to the SWAT leader.

"Don't see why not."

She went in, stopped short. The place smelled clean, and the living room off the front entry was tidy. She entered and looked around. It was sparsely decorated with two overstuffed leather couches, a boxy coffee table, a large flatscreen TV, and a bookshelf. The latter was dotted with bric-a-brac and a few coffee-table books, but Amanda danced her gaze over the spines.

She pulled a book that caught her eye. "Trent, look. It's a yearbook from the nineties."

"Huh. From the same era as the prom gown."

Amanda cracked it open, flipped some pages, and drew

back. "Whoa. Stinks like mothballs. Here, smell." She held it toward Trent's nose, but he batted her away.

"I can smell it from here, thanks."

She flipped more pages and found Leslie Hansen's grade twelve photo. "This was his graduating year. Or should I say, *her* graduating year. It looks like Leslie was much smaller then and dressed more feminine."

"Except there's the hair. It's short. It could be seen as masculine, then again, pixie cuts were popular if I recall."

Amanda nodded agreement. "Look at this." She'd spotted a photograph that, presumably, Leslie had scratched over with blue ink. Scrawled in messy handwriting was the word *Bitch*. Amanda angled the book and the glossy page gave up its secret. "Staci Gillespie."

"Obviously she and Leslie weren't friends."

"Or they were and something happened that hurt Leslie. I'd guess there's an association to prom."

"We theorized motive having to do with a traumatizing experience surrounding prom. Flip through and see if you can find pictures taken then."

Amanda turned pages, searching for Leslie's face. She eventually came to the photographs from the prom, but there was no sign of Leslie. Staci's picture was vandalized, though her name was left untouched in the column. "This girl was prom queen."

"I'm with you. I wager there's a long and hurtful story there."

"I don't care anymore. Not sure I ever did. No excuse for what he's doing. Now he has Ava." Rage pumped through her veins with a life of its own.

"Never said whatever happened to Leslie was a justification, just provides us some insight."

"Yeah, I know. I'm just frustrated. Ava's not here, SWAT cleared the place. But if she's not here, then where? Leslie doesn't have any other properties. I need to think." She paced the living room.

"Well, I just had an idea, but it might be a stretch," Trent said.

She stopped walking. "I'm all for hearing it."

"It seems that Leslie is afforded some flexibility when it comes to the work she does for Gray's Building Projects... and while he may not own any other properties—"

"Trent, you're a genius!"

"You don't even know what I was going to say."

"Oh, I think I do." She pulled her phone and called Robert Gray using the cell number he'd given her when they'd first spoken. "Mr. Gray, it's Detective Steele. I need to know if you have any long-term projects in the works—"

"Ones that may be on temporary hold even," Trent interjected, and Amanda nodded.

"You hear that?"

"I did. There are a few."

"Are any more remote or isolated than the others?"

"We're doing a rehaul on a building in the Woodbridge industrial park, but some permits have been delayed. The project's been on hold for a few weeks, and it will probably stay that way for another month."

Bingo! "The address?"

Robert gave her the specifics, and she thanked him as she was on the move. CSIs Blair and Donnelly were entering Leslie's home, and they'd do a thorough search for any possible trace that Reese Thompson had been there. But it was also possible that Leslie had killed her in this industrial building.

She directed the CSIs to collect the yearbook in the living room, and she and Trent started the drive to the industrial park.

Hold on, Ava! I'm coming!

FIFTY

He witnessed the shock play across the girl's features when she got a closer look at him. It was unspoken, but he was quite sure she had noticed the absence of an Adam's apple. Also reflecting in her eyes, he swore he detected judgment. It made her no better than the rest of them who ostracized him for who he truly was. Born with the anatomy of a girl, he eventually came to embrace his inner truth. It had been stirring for as long as he remembered, but *he* identified more with the masculine aspects of *herself*. As time passed, he chose to identify as being male—and this was long before it was "acceptable," prior to the multiple options now present on politically correct forms next to gender. His preference would always be he/him/his. At least this showed *some* progress to society as a whole. It was the individual that was the real problem, with their inherent habit of clinging to the familiar, the old-fashioned "ideals." Some reacted strongly—and violently—to what they didn't understand. Cowards really.

Though maybe if it hadn't been for all the cruelty and adversity, he would still be lost. In a way, his prosecution had served as a downpour and prompted the seedling of his true self to break ground. It was only then he could grow and accept his true identity, who he was on the inside. For what he'd failed to see clearly until more recently was his pain had been underlying all these years. Every time he saw Reese, this truth had built as a crescendo of clashing cymbals, alerting him that he could no longer tolerate the bigots. He had to make a stand, and without Staci here he'd grabbed on to the next best thing—an imitation but with stunning similarities. He harbored no regrets. Same with this girl he had captured. Given the fact she was trying to stop him, that alone screamed her disapproval. Just like his own mother.

She refused to see him for who he was, trying to make him fit in. The girlie clothes going back to the beginning, her insistence he attend prom wearing the blue poofy dress. He'd protested. He'd lost. But it was the battle, not the war.

He'd snuck in a trip to the hair salon and had his hair cropped short, which led to another screaming argument with his mother. But there was nothing she could do to bring back his locks. Score one for him.

And sure, he'd put on the gown, but he only pretended to go to prom. Instead, he hung out in the park and watched the Potomac River. He was heartbroken from Staci's rejection and the violence she had instigated toward him. More than the physical pain, she'd humiliated him and broken him mentally. That sort of bullying isn't something a person forgets, and for him it felt like it cut so deeply personal. But when he'd taken a few days to think about it, he realized he could no longer ignore or deny his own truth—even if that meant it was him against the world. Whether that viewpoint was reality, in his head it was truth.

He decided to come clean to his mother, which had been difficult but necessary. Her reaction only added acid to the wound that Staci and her band of cohorts had opened up. His own flesh and blood had tossed him out and disowned him. She yelled after him, "You are dead to me!"

Broken, but he eventually picked himself up. He'd held on to that prom dress all these years as a reminder of his commitment to himself, to his vow to never conform. He had to kill Reese once it became impossible to ignore all she represented—the years of brutality and ostracism that finally needed restitution. Being face to face with her, he was catapulted to the past. It was as if he were being choked all over again—his voice stolen along with his next breath. That suffocating feeling moved in and toppled him. He'd had no choice but to react, to save himself. To breathe freely.

Yes, dressing Reese in that gown had been a message, all right. A middle finger to the world. He had the right to be true to himself, and he refused to be the victim anymore.

He smiled, thinking that if they hadn't gotten the message yet, they would soon. When they found the body of Ava Rollins.

FIFTY-ONE

Amanda updated Malone on their status as Trent drove. She had him on speaker.

"Wait for backup, Amanda," Malone said. "I mean it."

Trent was there to hear the sergeant's directive and hold her accountable.

"We will." Her insides were jumping. This lead was the one that would return Ava safely home; Amanda could just feel it. She ended the call with Malone, just as Trent pulled to the side of the street a block away from the warehouse address. She turned to him. "What are you doing?"

"You heard what the sarge said."

"I can't just—"

"You don't have a choice, and we don't really know what we're walking in on, do we?"

"I need to get to Ava."

"Just hear me out. Leslie knows we're onto him. He also knows that you and I will come for Ava."

"You don't know that."

"Come on, Amanda. We both do. Leslie is getting desperate, or he wouldn't have taken Ava. She made him feel threatened. He's obviously been watching her every move to know when to act. Don't fool yourself into thinking he doesn't know about her aunt, the detective. We wait." He sat back, settling against the headrest.

Amanda licked her lips, stared into the distance, longing to run into that warehouse. But Trent was right. And they had to do this by the book.

Thankfully, they weren't sitting around waiting for too long. The SWAT command vehicle came up behind them. Amanda and Trent hopped out of their car and headed to talk to the SWAT leader.

"We're going to approach quietly, probably from here. Uniforms are on their way, sirens off so as not to alert the suspect, if she is inside. And they'll be setting up a perimeter."

"*He*," Amanda corrected. "If *he* is inside."

"Yes, *he*."

Amanda peacocked her stance, looking up at the man who towered inches above her. "We're going in with you and your guys, not up for debate."

"I'll allow it, but you follow my directions. I see you're wearing your vests already, but go back and see Tank, and he'll get you equipped with radios and NVGs. We suspect it may be dark in there."

Night-vision goggles. She would have loved a huge automatic gun too but knew better than to ask. The request would be denied. "And Tank is?"

"You'd figure it out quickly, but Tank's the biggest guy on the team. Shaved head, tattoo sleeves."

Amanda hustled to the vehicle and climbed inside. The SWAT command vehicle was essentially an RV, but it was decked out with a number of computers, surveillance equipment, and a meeting table. Next to it was a man, who must be six foot seven, talking to a few other officers. They all stopped when Amanda and Trent entered.

"Guessing you're Tank?" she directed this to the behemoth. Though it wasn't much of a guess, more educated observation.

"Yeah."

"Detectives Steele and Stenson." She gestured toward Trent. "Your boss sent us back here. We're going in with you."

"Sure thing. Let me get you radios and on the right frequency."

One of the other officers snickered at that, and while Amanda knew Tank's words enclosed an insult, she didn't give a crap right now. She'd get along to move along...

"We were just discussing approach," Tank told her and flattened a blueprint out on the table. It must have belonged to the building they were about to breech.

She leaned in and committed what she could to memory. "Two floors?" she said. "Main level and a basement?"

"Uh-huh."

Just more nooks and crannies to hide Ava away...

It took about a half hour for the SWAT team to cement a solid approach, and every passing minute was agony.

"All right, let's move," the SWAT leader said.

Amanda and Trent were to stay behind the SWAT officers on the way inside.

They set out toward the building. It was surrounded by a chain-link fence, but the gate was open. From the look of it someone had cut the chain that had secured it; the padlock was still closed but on the ground.

There were a number of bay doors for transports to back up against for loading and unloading. The group crept inside. The SWAT leader's suspicion was off the mark. Every light was on. She and Trent removed their NVGs.

Amanda kept her gun at the ready as she and Trent moved in unison with the SWAT officers deeper into the building.

With each step, Amanda was taken back in time to when Zoe had been taken and held in an industrial warehouse. She and Trent had joined the SWAT team then too and were ambushed by overhead fire. There had been an upper walkway looking down over the main bay. At least here it was single story. The blueprint showed two staircases that led to the basement level. One was located near the front—their point of entry—and the other at the rear. There was also another man door that exited in the back. All these egress points would have been mandated by fire safety laws.

Police officers were posted outside and two SWAT officers hung back at the front staircase. The plan was to go down once the rest of the SWAT team cleared the main level. Then both segments would use the staircases and move toward the center of the building or the lower level.

Leslie Hansen would be trapped.

At least that was the plan.

Amanda knew that plans didn't always work out. She and Trent remained with the first pairing of officers, and when the word came, they would accompany them downstairs.

That directive came about fifteen minutes after entry. Once they reached the basement, the hall continued straight and immediately branched off to the right. Amanda and Trent took the turn while the SWAT officers continued ahead.

Amanda and Trent cleared each room they passed in quick succession, but it wasn't quick enough for her. She feared the time to save her niece may be running out.

"This feels like Zoe all over again," she said lowly to Trent.

"Well, we saved her, so remember that." He looked over at her.

She could always count on him to see the upside. "Thanks for that." The end of the hall was a long way out. The footprint of the building was massive.

From the chatter coming over the radios she knew the SWAT members working toward them were still a distance away.

She entered the next room on the right while Trent hit the one on the left. The room was large, and it had a few construction items stacked up in the far-left corner. To the right was a wheeled toolchest. Another room fed off this one to the back right. Its door was shut.

Amanda moved farther in.

Her radio went quiet. *What the—*

Then the door behind slammed shut, and a lock *thunked* into place.

Shit! She pivoted and was face to face with Leslie Hansen. He must have been standing behind the door, out of sight. Leslie was larger in life than any picture did him credit for and could probably pull a monster truck or tractor.

Amanda's throat thickened, and her breathing slowed. But if Leslie was here, it probably meant that Ava was in the adjacent room. The deafening silence rang with fear.

She raised her gun higher. "Prince William County PD! Surrender."

Leslie stood there, legs shoulder-width apart, as if he were prepared for Amanda to rush toward him. Amanda stayed put.

Amanda fingered her radio, hoping to rouse it.

Leslie showed Amanda a small device in his palm. "It's a signal jammer. I wanted you all to myself."

"Where is the girl?"

"You mean the nosy little brunette?"

Leslie's smirk had Amanda tensing and fueled her with adrenaline. Her mind was flooding her system with warnings, that in a fight, she wouldn't stand a chance. But that seemed to be exactly what Leslie wanted. "Let her go."

"That's not going to happen."

"I have the gun, Leslie. Whatever this is, it's over."

"No!" Leslie rushed toward Amanda and bowled her over.

Her gun went flying across the room, and Amanda slammed

against the floor, her head just missing impact. Every bone in her back and hips throbbed.

"You and that girl should have left me alone! I was finally happy." Leslie stood over her, and Amanda screamed for help.

"That won't do you any good here."

"My partner's right outside this door and several SWAT officers are moving in on this room. You have nowhere to go."

"Your threats don't scare me, Detective. And they're not getting past that reenforced steel door anytime soon. That leaves us plenty of time to get acquainted."

He's going to kill me!

Instinct took over, and Amanda kicked Leslie, hitting him in the shins, but there was no indication it had even been felt.

"You're making me do this to you... Not that I won't have fun."

You sick bastard!

Leslie grabbed Amanda's hair and dragged her across the floor.

Amanda slapped at his hands, but it was pointless. Leslie kept moving, carting Amanda behind like a rag doll. The pain was blinding and had Amanda's vision flashing white. It felt like her hair was being ripped from her scalp.

She had to do something to break free of Leslie's grip... but what? There was nothing around to use in her defense. Without her gun, Amanda didn't stand a chance against Leslie in a physical altercation. She needed something to level the playing field. If she startled him, that might work.

Amanda let out a string of ear-piercing screams, and Leslie stopped and spun. He loomed over Amanda and threw a right hook that glanced off Amanda's jaw. Even the glance had her head swooning.

But she rolled with the vertigo and shimmied across the floor. A makeshift weapon might lie in the corner among the construction supplies.

"Oh no, you don't." Leslie grabbed the back of Amanda's head and bashed her face into the floor. Thankfully he must have shown restraint or the impact could have been fatal. Still, Amanda's mind floated away, and darkness loomed. But she refused to succumb. She had to fight for Ava!

She spit blood, her mouth coated with its coppery metallic flavor. She swept out a leg, but like before, it met with Leslie as if he were the trunk of a tree. But this time it registered just enough that Leslie drew back, giving Amanda the precious few inches she needed.

Amanda fumbled, fighting the dizziness, and tried to stand. She crumpled to the floor. But Leslie was quickly moving in on her.

Amanda mustered all her strength and stood. She grabbed a can of paint and swung it, hoping to connect with Leslie's head, but her limbs were too weak to follow through.

The room was spinning. *I can't surrender...*

She searched the construction items, desperate to find something to wield in defense. Nothing. Desperation overtook her. *I'm going to die!*

Leslie picked up Amanda and tossed her across the room.

Amanda's back slammed into a wall and her head spun even faster. Her vision was going fuzzy, but she made out Leslie's bulk as a black form coming toward her. It was apparent he wasn't going to let Amanda slip into the darkness; he wanted to send her there, to watch the light leave her eyes.

She thought of Zoe and how that little girl would be when she found out about her death. How she'd already suffered so much tragedy and loss for a child, enough for several lifetimes. Zoe's face floated into her consciousness. "I love you," she mumbled, all she was capable of in this moment.

Then Logan entered her mind. His soft touch and how comforting it was to be wrapped in his arms. His smell, that of a campfire. And he loved her. He wanted something more with her. How it had scared her when he said that. She was afraid to love fully again in fear it would be stripped away. But, in this moment, she realized that was no way to live.

Images of Trent flashed through, how devastated he'd be if she'd died mere feet away from him. He'd go on to blame himself, and his life would be over too, in a way.

Leslie hunched down in front of her. "Time for you to die."

FIFTY-TWO

Amanda had to hang on, just for a few more minutes. Surely, Trent and SWAT would be storming in here to save her, to save Ava.

Ava.

She needed to fight, fight, fight.

But she was barely able to see and most likely concussed. Through squinted eyes, she discerned that she was close to the wheeled toolchest. If she could just get to it...

Amanda drew in a deep breath and stared into the Devil's eyes as she curled in her legs, reached out and tugged on the unit. It rolled across the floor, smacking into Leslie. He batted it aside and it toppled over, drawers and doors opening.

Finally Amanda's luck seemed to be turning. A screwdriver skittered across the floor and stopped in front of her. She snatched it just before Leslie moved in.

The screwdriver burrowed through his flesh, meeting no resistance from bone.

Leslie stopped, jaw going slack, blood dripping from his mouth. His eyes remained wild but filled with shock as he looked down at the screwdriver in his chest. He pulled it out, blinked, groaned, and fell forward.

Amanda tried to move out of Leslie's path but found herself pinned.

He was either dead or unconscious. In this moment, Amanda didn't care which. She needed free, or she'd suffocate.

Just then came the loud bang of a breaching charge, and the steel door clanked open. Trent and SWAT flooded the room.

Two officers pulled Leslie off Amanda. Her lungs fully expanded in appreciation.

"You all right?" Trent asked her.

"Do I look all right?" Her head was throbbing, and it hurt to keep her eyes open.

"You look better than him." Trent nudged a head toward Leslie's still form.

One of the SWAT officers was checking Leslie for a pulse. "He's still alive," he said.

More chaos followed as calls were made for paramedics to get there. "We have an officer down and a stab victim."

"Ava," she said, projecting what she'd intended to be a shout, but it returned to her ears a dull whisper.

"Just stay put," Trent told her. "We've got this."

She stubbornly moved to get up. Her head spun wildly but she persisted, even as her vision fell in and out of focus.

"What's with you?" Trent helped steady her. "Can't you just let other people step in?"

"No." She tried a smile and felt a cut in her lip crack farther open. She hobbled across the floor toward the offset room.

Just keep your eyes down. Steady goes it. One step at a time....

"Ava." She didn't know why she bothered calling out when she couldn't project her voice.

A tsunami of vertigo crashed over her, and Trent buoyed her as he turned the handle on the door.

It was unlocked.

Inside, Ava was restrained to a plumbing pipe that jutted out of the floor and duct tape was plastered across her mouth. But she was still alive, looking back at Amanda, tears falling down her cheeks.

Amanda worked to free her, but her fingers fumbled, unable to get a solid grip. Her head was spinning out of control. Trent stepped in and cut the restraints.

The last thing Amanda remembered before all became dark was throwing her arms around her niece.

FIFTY-THREE

The next time Amanda opened her eyes she was in a hospital room surrounded by her blood family and Logan, Trent, and Malone. The latter three her chosen family. And as the thought entered in, she remembered what she'd decided about her future with Logan. But now, not directly facing death, the fear of taking that next step in their relationship was rising again.

Zoe was next to her holding her right hand, an awareness snaking its way through her fingertips to her brain. She hated the thought of Zoe seeing her like this. Leslie had treated her as a punching bag, and she must have looked hideous.

"Mandy? She's awake!" Zoe was smiling and lunged forward to hug Amanda, but Amanda's mom held her back.

"Just go a little easy for a bit, sweetheart. She's a little banged up." Amanda's mother put a loving hand on the top of Zoe's head.

"Okay." Zoe sounded disheartened, and Amanda squeezed her hand.

"Don't go anywhere," she said to the girl.

Zoe nodded and smiled.

"Ava? Is she—" She looked around, searching, and then her

niece stepped in front of her grandfather, who was at the bedside opposite Zoe.

"I'm here," Ava said. "And I'm okay, thanks to you."

"Oh, thank God." She let out a deep exhale, and every inch of it was excruciating. She winced and put a hand to her torso.

"Two broken ribs, one fractured," her mother told her.

Amanda believed it. She felt like she'd been run over. But *thank God?* Where had that come from? He or She proved themselves absent in the past, but she gave them credit now? No, it had been the hard work of herself, Trent, and SWAT.

Ava leaned over and tapped a kiss on Amanda's forehead.

"Will you please stop playing detective now," Amanda said.

Ava held up her hands. "I promise!"

"We should probably go now so you can get some rest," Amanda's mom said on everyone's behalf, and the mass started toward the door.

"Wait." Her head was groggy, like she'd slept for a month already but needed another. "How long have I been in here?"

"Just overnight." Logan swept some of her hair back from her forehead. "You have a concussion too, and they wanted to keep an eye on you."

"Leslie Hansen?" Amanda asked, seeking out Trent.

"He's going to live," Trent said.

"And spend his life behind bars," Amanda's father inserted. "I'll be back later to check on you, Mandy Monkey."

Her heart swelled at her dad calling her by her family's assigned nickname, one she normally detested. Her father, her brother and sister-in-law, three of Amanda's sisters, and Malone left the room. Kristen and Logan stayed, and Trent moved toward the bed.

"I need to question him, Trent." Amanda made a motion to get up, but her body wasn't cooperating. It felt like an invisible hand was holding her down.

"That's already been taken care of," Trent said evenly.

"Why did he do it? How did he know Reese?"

Trent's gaze flicked to Zoe, who was standing vigil, and Amanda's mom took the girl by the hand. "Come on, sweetie. We'll come back later."

"Okay." Zoe was sulking. "I love you." She kissed Amanda's hand.

"And I love you."

Once Zoe left the room, Trent filled her in on Leslie Hansen. "He said that he killed Reese to ease his own pain."

"Come again?"

"He blamed that girl we saw in the yearbook, Staci Gillespie, for ruining his life. Leslie's trust in the girl had backfired, and at her prompting Leslie was violently assaulted. His mother didn't provide a safe haven either and kicked Leslie out of the house when he told her he wanted to be identified as male. Sadly, this wasn't as accepted in the nineties."

"I can't even say that everyone's openminded these days."

"Suppose that's true."

"You bet it is." Amanda's mind drifted to how anyone who was perceived as different, for whatever reason, scared insecure people. The result was ignorance at best, hate crimes at worst. Of which, from the sounds of it, Leslie was a victim. "The dress, tiara, and makeup...?"

"It was all Leslie's. His mom insisted he go to prom. I asked him why he'd held on to the items if the memories of that time caused so much pain, and he said it was to remind him to stand up for his truth."

"The mind is mysterious. How did Leslie know so much about Reese, her successes, her popularity?" It was taking all her concentration to think coherently.

"Apparently, Leslie would go to Prince William Forest Park a lot too, and he and Reese made unlikely friends. They'd talk sometimes, and Reese had told him about being voted prom queen. But that fateful Wednesday, Reese berated Makayla, apparently making it very clear that she saw herself as better than her. Leslie said something shifted inside, and he returned to high school. He took advantage of Reese's vulnerable state—aided by the oxy. Leslie said it was easy to get Reese to go along with him. He took pride in that."

"He might have felt powerful to be the one doing the betrayal."

"Wouldn't doubt that. Leslie confessed to dosing Reese with Xanax to keep her subdued while he tortured her. Said he had a prescription from the start of the year and had leftover pills. The real sick part about all of this is he doesn't regret his actions. But the case we have against him for the murders of Reese Thompson and Susie Valentine and the kidnapping and holding of Ava are rock solid. And CSIs Blair and Donnelly found forensic proof that Reese Thompson had been held in Leslie's basement—something he didn't deny either. Reese's street clothes were found in the house too."

"I hope Leslie Hansen rots in a prison cell."

"Me too. And if we didn't catch him, I don't think he'd have stopped killing. It's like he developed a longing for it."

Amanda might have said something in response, but her eyelids dipped.

"Well, I'm going to go," Trent told her. "Get some rest."

She tried to nod, but wasn't sure if her head moved. Kristen came to her side, and Amanda braced herself for a lashing out, but Kristen hugged her gently.

"Thank you for bringing our girl back to us."

"You're not mad at me anymore?" Amanda's mind must not have been working right if she was arming her sister with artillery to use against her.

Kristen shook her head. "Erik helped me see that was on Ava. You did what you could to discourage her. And because of you, she'll be all right."

Tears snaked down Amanda's cheeks as she held eye contact with her sister for a moment before she left.

Logan remained by her side and reached for her hand. Pain danced in his eyes.

"You really scared me this time, Steele," he said, trying to brush off the impact it had on him by tossing out her last name.

"I'm sorry." She studied his face. They had broken up before because her job scared him. Best if he was going to end things that he do so now and not after she spilled her feelings. "I understand if it's too much..."

He squeezed her hand tighter and trailed the tip of a finger down the back of it. "Actually it made me realize something." He licked his lips, tightened his jaw.

"What's that?" Her heart was pounding, and her mouth thick with saliva. She, who, always asked for the bad news first, boasting to the world she could handle anything after losing Kevin and Lindsey, feared this man breaking her heart. She'd grown attached to him, allowed herself to become vulnerable. She loved him, and she wanted him in her future.

"There's no way I'm letting us go ever again." He kissed her hand. "And I know I scared you when I said I wasn't going anywhere. You're not good at hiding how you feel. If you need to keep things as they are, I accept that."

Her heart fractured at his declaration of understanding, at his consideration for her feelings. Her breathing was quickening as she thought of the right words to say. "You might have noticed, but I started to work on clearing out the garage. I still need to organize all the totes out there into piles of what's garbage, what will be donated, what I'll keep. But facing the end of my life, I realized something."

"And what's that?" Hope mingled with trepidation in his eyes.

"There's room for you in my life, Logan, now and moving

into the future. I just needed time to make the space in my heart. And you gave me that." A warm tear splashed her cheek. "I love you, and I'd love it if you moved in with me and Zoe."

He smiled and hugged her, just a little too tight. But she winced through the pain, refusing to let him go.

A LETTER FROM CAROLYN

Dear reader,

I want to say a huge thank you for choosing to read *Taken Girls*. If you enjoyed it and would like to hear about new releases in the Amanda Steele series, just sign up at the following link. Your email address will never be shared, and you can unsubscribe at any time.

www.bookouture.com/carolyn-arnold

If you loved *Taken Girls*, I would be incredibly grateful if you would write a brief, honest review. This book touched a personal note for me. Leslie's story is fraught with pain and hurt, all because he wanted to listen to his own voice. People of all walks of life and backgrounds are subjects of bullying from the ignorant. Maybe some find it easier to disregard the impact this has on society or even refuse to accept this behavior still exists. But the sad truth is, it does.

Hate crimes hit the news all the time, but even on a less violent scale, those who are viewed as different, for whatever reason—including those who have made choices others do not agree with—are segregated. This can result in victims of such treatment feeling rejected, abandoned, and betrayed. Others might become angry or vengeful. The truth is that reactions are as unique as the individual. And just as someone bullied in life may not show repercussions later in life, for others, it stays with them, haunts them, and it affects the trajectory of their lives. In extreme cases, it can make them violent, a protective mechanism to hurt before being hurt again. Their hearts become shut off, the level of pain too high to tolerate. They can lash out, and in fiction this real-life reaction has been the fodder for crime authors from the beginning of time.

In fact, it wasn't until I was discussing the theme of this book with my publisher that I realized how I have been personally affected by ignorance. And I don't believe this story is one that I've shared publicly before, so here goes... I was raised in a certain religion (which I prefer to leave unnamed) and in what I thought of as a loving and accepting home. My parents provided for me and kept me safe, loved me. They were doing the best they knew how, just as we all do. And I bare no ill will toward them, even send them love, but it took some time to get here. You see, they view this religion as "the truth," and when my husband and I decided that we didn't want to be associated with it anymore, they cut all ties. My parents and two of my three sisters decided to excommunicate us. Just. Like. That. The reason? They didn't agree with our choice to leave a religion that we no longer believed in. Their decision had left me devastated—I overdrank and at times was suicidal—and it took years to fully heal and recover. I realized the importance of extending forgiveness. To them, even though they'd never know; it wasn't about them at that point. Also to myself to release the buried guilt I carried from choosing what I wanted from my life.

I say to everyone out there who is struggling, who is the victim of bullying, there is light to be found. To society as a whole, I ask that we look inward and examine our hearts—are they big enough to love and accept everyone unconditionally?

And I realize this might be a deep topic for a fiction novel, but Deep is my middle name. Well, not really, but if I told you what it really was... well... you can piece together the rest.

On another note, in the vein of shameless self-promotion, if you'd like to continue investigating murder, you'll be happy to know there will be more Detective Amanda Steele books. I also offer several other international bestselling series for you to savor—everything from crime fiction, to cozy mysteries, to thrillers and action adventures. One of these series features Detective Madison Knight, another kick-ass female detective, who will risk her life, her badge—whatever it takes—to find justice for murder victims.

Also, if you enjoyed being in the Prince William County, Virginia, area, you might want to return in my Brandon Fisher FBI series. Amanda's best friend, Becky Tulson is dating Brandon, but you'll be able to be there when they meet in *Silent Graves* (book two in my FBI series). These books are perfect for readers who love heart-pounding thrillers and are fascinated with the psychology of serial killers. Each installment is a new case with a fresh bloody trail to follow. Hunt with the FBI's Behavioral Analysis Unit and profile some of the most devious and darkest minds on the planet.

And if you're familiar with the Prince William County, Virginia area, or have done some internet sleuthing, you'll realize some differences between reality and my book. That's me taking creative liberties.

Last but certainly not least, I love hearing from my readers! You can get in touch on my Facebook page, through Twitter, Goodreads, or my website. This is also a good way to stay notified of my new releases. You can also reach out to me via email at Carolyn@CarolynArnold.net.

Wishing you a thrill a word!

Carolyn Arnold

KEEP IN TOUCH WITH CAROLYN

www.carolynarnold.net

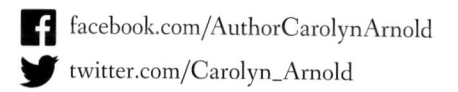

facebook.com/AuthorCarolynArnold
twitter.com/Carolyn_Arnold

Made in the USA
Monee, IL
22 June 2024